THE ROAD HOME

Book Two of The Winding Road Series

By Kerri Davidson and Mark Gelinas

A Bee and Badger Books Publication

This is a work of fiction. Names, characters, businesses, places, events, locales, and incidents are either the product of the author's imagination or used in a fictitious manner. Any resemblance to actual persons, living or dead, businesses, or actual events is purely coincidental.

ISBN 978-1-7779575-0-6

First Edition.

This book is dedicated to the many places we have called home.

ACKNOWLEDGMENTS

Many thanks to:

Our beta readers, Chris, Sam, and George.

Our editor, Joanne.

Our cover artist, Jamie.

Our Bee and Badger Books logo creator, Tropi.

The Ask Bathurst Facebook group.

Chapter 1

In Which They Cross That Bridge
Wednesday, August 23, 1995

"Left or right, Josh?"

Morgan's question roused Josh from his reverie. They were stopped at the end of the street. Not even a block into their trip back to Bathurst, he was already brooding over the implications of returning there.

"Left. Go left," he said.

Morgan eyed him before turning onto Silverdale Way. "You seem distracted. What were you thinking about?"

"A bit of everything." Josh chuckled. "It'll give us plenty to talk about on the ferry."

"Are you sure you want to take the ferry? The waters were kind of choppy this morning."

"It's either take the ferry or drive around to Seattle," Josh said.

"We'll drive. But why go back to Seattle? I'm done there. I said my goodbyes to Randy and my stepbrother this morning. I don't need to see them again. At least not right away."

"Whichever way we go, the road goes through Seattle. I mean, we could go farther south to cross the States, but it would take longer."

"Well, we definitely don't want to go that way then. So give me some directions, navigator," Morgan said.

They passed the plaza that included the Marine recruiting station for Silverdale. Although he couldn't see the office, Josh felt a twinge of bitterness, still stung by the Corps' rejection.

"Josh?"

"Hmm?"

"Directions?" Morgan reminded him. "Don't make me stop the car to look at the map."

"Stay on this road and it'll take us to State Highway 3."

Morgan nodded. “Were you thinking about home?” she asked.

“Among other things. Home, the trip back, the future, and you, of course.”

She laughed. “You sure you can handle all that? Do you need to loosen the band of your ball cap?”

“Very funny.” He removed the hat Morgan had given him and put it back on. “Fits just fine.”

“Let’s start at the top of your list,” Morgan suggested. “What’s troubling you about going home?”

“Who said I was troubled?”

“Two weeks. You and me in Zinger.” Morgan patted the steering wheel of her car. “I know you well enough by now to tell when something’s bothering you.”

Josh sighed. “I wasn’t expecting to return home until after boot camp months from now. Even then, it would’ve just been for a visit.”

“I’m sorry you couldn’t enlist. But at least you’ll have a roof over your head. You were living in your truck right before we left,” Morgan pointed out.

“I apologized, so now my father will allow me to live at their house again, even if it’s in Rab’s old room.”

“Your sister didn’t take long to snag your room,” Morgan said with a small laugh.

“She didn’t snag my room. I told her she could have it.”

“Only because you weren’t planning on coming back.”

“Ah, the best laid plans of mice and men,” Josh said with a tight smile. “We’re coming up on Gorst. Watch for Highway 16; we want to take it going east.”

The sky was overcast and a wind coming off the Puget Sound brought with it the smell of the sea. Somber gray vessels were moored at the Bremerton shipyard, visible for a brief moment as they rounded the inlet.

Morgan wore her curly blond hair short enough it didn’t blow in her face while she drove with the windows down. Josh liked that Morgan was a low maintenance type of girl – woman, now that she had turned eighteen.

He pointed to the sign for Highway 16, but Morgan already had her turn signal on. She smiled at him as she slipped into the light traffic heading east, her dark green eyes sparkling as a ray of sunshine broke through the clouds.

"You're right about those plans," Morgan said. "Both of ours went up in smoke. But I'm happy with the way things worked out for me. I don't think I really expected to live with my biological dad or work at his nightclub. Hell, I probably wouldn't even have left home if you hadn't offered to share expenses for the trip. I'm glad I met Randy and all, but I'm looking forward to getting back."

The clouds obscured the sun and with them, Morgan's face. Josh bristled, thinking of how she'd been kept in the dark about her biological father marrying and siring another child. Josh wondered briefly how many other half-siblings the man had left strewn across Canada and the States. He refrained from sharing the notion.

"Do you have any idea which route we should take back to Bathurst?" he asked, hoping to lighten her mood.

"Maybe we could go straight up to B.C. and take the Trans-Canada all the way across."

"Had enough of the States, have you?"

"It's nice and all, but let's face it, we're Canadians," Morgan said.

"I'm an American too."

"Only on paper, Josh. How long have you actually lived in the States, a week or two?"

"Point." He grimaced. She was right, as usual.

"Besides, I have no desire to cross the border at Sault Ste. Marie again," Morgan said, wrinkling her nose.

Josh shrugged. "We'd be going through the Canadian entry station. We wouldn't see that agent again."

"You can't seriously be thinking about going there."

"No, I was just saying we wouldn't see him," Josh said.

"But we'd know he was there," Morgan insisted.

"Eyes on the road, Angel."

Morgan laughed. "Are we still going to say that?"

"Maybe not as often. We've grown some this past month."

"Don't I know it. But we do need to decide which way we're going by the time we reach Seattle."

"Speaking of Seattle," Josh said, "I'd like to spend a couple of days in the city."

Morgan snapped her head toward him just long enough to ask, "Are you crazy?"

"I didn't get to see much of the city while we were there. Besides, the Yankees are playing the Mariners in the Kingdome tomorrow."

"Since when are you a baseball fan?" Morgan asked.

"Since I was on the team in high school. The ball cap should have been a clue."

"I thought you wore it to look taller."

Josh cringed a bit. Morgan was right again. He was slightly taller than her, but not as tall as he would like. "Did I tell you that?"

"I don't remember, but I can figure things out too, you know."

"I'm starting to realize this," Josh said.

"How about a compromise? We spend one day in Seattle, not two. We can stop early enough tomorrow to catch the game on TV."

Josh pursed his lips and considered it. After a moment he said, "I suppose that's reasonable."

"Any particular place you want to stop? We've already been to the Space Needle."

"My cousin told me about a crazy place called Pike's Place Market."

"I think I know where that is. Randy pointed it out to me on the way to visit his club."

"Is it right near the interstate with a big sign?" Josh asked.

"Yeah. But it says Public Market, not Pike's," Morgan said.

"That's the one."

"Okay. We'll go there, do some shopping, and maybe have a late lunch after. We can firm up where we'll cross the border at lunch."

"Sounds like a plan," Josh agreed.

With a plan in place and his list of concerns momentarily forgotten, they chatted happily about their time in Washington until signs informed them they weren't far from Tacoma.

"We should find a place to stop for gas," Morgan suggested. "It should be cheaper than in the city."

"We're coming up on an exit." Josh pointed at the sign.

Morgan took the exit and found a station. No other cars were at the pumps as she drove up.

They both got out and Morgan popped off the gas cap. "I'll pump," she said as she pulled the nozzle from the bracket. "Go pay and see if they have any coffee that smells reasonably fresh."

A strong breeze tugged at Josh's ball cap as he waved and went into the store. An older gentleman wearing a gray shirt bearing the company logo sat behind the counter reading a newspaper. A small TV flickered noiselessly behind the attendant.

Josh sniffed the coffee and believed it had been brewed sometime that morning. He poured two cups and waited for Morgan to finish. When the inside counter dinged, the man set the paper aside and shuffled to the register.

"What kind of car do you have there, sonny? I don't reckon I've ever seen its like before."

"It's a 1986 Pontiac 6000 coupe."

"That would explain it. The two-door model threw me off. You heading south?"

"Yeah, around to Seattle. How much?"

"Ten-fifty with the coffee. The wind's up today. The ghost of Old Gertie will be moaning."

Josh gave the man eleven dollars. "Ghosts in the daytime?"

"The bridge lies in a water grave. Day and night are meaningless."

Josh gave the man a strange look but didn't want to tell him he was talking nonsense. "Well, I need to get going. My girlfriend's waiting."

The attendant's voice went low and conspiratorial. "The first bridge, Galloping Gertie, liked to dance when the wind was up. One day she danced too hard and died. You'll be driving over her grave."

"Thanks for the warning." Josh collected his change and the two coffee cups. He pushed the door open with his back.

As he walked out the old man said, "Stay in the inner lane. It's safer."

Josh lifted a coffee cup as a sort of wave at the clerk.

Morgan stood next to the car with the door open. She had her arms crossed on the roof and leaned her chin on them. "You took long enough. Did you have to grind the beans?"

He shivered. "The attendant was telling me about a ghostly bridge."

"Sounds creepy."

As he handed Morgan a cup of coffee, the wind took his hat away. He set his cup on the ground and chased it down. Morgan was already in the car when Josh slid into his seat, holding cup and cap in his hands.

"Am I going to have to get you a leash for your hat?" she asked.

He leaned over for a quick kiss and then strapped in. "Let's get back on the road. I've had enough of this place."

They were soon back on Highway 16. After three miles, the road turned left and the towers of a suspension bridge came into view, grabbing at the low scudding clouds.

"*Merde*." Josh's eyes widened and his breath caught. "Inner lane," he sputtered.

"Are you okay?"

"Bridge. Big bridge."

"How did you expect to drive across the water?" Morgan chuckled.

As soon as the car cleared the last of the trees, the winds began to buffet them. Morgan didn't look too confident as she checked her mirror and moved to the inner lane. "There's no barrier between the lanes," she muttered.

Steel grating ran along the roadbed between each lane. Josh regretted his curiosity as soon as he glanced through them. The gray waters churned up whitecaps far below. In that moment, the old bridge became visible beneath the waves.

It had to be his imagination.

Morgan's knuckles were white as she gripped the wheel, her face scrunched up in intense concentration.

The car rocked when the wind hit it. Josh pointed to the oncoming lane. "Semi coming."

"Hang on," Morgan said, her voice shaky.

The semi approached quickly without wavering. As it passed Zinger, the winds it created buffeted the car harder than the natural ones. It pushed them toward the outer lane, but Morgan managed to stay between the grates. A pickup coming up on their right sounded its horn before speeding past.

By now they were between the two towers. The wind wasn't any stronger, but with no other vehicles nearby it could be heard moaning through the suspension wires.

Josh gripped the center console with one hand and grabbed the dash stiff-armed with the other. "We're almost across," he said, more for his benefit than hers.

Morgan nodded tersely. Neither one said another word until they left the bridge behind.

Morgan guided the car to the right lane and pulled off the highway at the next exit. She stopped at the first parking lot they came to in front of an apartment complex. She took a few deep breaths before turning to Josh. "Are you okay?"

He was panting but managed to say, "I'm okay. Tall bridges freak me out some."

"Can't say I enjoyed it either. Good thing you weren't driving."

"I actually think I would've been okay driving. I would've felt more in control."

Morgan watched him for a moment, took some more deep breaths, then drove back to the highway.

Josh studied the map for far longer than was necessary.

Chapter 2

In Which the Fish Fly
Wednesday, August 23, 1995

Morgan glanced at Josh in the passenger seat and supressed a chuckle. The trip over the bridge had unnerved her – so much so she'd nearly dug out her crusty pack of Camels from the glove box afterward – but Josh was clearly struggling more. He'd been studying the same spot on the map for the last ten minutes.

"Still up for a day at the market?" she asked, breaking the silence.

Josh started and pushed the map aside. "Of course. Are you still set on fleeing town tomorrow?" he countered with a weak grin.

Morgan laughed. "I am. I really don't mind going to the market; I'm just anxious to get home."

"Right. You said that." He grimaced.

"Come on. I know you still have things to work out with your family – so do I – but there must be something you're looking forward to back home."

"I'll be happy to see Rab. And I'm eager to get back to work so I can fix Old Blue." Josh took off his ball cap and ran his hand through his hair.

Morgan smiled as she stole another peek at him. He seemed to be perking up. She'd never tell him how much she loved the way his light brown hair stuck out in all directions – kind of messy-casual like – because he'd be sure to go and hack it all off.

"That's the spirit," she said. "You'd better be nice to me on this trip back then. I still have the keys to your truck." She flashed him a wicked grin.

"Oh, I'll be nice all right. I learned a thing or two on the way here." He snickered.

"We're not far from the market. What's the big deal about it anyway? Randy told me they throw fish around in there or something."

Josh laughed. "There's a lot more to it than that. There are several levels with loads of shops, street performers, and places to eat."

Morgan shrugged. "We never had a chance to really enjoy ourselves after we got here, what with all the unexpected things that were thrown at us. You're right. We deserve to celebrate a bit."

"I'll pay for parking and lunch," Josh said.

"Thanks. Money's not that big of a deal for me this time. My parents wired me enough to get home. But I'll accept your offer. What about you, though? Don't you have to pay your mom back for the money she gave you?"

"No. She only transferred money from my savings account because I couldn't access it with my bank card. She'd never lend me money. Hey, look!"

The clouds had cleared somewhat since their drive across the bridge. Josh didn't have to tell her what she was supposed to be looking at. Morgan gasped at the sight of Mount Rainier dominating the sky.

"It looks so close," she said.

A honking horn reminded Morgan she was supposed to be driving, not gawking. She shot Josh a sheepish look and put both hands on the wheel, correcting her drift. "Go ahead and say it."

"Nah, your eyes are clearly on the road now. And we decided we needed a new phrase, remember? How about on to the next?"

"That could work." Morgan laughed. "That's real growth. Man, we didn't have a clue coming here did we? Well, especially me. I had no idea what to expect when I met Randy. You had a solid plan."

Josh snorted. "Yeah, but no Plan B. At least we've got things figured out now."

He turned his attention to the Boeing runway off to their left, examining all the weird-looking airplanes. "Hey, that one looks like it's pregnant."

Morgan listened with half an ear as her thoughts drifted to Josh himself. Her first real boyfriend. She couldn't wait to tell her best friend Mel about him. As soon as Mel would talk to her again.

Morgan had been a few days shy of her eighteenth birthday when she decided to take Josh – a virtual stranger – up on his offer to share traveling expenses to Seattle. He'd been on his way to visit his uncle and join the Marines while Morgan was chasing the dream of meeting her birth father. Long story short, Morgan had basically run away from home in order to avoid a confrontation with her parents, and Mel had taken the brunt of her secret-keeping.

Never in her wildest dreams did Morgan expect to have feelings for Josh. Their personalities clashed right from the start. It wasn't until the night of her birthday when things really started to change. Josh had taken her out for dinner and been a right proper gentleman. He'd given her the most thoughtful presents and agreed to have a drink with her back at her hotel room.

She would never forget their first kiss that night. Sure, he was a bit tipsier than she'd been, but she would always remember gazing into his ice-blue eyes as their faces drew closer and –

"Earth to Morgan. You need to turn."

Morgan blushed and flipped on her signal. She'd nearly driven right past the market. "I know. I was just thinking."

Josh raised a brow. "I thought we put that on hold. What were you thinking about?"

She pulled up to the ticket machine and took the slip of paper indicating their time of entry. She drove through the parking garage pretending to be super engrossed in her search for a spot. What *was* she thinking about? Her boyfriend Josh? She couldn't very well say that. Because really, neither one of them had referred to each other in such a way before. What would he think if she said it? Oh hell, what if he thought she was delusional?

Realizing Josh was still waiting for an answer, Morgan said, “I was thinking about you. I kind of like you in case you hadn’t noticed.” She pulled into an empty space and shut off the engine. “Now, on to the next if you don’t mind.”

Josh grinned and said nothing. Morgan was grateful. They got out of the car and Josh came around to take her hand as they walked to the building.

“Oh wait!” Morgan exclaimed. “I forgot my camera.”

Josh waited while she ran back to the car to get her disposable camera. She cursed under her breath as she grabbed the door handle. Locked. Josh had the most annoying habit of locking the doors every time they left the car for five minutes.

After unlocking the door and rooting through the bag she kept in the back seat, Morgan emerged victorious and hurried to join Josh.

“Have you ever been here before?” Morgan asked as they approached the entrance. The sounds of people yelling and cheering inside already assaulted her ears.

“Nope. But Sally has. She made me promise to stop if we had time.”

Morgan smiled at the mention of Josh’s younger cousin. She hadn’t had the chance to spend much time with her during their visit, but the bubbly teen had totally won Morgan’s heart.

Inside the market, Morgan tossed out a mental “what were you thinking?” to Sally. She stood next to Josh, mouth agape, taking in the booths and crowds of people around them.

The central attraction was indeed the fish-throwers. Men in aprons laughed and shouted as they chucked gigantic fish back and forth across the hordes of people gathered round. Morgan took a step back as one of the customers was whacked in the face with one of the fish. Everyone, including the victim of the fishcapade, broke out in laughter.

Except for Morgan. She tugged on Josh's arm.

"What's wrong?" he asked. "That was hilarious."

"That was disgusting." She took a good look at the hat she'd bought him to replace the one he'd lost on the ferry. It read, "Mechanic by Week, Fishing Legend by Weekend."

He caught her stare. "Yeah, I've never done much fishing, but I still like the hat."

"I don't. I'll get you a new one."

Josh led Morgan away from the seafood and produce displays. They descended the stairs to a level that was a bit quieter and way less fishy. At least there were cool shops down here.

They stopped to watch one of the many street performers. An older fellow who looked like a cowboy played a melancholy tune on his guitar, his hat pulled low over his eyes. When he began to sing, Morgan was entranced.

She was sad when the song ended too soon and reached for her wallet on a string that served as her purse to toss a few dollars into the man's basket.

"How about we grab something to eat?" Josh asked.

"That bakery smells amazing. Can we get something to go and start shopping?"

Josh shrugged. "As you wish."

Morgan let Josh pick their sandwiches and they strolled along while munching them. She couldn't tell what exactly was in hers but she didn't care. The meat may have been a mystery, but it was far better than the prepackaged truck stop sandwiches. The bread itself was her favorite part.

"I can't remember the last time I had fresh bread," Morgan commented. "It would've been back before my grandma moved to the retirement home. I might have to figure out how to make this myself."

"The sandwich or the bread?"

"The bread," Morgan said through a mouthful. "But I was just kidding. It's all I can do to toast the stuff."

"You never learned to cook?" Josh laughed.

She shrugged. "Never needed to. I know how to warm stuff up."

They found a trashcan and deposited their wrappers. Josh went over to a coffee vendor while Morgan waited off to the side. She fiddled with the camera she was carrying, wondering what she might want to take a picture of. Nothing caught her eye as she looked through the viewfinder. The place was too crowded. And noisy.

Nevertheless, many heads turned when she screamed.

"Sorry, miss. Didn't mean to startle you. What's your pleasure?"

The balloon-making clown backed away when he noticed Morgan's balled fist. She checked herself and relaxed her hand just as Josh came running over with the coffee cups.

"What happened? Did that guy do something to you?" Josh asked, his head whipping between the retreating balloon man and Morgan.

"No. He just startled me."

"Not a fan of clowns?" Josh asked and relaxed.

"Balloons," Morgan practically whispered.

"You're scared of balloons?"

"Yeah, well, you're scared of bridges," she snapped and immediately regretted it. "I'm sorry. I know it's stupid, but I really don't like balloons. They . . . pop." She grimaced. "Honestly, I'm not a fan of crowds either, unless there's liquor being served."

"Do you want to leave?"

"I'm okay now. I'm glad we stopped. I really do want to check out some of the shops. Let's split up for a bit and meet back at the guitar guy? I might want to get you a surprise."

"So long as you're sure you're okay." Josh checked his watch. "Meet back here at noon?"

Morgan checked her watch as well and groaned. "I forgot about all the time changing we'll have to do on the way back. You're still in charge of that?" she asked sweetly.

"I'll take care of it," Josh assured her.

"Great. See you soon." Morgan pecked his cheek and took off toward one of the artsy shops, avoiding the tourist traps. Who wanted a mug with the space needle on it? Or worse, one with a picture of those gross fish. Come to think of it, Morgan realized she'd never had a coffee mug of her own. She decided when she did get one it would not be crappy.

Morgan wandered through the shops that caught her eye, considering and dismissing potential gifts for her mom, dad, brother, and Mel. She ended up buying herself a cool tie-dyed T-shirt and a plain black hat for Josh.

By the time she arrived at their meeting spot, Josh was waiting for her with a sack full of items.

"I thought girls were supposed to be the shoppers," she teased.

"I thought girls were supposed to know how to cook," he said.

"On to the next?" Morgan laughed.

"We need to come up with a better line. You ready for a real lunch?"

"Kind of. But is it okay if we get out of here? I've really had all I can take of this." She waved her arm to encompass the mobs of boisterous patrons and sideshows.

"No problem. Let's go."

Josh took her hand and held it all the way back up and out to the parking garage.

"Any idea where you want to eat?" Josh asked as they got to the car.

Morgan walked over to the passenger side. "Not really. Just someplace a bit quieter. You can drive."

She opened the door and went to put her unused camera and purchases in her duffel bag as Josh put his stuff in the trunk with his gear. She was still looking for her duffel bag as he opened the driver's side door.

"Can you move your seat up?" she asked him. "I think my bag may have fallen."

Josh pulled the seat forward as far as it would go.

Still no bag.

"Would you have put it in the trunk?" Josh asked. "I didn't notice it in there."

"No. You know I always keep it right here," she said, digging under the seat. Panic began to rise as she noticed a few other things out of place. Her car was messy but there was no denying her bag was gone.

"My library books are missing too." She pulled herself from the car and plunked down on the ground.

"Morgan, don't worry. We'll find it." Josh said, coming around the car.

"No. No we won't." Her eyes filled with tears. "Dammit."

"I'm sorry, I was sure I locked the car."

"You did," she moaned. "I must have left it unlocked when I came back for the camera. It's my fault."

"Look, it doesn't matter who's to blame. I'll take a look around the lot."

Morgan remained sitting where she was with zero hope of her bag reappearing. She cursed whoever would be rude enough to steal it. She cursed Seattle for allowing such people in their city. Mostly, she cursed herself for cursing Josh about locking the doors.

She was still cursing when Josh returned empty-handed, concern etched on his face.

Chapter 3

In Which Plans Get Changed
Wednesday, August 23, 1995

Josh gazed down at Morgan, who was still sitting by Zinger, and his heart ached for her. She'd stopped cursing and her eyes were cast down to the pavement.

"Sorry, Angel." He extended a hand to help her up. She looked up at the sound of his voice. Her cheeks showed no tears. "There's no sign of it."

Morgan accepted his hand and stood, moving smoothly from standing next to Josh to wrapping her arms around him. Several sobs wracked her chest.

"We can . . ." Josh started to say.

"Shh . . . just hold me for a minute. Right now, you and Zinger are all I have in the world, and Zinger doesn't hug."

They stood in the embrace for a long time. Morgan rested her head on Josh's shoulder and used his shirt sleeve to dry the few tears she'd shed.

Thunder rumbled and a few fat raindrops splattered on the top level of the parking garage.

Morgan finally broke the embrace. "Well, I guess we should get going. We can hug later when it's not costing us money to park."

"We should call the police."

Morgan studied the sky silently before stepping into the car.

He joined her to get out of the steadily increasing rain. "We should tell them we were robbed."

"There's no point," she said. "Besides, we weren't robbed; it was a theft. There's a difference. It's not like they're going to put out an APB out on some stolen underwear."

"They took more than that," Josh said.

"I can replace the clothes," Morgan replied tersely. "Let's just go."

Josh thought briefly of Morgan's sketchpad and the drawings she'd shown him on the way to Seattle. Those weren't replaceable. He started the car and drove to the attendant, his heart heavy. However, he didn't mention the lost work to Morgan. She was keeping herself together quite well.

With parking paid for, they left the lot and made their way to Western Avenue where Josh turned north.

"Here's what we'll do," he said, turning the windshield wipers on high as the rain fell harder. "We'll find someplace to go shopping so you have something clean to wear tomorrow."

"Oh God, yes. I don't want to end up like you on our first day driving, no offense." Morgan wrinkled her nose.

"I was pretty stinky on the day we left. I'm thankful you even let me in the car."

Morgan's chuckle turned to an exasperated sigh. "At least I bought one damned T-shirt at the market but I can't wear it all the way home." She fumbled around the dash area just inside Josh's peripheral vision. "Well, shit. They took all my cassette tapes too. Is there anything they didn't steal?"

"They didn't steal Zinger, so that's a good thing."

"They're lucky they didn't, or I'd have hunted their asses down and dragged what was left of them to the police myself. At least your stuff was locked in the trunk."

Josh considered asking how she'd managed to make such a mess of her car again during the few days they'd been apart, but once again thought better of it. "Okay, so we'll stop and go shopping."

"Sounds good so far."

"After that, if you're hungry, we'll get some food and decide where we're going to cross the border." A cluster of shops appeared ahead of them. "Do you have a preferred place to shop?"

"Someplace mid-range. Not K-Mart, but not JC Penny either," Morgan said, patting her purse.

"So a thrift store is out of the question?"

"Thankfully, I had all my money on me. We'll leave the thrift store for those who want to be thrifty."

"There's a Red Dot store. That should work," Josh said.

"Yeah, that looks good."

Josh pulled into the parking lot and found a spot.

As they left the car, Morgan tugged the strap of her purse up over her shoulder. "Let's go shopping," she said, striding toward the doors.

Josh hurried to catch up with her. "While you shop for your personal things, I'll find a bag for you to put them in. Okay?"

"Okay, but nothing goofy or fancy or I'll make you take it back."

"Plain and simple it is," Josh said.

Morgan took a cart and Josh went looking for luggage.

He didn't find anything suitable in the luggage area, so he went looking for a sports department. He found several duffel bags there. They all had brand names. Frowning, he chose an unfamiliar brand and hoped Morgan wouldn't consider it fancy.

She had several items in her cart when he found her. She was looking at a purple blouse as he approached. He held up the duffel bag he'd chosen. "Will this do?"

"That's not bad. Is that the only color they had?" she asked.

"They had others, but this seemed to fit you the best."

She examined the gray bag again. "Okay, toss it in the cart."

"I've got this. Consider it a gift if you want," Josh said.

She laughed. "What's the special occasion?"

"How about the occasion of Morgan buying a nice purple blouse?"

She picked up the sleeve and checked the price tag. "I'm not sure I should."

"Come on, I can tell you like it. Besides, I'm buying the bag, so you can afford the blouse."

Morgan tilted her head down and smiled as she put the blouse in the cart. “Thanks. I think I have everything I need.”

“Toothbrush?”

“Oh, I knew I forgot something.”

“I’ll take the cart to the front while you go get that,” Josh offered.

“Okay, but don’t be looking at my underwear.”

“Promise.” Josh snickered. “I’ll meet you by the registers.”

Josh took the cart to the front and browsed the latest movie releases on VHS while he waited.

Morgan appeared with a handful of toiletries and asked, “Anything interesting?”

He shook his head. “Nothing I’m itching to see. Some of these I watched in the theater.”

“Well, I’m done, and hungry.”

Josh went to the Express Lane while Morgan unloaded her cart. He paid for the duffel bag as well as a deck of cards snagged from the impulse-buy rack.

After packing everything in the trunk, they walked over to a fast-food restaurant for Buffalo wings.

As they munched on the wings and celery, they looked at the map spread out on the table between them.

“There are three major highways going from Washington into Canada,” Josh said, pointing to where each crossed the border.

“Hmm. It looks like Interstate 5 curves to the west before crossing.”

“It does, but because it’s an interstate the travel will be faster. That’s one thing I’ll miss when we get back to Canada.”

“I’ll miss the speed limit, or lack of one, in Montana,” Morgan said.

Josh took another wing. “These things are hot.”

Morgan laughed. “And you got the mild ones. Try dipping them in blue cheese dressing; it takes out some of the heat.”

Josh managed to finish his wings with copious amounts of dressing and soda.

Back in the car, Morgan took the wheel and they searched the area for a hotel. She decided on one that was a little fancier than their usual choices.

"You sure you don't want to look around for something less expensive?" Josh asked.

"I already broke open the piggy bank today. Besides, I'm a bit worn out and I still need to call my mom. It's already getting late there."

They checked in, getting adjoining rooms. Josh gave Morgan both room keys and parked the car while she took her stuff up to her room. By the time he arrived, she'd propped his door open and had already opened the doors between the rooms.

Josh dropped his gear in his room and stopped before entering Morgan's because she was on the phone. She motioned for him to be quiet but to come in. He did so and sat at the desk.

"It isn't even dark here, Mom." Morgan turned to Josh and rolled her eyes as she spoke.

He couldn't hear the other end of the conversation, but from Morgan's responses, he could guess what her mother's questions were.

"We're still in Seattle," Morgan said. Another eye roll and she held the phone slightly away from her ear.

The squawking reached Josh's ears now.

"Mom! We did some sightseeing. Relax. I appreciate the loan, but I'm not going to be calling you every night if you keep going on like this. We'll be on the road tomorrow."

Morgan tapped her foot as she listened and then sighed. "No, Mom, we have separate rooms."

Josh waited until Morgan finished her less-than-pleasant conversation and grimaced as she hung up the phone. "Sorry to get you into trouble with your mom."

"It's just Mom being Mom. I could really use a smoke. I wonder if they stole those too?"

Josh hoped they had but kept his opinion to himself. He was doing that a lot today.

While Morgan took a shower, he sat in her room and wrote a postcard to Rab. He marveled at how different this trip was from the last. Three weeks ago, they barely knew each other and the door to her room would have been locked and chained at this time of night.

Morgan was dressed in shorts and a tie-dyed T-shirt when she came out of the bathroom, her hair wrapped in a towel. "Writing a card to your sister?"

"Yeah. I figure I'll write to her today and tomorrow, but then anything I send won't get there until after we do. I have a few extra postcards if you want to send one to your brother."

Morgan laughed. "Matthew is only eighteen months old. He can barely put a sentence together, much less read."

"No other brothers or sisters at home?" Josh asked, surprised he was only learning this now.

"Nah. They seemed content to raise me. I think Matthew was a happy accident. Maybe it'll keep the pressure to have grandchildren off me for a few years." She laughed at the thought.

"So you're in no hurry to have children?"

"After babysitting Matthew, no hurry at all, if ever," Morgan said.

Josh wasn't sure how he felt about the revelation, or why he should be having feelings about it to begin with. It wasn't like he was thinking of having children with this woman – or any woman, for that matter – at least not right now.

"My turn to shower," he said.

"You can use mine if you want," Morgan offered.

"I might take a long one. I'll use mine in case you need to use the bathroom."

"More heavy thinking?"

He nodded. "Yeah, you could say that."

Josh returned to his room and took a long hot shower. He turned off the hot water and let the cold water run for a minute before getting out. He'd discovered that simply the sight of Morgan had an effect on him.

He put on his jeans, because she had a thing about him running around in his boxers, and pulled on a clean T-shirt.

When Josh stepped into her room, Morgan was already in bed. He crossed the room and placed a gentle kiss on her forehead. She reached up and put her hands on his head, drawing him back down for a proper kiss. "Good night, Josh."

"Good night, Angel," he said when she released him.

Josh returned to his room, pausing at the doorway for one last peek at her.

He undressed and climbed into bed. He had no sooner pulled the covers over himself when she called loudly enough for him to hear, "Josh?"

"Yes? Do you need a glass of water?" he asked and chuckled.

"Funny. Do you have anyone waiting for you when you get home?"

"Just my *maman* and Rab, I guess. I'm not sure how my father feels about me returning."

"Hold on," she said.

From her room there was a thump and then the sound of something being dragged.

"Are you okay?" Josh sat up in bed.

"Yeah, I just moved my mattress closer to the door so I don't have to yell."

"Good idea. Hang on."

A few minutes later, Josh had his mattress off the box spring and placed by the adjoining door next to Morgan's.

"I meant, do you have anyone like a girlfriend back home?" Morgan clarified.

"No. I said goodbye to Trixie the day before we left."

"Who's Trixie?" she asked stretching a hand toward him.

He reached out and held it. "Trixie is Rab's best friend. Sometimes we would go places together. I suppose she's the closest thing to a girlfriend I've ever had, but I never called her my girlfriend."

"Would you call me your girlfriend?"

Josh refrained from laughing, it was a dangerous question. "You're a wonderful girl . . ."

"Woman," she corrected.

"Woman, and yes, the thought has crossed my mind, but I want to take a little more time before I'm sure."

She released his hand. "So you can check to see if Trixie will take you back?"

A loud crack of thunder sounded.

"Hey, what time is it?" Josh asked.

"You're avoiding my question."

"No, the thunder reminded me I wanted to check the weather."

"Likely story," she said.

"Serious." He stood. The room's alarm clock showed it was just after eleven.

"Boxers!" Morgan complained.

"I'm not going to sleep in my jeans," Josh said.

He turned on the TV in his room and found the local weather channel.

Morgan leaned on her elbows and looked up. "Why check the weather now? We haven't before."

"We had good weather all the way here but now we're starting to see rain. When was the last time you got new wiper blades?"

Morgan sat up and pulled the blanket around her. "Hell if I know."

"Exactly." Josh stared at the TV. "*Merde*, that's not good."

"What isn't good?

"There's a travel advisory for eastern B.C. and northeastern Washington," he said.

"Travel advisory? What's going on?"

"Smoke from a big forest fire is making driving hazardous."

"Well, that puts a kink in our plans," Morgan said and flopped back down on her mattress.

"We'll go back the way we came, at least until we get past the fires, then we can cut up to Canada."

"Well, I'm going to try sleep now and do my best not to worry about this Trixie person."

Josh turned off the TV and got back on his mattress.

Morgan pulled the blanket up over her shoulder but extended her hand again. He took it.

Despite their weariness, they talked late into the night about silly little things. It was just nice hearing her voice.

They fell asleep hand in hand through the open door.

Chapter 4

In Which Morgan Goes Around the Bend
Thursday, August 24, 1995

Even though they'd been up late, Morgan found herself wide awake at six in the morning. Spending the night in Seattle hadn't been all that bad, but she couldn't wait to finally get on the road.

She smiled at Josh snoring on the mattress next to her. He'd thrown off his blankets sometime during the night so she covered him up before making her way to the bathroom. She should have bought him pajama pants at that dastardly market instead of a ball cap. Maybe she'd get him some for Christmas.

Morgan crept back out from the bathroom to retrieve the bags of clothing and toiletries she had yet to go through, cringing at the rustling of the plastic bags. She jumped when Josh let out a loud snort and laughed, remembering the day she picked him up when they first left Bathurst. He'd been sleeping in his truck with his feet hanging out the window and she'd needed to do a lot of thumping to wake him. Some things never changed.

But a lot of other things did.

No longer worried about disturbing Sleeping Beauty, Morgan dragged her bags into the bathroom and shut the door. She turned on the shower and sat on the edge of the tub, waiting for the water to run hot.

Trixie, Trixie, Trixie . . .

She'd been half-joking when she asked Josh if he had a girlfriend waiting for him back home. The only reason she'd mentioned it was to open the subject of the boyfriend/girlfriend issue.

While he didn't seem to technically have a girlfriend waiting for him, he certainly had something. Morgan frowned and bit down on her lip. At least he said he'd sent the cheap little Trick on her way before leaving.

No, that wasn't fair, Morgan chided herself as she got into the shower. She didn't even know who the girl was. What was with the jealousy? Morgan had never seen herself as the jealous type.

Then again, Morgan had never had a guy to be jealous over. Not that she had one now . . . her suspicions had been correct. Although he'd done it tactfully, Josh had basically balked at the idea of calling her his girlfriend the night before.

Which made no sense at all.

Morgan turned off the water and wrapped herself in a towel. She rummaged through the bags until she found a suitable outfit – her old ripped jeans and a new plain white T-shirt. She wasn't ready to try the new jeans yet. They weren't bad looking, but she sure as hell didn't relish the thought of breaking in a new pair in the car all day.

Morgan sat on the tile floor and began placing her new things into the duffel bag Josh had bought, setting aside the ball cap she'd purchased for him.

It was things like this that should have made their relationship status a no-brainer. When was the last time she'd walked through a store and hadn't thought to pick up something for him? He was always attentive, holding open doors, making sure she was all right – and yeah, they'd had their fair share of kisses. Plus they'd just spent nearly the entire month together.

Morgan placed the last of her things in the duffel bag and stopped in the middle of zipping it up, a disturbing notion forming in her mind.

Maybe Josh was just a nice guy. Maybe what she viewed as boyfriend-like behavior was nothing more than his chivalrous personality.

Morgan gave her head a shake and finished zipping the bag. No. There was more to it than that. Fine, he wasn't ready to take their budding whatever-it-was to the next level, but surely she meant more to him than just some girl he was road-tripping with. And hopefully his kisses, at least, belonged only to her. For now.

Trixie, Trixie, Trixie . . .

Morgan didn't bother being quiet as she exited the bathroom. In fact, she turned on one of the lamps in her room and threw her newly-packed bag on the box spring.

Her dark mood evaporated as she turned to Josh and found he'd once again tossed his blankets off. She giggled and went over to throw another blanket on him. Christmas wasn't coming fast enough. Maybe she'd have to get those pajama bottoms for his birthday instead.

Morgan squatted to look more closely at him as he slept and was hit with another realization. She had no clue when his birthday was. Maybe he was correct about not wanting to rush things. There was still so much they had yet to learn about each other.

However, if Morgan had learned one thing about him, it was that he was a man of honor. If he said Trixie was out of the picture, she should have no reason to doubt him.

Morgan allowed herself one last green-eyed thought about what a ridiculous name Trixie was before dismissing her from her thoughts altogether. She leaned over Josh and kissed him gently.

"Good morning, sunshine."

Josh groaned and swatted the blanket off yet again.

Morgan groaned and pulled it back up.

His eyes opened and a smile lit up his tired face. "Good morning, Angel. Wait, it's already morning?"

"It's early, but yep. Come on, get your butt in gear. I want to get on the road."

"What's the hurry?"

"You had your way yesterday. Now it's my turn. We're gonna drive until the damned sun sets."

Josh gave her a wary look before getting up. Morgan sighed at the futility of trying to keep him covered.

"It's not even seven in the morning," he said, looking at the clock. "You want to drive for twelve hours in a row?"

"It won't be twelve hours once we put these rooms back together and you get moving," Morgan pointed out.

Josh sighed. "Okay, just give me a chance to wake up. You're driving today?"

"No. You can drive until we get through those mountains. I'll take over when we get to Montana." She grinned wickedly.

"Of course you will." Josh laughed and headed for his bathroom.

Morgan had the beds mostly back together by the time he came out.

"Good enough," she declared. "Housekeeping can do the rest for the price we're paying here."

"Want to go down for breakfast?"

"Not even a little bit. It's a restaurant, not continental. Can't we get something on the road? It wouldn't be the first time. Don't you remember feeding me fries and sticking them in my nose?" Morgan chuckled.

Josh chuckled too. "I sure do. But I don't think you want fries for breakfast."

"Actually, that sounds like a great idea. Good luck finding them though."

Josh gave her an odd look.

"Seriously, what's wrong with fries for breakfast?" she asked.

"Nothing, I guess. I'm just learning more and more about you each day."

"Ditto," Morgan muttered, determined not to speak the name she wasn't allowing herself to think of. Trina, Trampsley, T-Rex, was it? Exactly. Not worth her time.

"Are you all right? You seem a bit off this morning."

"Sorry. I'm just excited to get on the road." Morgan widened her eyes and looked pointedly at Josh's half-packed bag.

He held up his hands in surrender. "As you wish."

"Here." Morgan chucked the black ball cap at Josh. "I bought it yesterday. I don't want to see that fish hat at all today."

"Thanks," he said, putting the hat on.

They checked out in a flurry and stopped at a drive-through for breakfast pastries. No rain today; it looked like it was going to be a scorcher. Josh pulled down the sun visor and turned on Zinger's air conditioning as they left the city behind them.

"*Merde.* Traveling east is hard on the early morning eyes."

"Agreed." Morgan pulled down her own visor. "How can you even see?"

"It's tough, but at least we're still in the mountains."

Morgan settled back in her seat and closed her eyes. She was incapable of sleeping in a moving vehicle, but it blocked out the sun.

The sun was high enough in the sky by the time they left the mountains behind them. The last time they'd driven through the Cascade mountains, it had been in the middle of the night. She hadn't realized the country was so barren and dry on this side of them.

The drive itself was boring, but they passed the time playing the license plate game, reliving moments from their previous trip, and teasing each other mercilessly.

Morgan and Josh were returning to the car after a quick lunch at a roadside diner not far from Montana when Morgan thought to ask, "When's your damned birthday?"

Josh dropped the keys as he went to unlock the passenger door. "What?"

Morgan laughed as he bent to pick them up. "Sorry. I didn't mean to swear. I just realized this morning I didn't know when it was."

"It's in December," Josh said as he climbed into the passenger seat.

Morgan frowned. Was he going to dance around this question too?

"The thirty-first," he added as she got in.

"New Year's Eve? You must have had some wild birthday parties over the years."

He shrugged. "Not really. In case you haven't noticed, I'm not a big partier."

"True." Morgan almost suggested they would have to fix that come his next birthday, but didn't. She didn't want to seem so presumptuous as to think they'd still be together by then. Her grumpiness settled back in as she set off down the highway.

"You sure you're okay with going back the same way?" Josh asked.

"Of course. It's not for long. And Montana, remember?"

"How could I forget?" Josh reclined his seat and pulled his new hat down over his face. Seconds later, he was snoring lightly.

That guy could sleep anywhere. And through anything. Morgan found a radio station playing the top hits and increasingly edged the volume up until she was satisfied. She liked her music loud. Josh did not. However, he didn't get a say in it today, being unconscious and all.

As soon as they entered Montana, Morgan gleefully stepped on the gas, sailing past slower moving vehicles and singing aloud to some of the songs she kind of knew the words to. Josh twitched once or twice but remained asleep.

Morgan was getting tired herself, having slept so little. A row of songs she didn't care for came on and her thoughts turned back to the theft of her bag.

She wasn't lying when she said she didn't care about the clothes she'd lost, but she'd been careful up until now to not dwell on the irreplaceable items that were taken.

Thankfully, she'd taken her birth certificate out of her bag and returned it to her wallet, but there were cards and letters from her biological father in there. Not as important now as they had been before she met him but . . .

The journal she'd written in for years to her late best friend was gone too. It was disturbing to think someone out there might be reading her words. Really, they weren't her deepest thoughts and feelings – only a misguided attempt to hang on to her beloved friend through writing. Still . . .

Her sketchpad, on the other hand, was something she sorely missed. Sure, most of her work had been trash, but it was her work, dammit. And there was that one portrait she'd drawn of Josh – the first drawing she'd ever finished that she'd been truly proud of. She'd promised to give it to him and now . . .

And now she'd just have to suck it up and draw another one.

Enough with the miserable thoughts. Morgan had plenty of things to look forward to when she got back home. No more babysitting; she'd find a great job and, with any luck, an exciting career. She was young, she was healthy, and she had a really cute maybe-boyfriend sitting right here next to her.

As if on cue, Josh stirred and took the hat off his face. Morgan turned down the radio and eased her foot off the gas pedal a bit.

"How long did I sleep?" Josh asked, rubbing his eyes.

"Don't you ever get tired of asking that question?" Morgan laughed. "You've been out all afternoon. The sun will be setting soon."

Josh straightened up and looked behind them. "Gee, sorry I've been such a boring traveling companion."

"Don't worry about it." Morgan noticed the sign for the town of Butte ahead and shivered. Their last stop here had not been pleasant. In fact, they hadn't been together at all. She'd kicked Josh out on the side of the road a few miles out of town.

Josh gave her a concerned look, probably recalling their not-so-insignificant spat from that day.

Morgan ignored the look and focused on driving around the town as quickly as possible. Of course, by sticking to the road they were on, she passed Harrison Avenue. That was the road where she'd spent the night in Zinger at a truck stop. It was also the same road that led to the dealership where she'd sold him. The emotions of that day, remembering Josh showing up in time to save her and Zinger, and the weariness of the drive caught up to her all at once.

Instead of staying on Interstate 90, she wrenched the steering wheel at the last minute, cutting off another vehicle that honked at her, and took the exit heading north.

"*Merde!* What are you doing?" Josh was holding the oh-*merde* handle above his door.

Morgan took a breath and wiped the tears from her eyes. "I don't want to go back that way, Josh." She knew she sounded hysterical but couldn't help herself.

Josh reached over and put his hand on her shoulder. "Morgan, please slow down. You need to calm down."

She nodded.

"Pull over when you can?"

She nodded again as tears continued to fall.

Soon enough, she eased onto the shoulder of the road and sat crying behind the steering wheel. Josh kept an arm around her but didn't say a thing until she finally stopped.

"Can you tell me what happened?" he asked.

"Maybe I'm having my period." Morgan sniffled.

Josh looked ready to flee.

"I'm kidding," she assured him. "I really don't know what happened. It was just driving through Butte and then remembering . . . I need a tissue."

Morgan reached over and pulled open the glove box. She started crying again when she saw her cigarettes were still inside. She yanked out a tissue, the Camels and lighter, and got out of the car.

She settled herself on the shoulder of the road and blew her nose before lighting a cigarette. Josh emerged slowly from the car.

"Happy tears?" he ventured.

Morgan laughed and took a deep drag from her cigarette. "That last batch kind of was. I think I've lost my mind."

"What can I do to help?" Josh came to sit beside her, upwind from the smoke.

"I just want to go home," Morgan said.

“We can’t get there tonight but I’ll drive until we find a place to stay.”

“North?”

“Yes, we’ll go north.”

Chapter 5

In Which Montana Never Ends
Friday, August 25, 1995

Josh rolled over and smiled at the sight of Morgan lying no more than five feet away. A gap separated the two beds of the hotel room. From the gentle rise and fall of the blanket covering her, he reasoned she was still asleep.

After a hard day's drive, they'd arrived at Helena well after dark. Once he'd taken over for Morgan, Josh had continued north on Interstate 15 until he found the Starlight Hotel just outside the city. Morgan had suggested they share a room as long as it had two beds because she didn't want to sleep on the floor again just to be near him.

Getting up quietly, Josh thought the sunlight stealing between the curtains was brighter than it should be for seven in the morning. Then he looked at the clock and saw the time was already after eight. He remembered they'd passed into Mountain Time yesterday but neglected to change their clocks. He also realized they should be entering Central Time today. Josh set his watch to Central Time and made a mental note to change Morgan's watch and Zinger's clock once they got on the road.

Josh didn't want to disturb her sleep, but they had another long drive ahead, especially since Morgan was feeling the need to get home soon. She had apologized profusely for the sudden change of plans, but he really had no reason to be upset.

He was with Morgan and that made him happy – happier than he'd been in years.

Josh was rather ambivalent about getting home. Sure, he wanted to get back to work at Cal's garage, but he would have to pay rent to live at home. The amount had not yet been named, but he hoped it wouldn't be so much that he couldn't save for school.

Not wanting to startle Morgan by touching her while she was asleep – she could hit hard – Josh leaned close to her ear. "Good morning, Angel. It's time to get up."

She murmured something and rolled onto her back, opening her eyes as she did. "How long did I sleep?"

"Hey, that's my line."

"Well, I'm stealing it for this morning."

He closed the space between their lips and kissed her softly. "You don't have to steal it. I'll loan it to you for today. But it is already eight, and we should get on the road."

She sat up and dropped her legs over the edge of the bed. "Well get some clothes on, boxer boy. I've got dibs on the bathroom."

"Do you need to call your mom this morning?" he asked.

When Morgan had made her call home the night before, her mom had chewed her out for calling so late and told her to call in the mornings, at least until they got to Quebec. Morgan had said very little in reply and Josh was surprised she hadn't blown her stack.

"Nah," Morgan said. "I just talked to her. I'll call tomorrow morning from wherever we are."

She scooted off to the bathroom, snagging her duffel bag on the way. When the shower started, he finished dressing.

Ten minutes later, they were checking out.

A young woman with short dark hair worked the desk. "Good morning. Did you and your girlfriend enjoy your stay?"

"It was short but pleasant enough. We're on our way home after almost a month of being away and have a long way to go," Josh said and smiled at Morgan.

"Almost a month? Well, you know what they say; you can't go home again." She pulled the bill off the printer and slid it over to Josh. "Where're you headed?"

"We live in a little town on the coast of New Brunswick," Morgan said while Josh signed the bill.

"That's in Canada, right?"

"It is," Josh said. "Thank you for your hospitality."

"Thank you for visiting. Have a safe trip."

Josh put his wallet away. "We'll give it a good try."

The clerk waved and said, "Good luck," as they walked out to Zinger.

Josh put his gear in the trunk and Morgan offered to drive.

"Sure you're up for it?" Josh asked.

She nodded. "I'm better now. We're past Butte and that much closer to home. Thanks for letting me sleep in."

Josh laughed. "You're welcome, but I woke up only a few minutes before you did."

"Well, thank you anyway."

After another fast-food breakfast, Josh reset Morgan's watch and Zinger's clock. It didn't take Morgan long to get back on Interstate 15 heading north, but she didn't drive quite as fast as she had yesterday.

They crossed the Missouri River several times. Josh reflected on how the waters below them would someday enter the Gulf of Mexico many thousands of miles away.

And here they were, still over two thousand miles from home. Again, the thought came to him that home was wherever Morgan was. If she had decided to stay in Seattle, he would have stayed as well.

Morgan didn't seem to be in a chatty mood this morning, but she didn't seem particularly unhappy. Josh had tried to strike up a conversation several times, only to have it drift off.

As they neared Great Falls, Morgan said, "Josh?"

"Yes, Angel?"

She smiled. "You called me your girlfriend this morning."

"No, the clerk called you my girlfriend," Josh replied.

"But you said nothing to correct her."

"Well, we didn't have time to tell her about our relationship and . . ."

"And?" Morgan let the question hang.

"And . . . it's pretty obvious to everyone we meet that we're a couple. I mean Sally sees it, Aunt Peggy sees it . . ."

"We do seem to get that a lot," Morgan said.

"We seem to be the only ones that don't see it," Josh said.

Morgan smiled slyly. "Maybe we ought to do something about that?"

"Maybe we should."

"Okay, and . . . " Yeah, she let the question hang again.

"Do you want me to do this while you're driving?"

"I'm not expecting you to propose to me. You're not, are you?"

"No. I mean not now, but maybe someday." Josh turned red as he stumbled over his words.

She laughed but then said, "Sorry. It's okay, go ahead. If I get too emotional, grab the wheel and get us to the shoulder."

"Er, okay." Josh cleared his throat and his mouth was suddenly very dry. "Morgan Parker, Angel, will you be my girlfriend?"

Morgan started blinking hard. A few tears rolled down her cheek. She gripped the wheel with one hand and brushed away tears with the other.

Josh put his hand on the wheel but she said, "I'm okay."

Nevertheless, she put the turn signal on and drove onto the shoulder. Once she'd put the car in park, Morgan threw her arms around Josh's neck and tugged him toward her.

"Yes, Josh. Yes I will be your girlfriend. You don't know how happy this makes me."

She drew her arms back and wrapped them around his head to give him perhaps the most passionate kiss to date.

"Remind me not to propose to you while you're driving," Josh said.

She let go and punched him softly on the shoulder. "Jerk."

"What?"

"You could have let me enjoy the moment a little longer," she said and put Zinger back in gear.

"We'll celebrate properly when we stop for the night early enough to eat at a decent restaurant."

"You have yourself a deal, Mr. Hampton."

They arrived in the Great Falls area ten minutes later and pulled off at the first gas station they saw.

Since there was no line at the counter inside and no one telling ghost stories, Josh made it back to the car before Morgan finished pumping the gas. He spread the map of Montana on the warm hood.

Morgan joined him and wiped her hands with some towels from the window washing station. “What are you doing?”

“Looking at the rest of our route for today.”

“We should have done that last night.”

“We got in late and by the time I took a shower, you were already asleep,” Josh pointed out.

“So, what are our options?” she asked.

He traced Interstate 15 with his finger. “We could stay on I-15 and cross the border here.”

She frowned. “That’s kinda going west isn’t it?”

“Northwest, but not that far west,” he said, but suspected it would be too far for Morgan’s liking.

“What’s this road? It’s going east. Highway 87?”

“Yes, US 87. It won’t be as nice as the interstate, but it’s not a country road.”

“Let’s take that one,” Morgan decided. “It’s going east, and home is east.”

“It’ll be slower than the interstate; the roads aren’t built for speed.”

“You drive then.”

Josh folded the map and dug into his pocket for his key to Zinger. Before he could walk far, Morgan drew him into a hug. “Hold on. I want to finish that kiss first.”

They locked lips and got lost in the kiss until Josh broke it off.

“We best get going or someone’s going to tell us to get a room,” he whispered with their lips only inches apart.

“Mm, yeah.” She smiled wider than the Cheshire cat and slid into the passenger seat.

Once they were back on the road after an uneventful early lunch, Josh was struck with an out-of-the-blue thought.

What have I done?

What he had done was acquired a girlfriend, one he acknowledged as such. And not just any girl; he had chosen Morgan. What amazed him even more was that she'd accepted.

But what did it mean, really? It meant they had committed to getting to know each other better without having to stress over the whole dating scene. Josh couldn't see a problem with that.

He liked the look of her. He liked the scent of her, her softness, and the taste of her lips. She was fun to be around. They joked about proposing, but it wasn't beyond the realm of possibility. They just needed to figure out if they loved each other first.

Wasn't that what his sister had said? Love is the most important thing?

He laughed when he imagined what his friend Shack would think about this. But Shack had his own priorities and, Josh suspected, a lot of heartbreak in his future – if not for him, at least for the women who had succumbed to his charm.

"What do you think she meant?" Morgan asked.

Her question pulled Josh out of his reverie. "What who meant?"

"The clerk this morning when she said, 'You can't go home again.'"

"Since we obviously can go home physically, she must have meant metaphorically," Josh said.

"You have a point. I guess the town will have changed since we left. Some babies will have been born, some people will have died, some people may have moved in, and some may have moved out. And maybe Matthew's damned tooth will finally be in." She laughed.

"True. It won't be exactly the same place we left. When we were in Bathurst, the changes happened around us; but because we were there, we were part of the changes," he said.

They spent the rest of the drive speculating about things that might have changed and things they hoped had changed back home.

At a small town in the northern part of Montana, they switched over to Highway 2. They followed it into North Dakota and a new time zone before stopping for the night in the sleepy little town of Minot.

There was no hesitation when they chose a single room at the hotel. The last thing Josh saw that night was Morgan smiling at him from her bed.

He smiled back. *I have a girlfriend now.*

His thoughts darkened as they turned to Trixie. She would see his return as an opportunity. And she was not likely to accept no as an answer.

Chapter 6

In Which Morgan Finds a Diversion
Saturday, August 26, 1995

Morgan could not have been happier as she lay in bed watching Josh sleep. The clock showed almost seven, but she wasn't in a hurry today. For the life of her, she couldn't recall why she'd been rushing to get home at all.

Ever since they started out on the road home, she'd been anxious to get back and begin her new life. But really, her new life was right here in this motel room, snoring softly just feet away. And her boyfriend had even managed to make it through the night without discarding his blankets.

Morgan sighed happily and leaned back on her pillow, enjoying a proper stretch. They'd be back in Bathurst soon enough. After yesterday's discussion about what may or may not be waiting for them there, she decided Josh was right. There was no harm in enjoying themselves a bit during this trip.

She was still a bit disappointed in herself for her nervous breakdown on Thursday, but it didn't seem to have fazed Josh at all. In fact, it was almost as if it strengthened their fledging relationship. Still, she was in no hurry to repeat the episode. How silly she'd been, thinking Josh was hesitant to commit to her. He was just nervous. She never should have doubted him.

Morgan turned back to find Josh awake and smiling at her.

"Good morning, Angel."

"Good morning." She grinned. "Ready for another day on the road?"

"With you? Always," he replied. "And you should be happy we're only about an hour from the border now."

"I am happy. But not just for that reason. Why don't you go ahead and use the bathroom first? I'll make my call." Morgan rolled her eyes toward the phone.

"Good luck."

Josh flipped the covers off, Morgan sighed, and he grabbed his bag on his way to the bathroom. She picked up the phone and dialed her home number. It was answered on the second ring by . . . Matthew?

She pulled the receiver away from her ear and grimaced. She did not miss the sound of his screaming in the slightest.

Morgan waited until it quieted down and she could hear her mom's voice before returning the phone to her ear.

"Mom?"

"Morgan, sorry. Matthew's a bit fussy today."

Just today, huh? Aloud, Morgan said, "He's answering the phone now?" and forced a laugh.

"He's chewing on the phone. Matthew, enough!"

"I won't keep you," Morgan said, wondering why her mom couldn't put her brother down long enough to talk to her. "I just wanted to give you a quick call. We're in North Dakota and should be crossing the border shortly."

"That's great news. You'll be home in no time."

"It'll be a while yet. I've decided I want to do some more sightseeing along the way. Might as well enjoy the trip."

Morgan's mom was silent. Was she going to start in on her?

Nope. Matthew had possession of the phone again. Morgan sighed and waited until her mom regained control of it. At least he wasn't screaming anymore, but Morgan hadn't called to listen to her brother's gibberish.

"Morgan, why don't you give me a call a bit later when your brother's calmed down?"

"No. I just called to check in. I've checked."

Morgan's mom either didn't hear the annoyance in Morgan's voice, or she chose to ignore it. "Okay. Drive safe today."

"Will do. Bye."

Morgan hung up the phone and heard water running in the bathroom. Was Josh showering? Weird. He normally did that at night. She got up and pulled the piece of cardboard with Mel's number on it out of her wallet. It seemed as good a time as any to give her a call.

Or not. As soon as Mel answered the phone and Morgan announced who was calling, she hung up.

Morgan sat staring at the phone, stung. How could she still be so mad? Sure, Mel had been angry because she'd gotten in trouble for keeping Morgan's travel plans a secret, but really? That was weeks ago. She'd moved out and started university since then.

Josh emerged from the bathroom and gave Morgan a concerned look. "Your parents give you a hard time?"

She placed the receiver back on the hook. "No, not them. I tried calling Mel."

"Was she not home?"

"Oh, she was home all right. She hung up on me."

"Are you sure? Maybe it was an accident."

"Oh, no. She pounded it pretty hard." Morgan shook her head and got up from the bed. "She'll get over it eventually. I guess today's just not the day."

Josh placed his bag on the bed and Morgan dodged his attempt for a hug. "No fair. I've got to brush my teeth first."

He laughed and flopped down on his bed while she took her bag into the bathroom to get ready.

When Morgan was finished, she made up for the delay by flinging herself at Josh and wrapping him in a tight embrace filled with minty-fresh kisses.

It was a few minutes before they parted, both slightly out of breath and flustered. Morgan hadn't realized how close they'd come to sinking all the way down onto the bed.

"I'm checking us out today," she announced, turning away to fix her hair and willing her flushed cheeks to cool.

"Want me to come?"

"No. Just take the stuff out to the car, okay? I think we could both use a minute."

She glanced at Josh, who looked a bit relieved.

"Sorry. I didn't mean to . . ." Josh trailed off.

"Heh. You weren't smooching yourself there. We should probably both watch that." Morgan turned back to him and gave him a peck on the lips and a sweet smile before grabbing her purse and the room keys. "Meet you at Zinger?"

"Absolutely."

Morgan had a spring in her step as she approached the counter to check out. The man at the desk was super friendly. He chattered on about the city of Minot and asked if they'd had time to see any of the attractions.

"What attractions?"

"Oh my, you mean you haven't enjoyed the city at all? Well, let me tell you . . ."

The man had a tourism pamphlet open on the desk and was listing off all the sights before Morgan could stop him. She was only half-listening and thinking of a way to stop him when something in the brochure caught her attention.

"Is that a zoo?" she asked, cutting him off mid-sentence.

"It certainly is," he said, not minding her interruption. He began to launch into a detailed history of the place, but Morgan placed her hand on the pamphlet and smiled sweetly.

"Would you be so kind as to give me directions? My boyfriend and I might like to check it out before we leave."

Morgan left the building with directions and a grin. Josh had brought Zinger around front and stepped out of the car when he saw her. She motioned for him to get back in and hopped in on the passenger side.

"What say we go to the zoo?" she asked with a grin.

"A zoo? Here?" Josh looked surprised but pleased. "Of course. Do you know where it is?"

She handed him the paper the man had written directions on and they were off.

It wasn't long before they were parked and heading hand in hand to the admissions booth. Josh paid for their entry and they linked arms to stroll through the grounds.

"So, I hope I don't regret asking this, but what changed your mind about getting home as soon as possible?"

Morgan leaned her head on his shoulder. "I guess I realized you were right. We should be enjoying our time together. And each other." She raised her head in expectance of a kiss. She wasn't disappointed.

"Oh, look at that!" Morgan took off running toward a pen.

Josh followed behind at his regular pace and stopped a few feet from the fence. "What *is* that?"

"I don't know. It doesn't have any signs."

Morgan stood touching the fence, face to face with . . . the creature. It looked a bit like a buffalo, but the horns were something else. They were curled but probably at least six feet long. The mangy brown animal would have towered over Morgan had they been on even ground, but the enclosure was low enough for her to stare straight into its mouth, which appeared to be curved in a smile. It hung slightly open, revealing boulder-sized chompers.

"Morgan, don't touch that thing," Josh warned as her hand began reaching out.

"Dude, it's standing right here. I'll never get a chance like this again. Not in Canada. They keep the animals all spread out so they can roam there. A lot more humane, yes, but there's no way I'm not petting this guy."

"He'll take your arm off!"

"Don't be silly. Besides, we're really close to the border if he does. If you have to, just floor it so we don't have to pay for medical attention in the States." Morgan reached out with a slight squeal and stroked the beast's fur on the side if its neck. "Josh! He's so fuzzy!"

"Okay." Josh had hold of her other arm and pulled her back ever so slowly. "You've pet it. Let's go."

Morgan relented and waved goodbye to her furry friend. Josh wiped sweat from his brow.

"Look at the duck pond!" Morgan was off again. She stopped at the duck food dispenser. "Do you have any change?"

Josh sighed and dug in his pocket until he found a couple of quarters. Morgan filled both their hands with duck treats, and they wandered along the edge of the pond where the ducks waited expectantly.

By the time they were down to their last morsels, Josh was relaxed and enjoying himself. Morgan was resigned to the fact she was not going to get to pet a duck. Unless . . .

She noticed another girl about her age with long dark hair leaning over the bridge in the middle of the pond. She was reaching out and she was so close.

Morgan gasped as the girl tumbled headfirst over the railing into the water. Ducks fled quacking as the girl sat waist deep in the water, alternating between laughing and screaming.

Josh had come running back from the other side of the pond at the sound of the first scream. He put his hand to his chest when he saw Morgan wasn't in peril, and the girl who had fallen was being helped up by a young bald man.

"You thought that was me, didn't you?" Morgan glared at Josh but couldn't hide a smile.

"You blame me?"

"Not at all. I was going to try it next." Morgan broke out in laughter. "Lesson learned."

Josh checked his watch. "How about we grab an early lunch and head out? Unless you want to see more."

"No, that's fine. I'm just glad we got to spend some time together that was not in Zinger and not in a motel room."

They linked arms again and walked over to a hot dog stand. They sat and ate at a picnic table in the shade.

"Looks like it's going to be another warm one," Josh commented as he bit into his hot dog.

"It sure does. We'll have to crank the air conditioning." Morgan snickered and wiped ketchup off Josh's cheek, letting her finger linger on the corner of his mouth, which she tapped. "Think you'll be able to control this thing when we cross that border?"

"Funny. But actually, I do have a plan for that."

"Really?" Morgan quirked a brow.

"Really. I'm going to let you drive *and* do all the talking."

The hour-long drive up to the border was indeed a hot one. There weren't many trees for shade and the sun beat mercilessly down on them.

This border crossing station was far different from the last one they'd gone through in Sault Ste. Marie. Morgan turned down the air conditioning that had been blowing full blast and rolled down her window as she approached the gate.

It was a yellow wooden gate that she figured she could easily drive around. A small building sat to their right and no one was in sight. Morgan looked at Josh and shrugged.

A moment later, a tall man in uniform came out of the building and sauntered over to Zinger's driver's side.

"Documentation?"

Morgan dug out her driver's licence and registration and handed them to the man. Josh pulled out his wallet.

"How long have you been in the States?" the officer asked.

"Um, a couple of weeks. We were visiting relatives," Morgan said, hoping to clear up some of the questions right away.

"Anything to declare?"

"Not really. I guess I bought some clothes and stuff, but how much does it have to be?"

"Over five hundred dollars."

"Oh, then no."

The man handed her papers back, tipped his hat, and walked over to the gate.

Morgan turned to Josh whose mouth was hanging open, his unopened wallet still in his hand. "If we ever come back to the States, we're crossing here," he said.

Morgan laughed and waved to the officer as she drove into Canada. "Remember, the U.S. agent would be a different person."

"Whatever. You're still doing the talking."

Josh opened the original map of Canada that had come with Zinger and found the quickest way up to the Trans-Canada Highway.

Happy to be back on Canadian soil, the drive flew by for Morgan. Josh had another one of his naps, and signs for Winnipeg soon appeared on the roadside.

"Josh!" Morgan squealed.

"What?" He sat straight up in his seat, his hat falling to the floor. "How long –"

"Don't you dare ask me how long you slept." Morgan laughed and ruffled his hair. "We're coming into Winnipeg and I saw a huge sign for the zoo. Please, can we stop?"

"Are you serious? Another zoo?"

"Yes, please? I had such a good time."

Josh shrugged. "I don't mind. I suppose we'll have to stop and ask for directions."

"Sure. We need gas anyway."

Morgan pulled into a gas station and asked Josh to pump while she went in to use the washroom, pay, and get directions.

When she emerged, Josh was back in the passenger seat. She threw herself into the driver's seat, hardly able to contain her excitement.

"You are never going to believe this!" Morgan squealed.

"They have two zoos?" Josh guessed.

"No. The zoo's closed."

"What's with the maniacal grin then? You're freaking me out."

"Drinking age here is eighteen."

Chapter 7

In Which They Drink Legally
Saturday, August 26, 1995

"I suppose you'll want to go to the zoo in the morning," Josh said, focusing on Morgan's recent obsession with zoos rather than the fact they could drink legally.

"Maybe. We can figure it out tomorrow, can't we?"

"It might mean another night in a hotel," he said.

"What's wrong with that? Are you worried about travel time or money? Do we need to be more careful with our funds?" she asked.

"No, no. Well, maybe."

"Which is it? Yes, no, or maybe?"

"We're doing well, but we want to keep a reserve for the unexpected. I don't think either of us want to call home and ask for more money," Josh said.

"I wouldn't mind seeing the zoo and comparing it to the other zoo, but we'll see how we feel in the morning. I may be too hung over to want to do anything but climb into Zinger and curl up in agony."

"I hope you don't get that drunk." *I hope I don't puke again.*

"Hey, let's enjoy the night and deal with the consequences tomorrow," Morgan declared.

Josh had mixed feelings about Morgan's proclamation. Although he'd been aware they'd crossed into Manitoba, it hadn't even crossed his mind that they could legally drink in this province.

It seemed, though, something was on Morgan's mind as she drove past several hotels that might have been suitable, even affordable.

"Are you looking for a particular color of hotel?" Josh asked.

"I'm looking for one that has a lounge – it should say on the sign."

"There are plenty of bars around."

"Yes, but if the hotel has a lounge in it, we can both drink," Morgan said.

Josh laughed.

"What's funny about that?"

"Shack would never be that considerate," Josh said.

"That's your friend back home, right? The one you were with at the party?"

"That's him all right. But he's off to college now."

"Let me guess," Morgan said. "You were always the designated driver?"

"Got it in one."

"Lucky for you, I'm a lot nicer than he is."

"A lot cuter too," Josh said, brushing the back of his fingers on her cheek.

"Hey, no distracting the driver," Morgan said, laughing. "Oh, here's one." She pulled into the entry of the Northwoods Hotel, which clearly advertised a lounge.

In an unusual act of trust, Morgan allowed the valet to park Zinger while they went inside to register.

Once registered, they went to their room to clean up and change.

While Morgan was showering, Josh used the room's ironing board to smooth out some wrinkles in his green button-down shirt.

Morgan came out of the bathroom in her purple blouse and new jeans. "I guess I should have gotten some nice pants to go with this shirt," she said, examining herself in the mirror.

"No one is going to be looking at your legs."

She looked down at the front of her shirt. "No one's going to be looking at my chest, that's for sure."

"There's more to beauty than a woman's cup size," Josh said.

Morgan laughed. "If I hadn't seen you in your boxers, I'd have to wonder if you're really a guy."

"Not all guys think like Shack."

"There's that name again. I hope he's not your sole source of knowledge about women."

"Thankfully, no. My *maman* gave me a lot of talks."

"I'm not sure that's any better. You're not a mama's boy, are you?" she asked, eyeing him carefully.

"I don't think so. She had to fill in where my dad failed. Wait, how did we get on this topic?"

"You were dissing my legs," Morgan said.

"I was trying to say you're beautiful and everyone will be looking at your face."

"Well, if you would have just said that we could have saved a lot of time. Come over here and kiss me before we go."

"As you wish," Josh said and complied with her request.

"You should think about leaving your hat behind for the night. I'm the only one you need to impress, and I've already accepted your short ass."

Josh hesitated before tossing it on the dresser.

Downstairs, the lounge was quiet. Soft instrumental music drifted from overhead speakers. Only a few other couples occupied the lounge where a big screen TV over the bar was tuned to a baseball game. Josh sat with his back to the screen.

Morgan frowned. "I thought there would be more action than this."

"Yeah. Even I thought it would be livelier. Tell you what, let's get something to eat and if it doesn't pick up, we can go somewhere else."

"That's reasonable, and I am kinda hungry," she said.

Morgan ordered a steak, extra rare, with a small side salad. Josh ordered the house lasagna without a salad. They each had a glass of wine to get the evening started but agreed they should probably stick to drinking beer the rest of the night to keep the bar bill down.

By time they set their forks on their plates, a middle-aged woman in a black jumpsuit took a seat at the grand piano. Most of Josh's wine remained in the glass.

Taking the initiative, Josh asked for the check. After paying for the meals, drinks, and tip, he noted that he'd just spent about a night's stay at a hotel.

As they stood to leave, Morgan picked up Josh's glass and downed it. "No sense letting it go to waste." She grinned.

At the desk, the concierge gave them directions to several nightclubs in the downtown area and offered to have the hotel van take them to one. Josh declined, but the gentleman handed him a card. "If you need a ride back to the hotel, just call. The ride is free."

The evening was warm enough for them to walk to the closest club. Music reached them from a block away.

"Now that's more like it," Morgan said. She grabbed Josh's hand and tugged to get him to speed up.

"Are you even listening to what they're playing? You said you didn't like country music."

"Oh come on, get that stick out of the mud. We're young, in . . . in a big city, and we're going to make this a night to remember."

Josh could only shake his head. He hoped it would be memorable in a good way, but there was no telling what an alcohol-fueled night would bring. He imagined she would want to dance, too. Well, he supposed he could press her body to his and shuffle around some.

At the door, the bouncer checked their IDs and stamped their hands. They had hardly gotten inside when Morgan let loose a "Yee-haw!"

Josh scanned the room and located an open table, tapping her on the shoulder and pointing. He was glad to see that not everyone in the crowd wore a cowboy hat. His ball cap would have had plenty of company, but he wasn't going to fuss about it.

The jostled their way to the table and ordered long neck beers. Josh wasn't sure how the beer would mix with wine, but Morgan didn't seem to care.

When the band began the next song, Morgan grinned at him. "Come on, let's dance."

Josh followed her out to the dance floor. An area by the stage had a dozen or more dancers performing some sort of organized, coordinated dance, which he believed was called line dancing. However, enough people were wiggling to the music that he didn't care. Although the lyrics had a country theme, there was enough of a tempo that he didn't feel entirely awkward.

In between songs, Morgan powered down her beer and replaced it with a fresh one.

They danced several more times and Josh became increasingly relaxed as he drank more of his beer.

The band wrapped up their set and Josh managed to find another table before they all filled up.

"Thank y'all for coming out tonight. While the High Country Heroes get set up, the management would like to invite the guests to try their voices. The karaoke mic is open for the next half hour."

The audience cheered and a brunette took the karaoke stage. As she sang, Morgan cringed. "I can sing better than that."

Before Josh could stop her, she was already plowing her way to the stage. She told the DJ her selection and took up the mic.

"I would like to dedicate this song to Josh, the man of my wife – life – I meant life."

The audience laughed and Josh ached for her. She looked like she was going to walk off stage, but the music started. As the intro finished, Morgan lifted the microphone and began to sing "Angel of the Morning."

A hush spread across the bar starting from near the stage and stretching across the room as Morgan poured heart and soul into the song. Josh had listened to her sing in the car, but this was something else. He was hearing the voice of an angel, his Angel. He may have fallen in love with her at that moment because she was singing every word to him.

The song ended and she raised the mic in the air. She had killed the song. She knew it and the audience knew it. The applause was thunderous.

Morgan beamed as she walked back to the table, giving high-fives to all that extended a hand to her.

Josh simply looked at her and asked, "How?"

She shrugged, lifted the beer bottle, and slaked her thirst.

"You were amazing, Angel," he said.

"Maybe I got something more from my bio-dad than these green eyes."

"Which are amazingly beautiful, if I may say."

"You certainly may." She scanned the room for a server, but they were all busy refilling drinks while the next band set up. "Dammit, I need another beer. Please go fetch us some, my handsome mechanic?"

"Woof, woof." Josh laughed and navigated through the crowd to the bar.

It took him several minutes to get the bartender's attention, grab a beer and a Coke, and return to the table. A tall man with a thick beard was talking and smoking with Morgan.

Josh's anger flared and he pushed the man aside, inserting himself between him and Morgan. "Excuse me, but this is my woman."

"Whoa, hey dude, I was just telling her what a wonderful singer she is and she asked for a cigarette. I meant nothing by it."

Josh turned to Morgan.

"Cool down," she said with a frown. "He's telling the truth."

"If you're the one she was singing for, you're one lucky dude," the interloper said, offering a hand. "No hard feelings?"

Josh accepted the handshake and tried to grip back as hard as he was being gripped.

"Thanks for the cigarette," Morgan said with a smile, and waved as he left their table.

"If you wanted a cigarette, I would have gotten some for you," Josh said, trying his best to keep the irritation out of his voice.

"Didn't know I wanted one until he came up with one." She shrugged. "Can we talk about something else?"

"Fine. Are you having a good time?"

"My God, yes. Thanks for bringing me here."

They shared a quick kiss as the High Country Heroes took the stage. They hadn't gotten three songs into their set when Morgan said, "This is the main band? The other band was better."

"I hope you don't expect me to try dancing to that."

"I'd rather try dancing to the lounge music back at the hotel. At least we could lean on each other."

"Shall we leave then?" Josh asked.

"Yeah. Go call the hotel while I finish my beer?"

Josh agreed. When he returned to the table, Morgan had finished his soda too.

"Sorry, I was thirsty," she said with an apologetic grin.

"It's okay, the van will be here in a few minutes."

"Enough time to run to the facilities."

She made it outside before the van arrived. The evening air was chilly, so Josh stood behind her and wrapped his arms around her.

Ten minutes later, they were back at the Northwoods Hotel.

Morgan was a bit unsteady and leaned on Josh as they peeked into the lounge. It had become a bit busier. The pianist was still playing and a couple was dancing to a slow tune.

"I don't want to dance to this either," Morgan declared.

Josh happily led the way back to their room.

"It's too early to go to bed," Morgan said as she sat at the table. "Hand me the stationery and a pen, please."

Josh pulled the items out of the drawer and passed them to her. Morgan started folding and tearing the stationery.

"What are you doing?" Josh asked.

"Making cards so we can play."

"Oh, no need for that. I bought some in Seattle."

"Ooh, even better," Morgan said, tossing the torn bits into the trash. She placed what was left of the notepad on the dresser. "Fish them out."

Josh put them on the table and she opened the box.

"You got cards with the Space Needle on them?"

"I thought my sister might like them," Josh said.

"Tourist. Hey, let's get a pizza – pepperoni with extra cheese."

"I'm still full. I don't think we can eat a whole pizza."

"What we don't eat we can have for breakfast. Get some beer too," Morgan said and started breaking in the cards.

Josh called the pizza place that advertised delivery to the hotel and then called room service for the beer.

"So what are we playing?" He asked as he sat at the table.

Morgan grinned and said, "Strip poker. Prepare to lose your shirt."

"What are the rules?"

"It's like poker, except when you lose, you have to remove an article of clothing."

"I know what strip poker is," Josh said. "I meant the specific rules. Is each shoe and sock a separate item?"

"I'll allow it for tonight."

"You're such a generous woman."

"It doesn't matter, I'm going to beat the pants off you," Morgan said.

"How about we wait until we get our deliveries before removing clothes?"

She agreed and they started playing. At first, Morgan won most of the hands, but by the time the beer and pizza had arrived, they were pretty even.

After consuming a slice of pizza and half a beer, Morgan shuffled the cards, slapped them on the table and said, "Cut. High card gets first deal."

Josh pulled the seven of clubs and Morgan got the ace of hearts. She waggled her eyebrows at him. "Time to get serious."

They played for a half an hour, during which time Morgan had finished her first beer and was well into the next. The piles of clothing next to each of them served as witness to the fact that they had both won their share of hands. Now, Josh sat with only his boxers on. Morgan still had her underwear and purple blouse.

Morgan dealt the next hand. Josh looked at his cards and felt confident he had the win. She had called for five-card draw. He'd taken only one card, but she'd taken two.

"Call," she said.

Morgan laid her hand down. She had two pair, aces over nines.

Josh placed his cards on the table. He had three queens.

"As you say, *merde*."

"It's okay, Angel. We can stop now."

"Would you have removed your boxers if I'd won?"

He nodded

"Fair's fair then," she said and unbuttoned the top button of her blouse.

Josh found he was holding his breath and took a shallow gulp of air.

She was removing the buttons slowly. She wasn't teasing him; her coordination was affected by the drinks.

When she reached the bottom button, she gave up and tried to pull the blouse over her head. When she got stuck she called, "Help?"

Josh got up and rounded the table. He pulled the blouse free and dropped it to the floor. She looked up at him as he looked down at her. Josh had seen a woman's bare breasts before, but only in the magazines in Shack's car. It was nothing compared to this. His body reacted instantly.

Morgan stood and wrapped her arms around him. They remained standing skin to skin, studying each other's eyes before pushing their lips together in a passionate kiss. He picked her up and carried her to her bed, tossing the covers aside.

He settled her on the bed as she clung to his neck. She drew him down and he began covering her face and neck with kisses.

Their desire rose as they caressed each other. Josh started to remove his boxers but stopped. “*Merde*.”

“What?”

“I’ll be right back.”

“Hurry.”

Josh reluctantly climbed out of the bed and went to find his wallet. It wasn’t in his pants. He dug around the mess of clothing and beer bottles before he remembered setting it down after paying for the pizza. He trudged to the door where he found his wallet and removed the condom he had there.

By the time he got back to Morgan’s bed, she had fallen asleep.

Josh pulled the covers over her. He took a long shower before going to his own bed.

Chapter 8

In Which the Road is Treacherous
Sunday, August 27, 1995

Morgan poked her head out of the bathroom door. Thankfully, Josh was still asleep. She wasn't ready to get into all the talking yet.

Morgan finished drying her hair and draped the towel around her neck. She left her bag in the bathroom and took only her comb back to bed with her. She sat on the bed, studying Josh in the near-dark room.

Morgan ran the comb through her hair as she gazed at her slumbering boyfriend. She was pretty sure she was falling in love with him.

She was also pretty sure she'd come close to screwing everything up last night.

What the hell had she been thinking?

The answer was simple. She hadn't been thinking. She'd been determined to drink and dance the night away, consequences be damned.

If Josh hadn't stopped when he did, she could have been waking up to some pretty severe consequences instead of just a throbbing head.

Josh stirred and Morgan's heart leapt. His eyes opened and she sat frozen, comb poised above her head. He looked at her and smiled a sleepy smile before his eyes focused and then grew dark.

They both spoke at once.

"I'm sorry."

Morgan started to laugh and grimaced as another pain shot through her head. She set the comb down on the bed. "What in the world are you sorry about?"

"I . . . I almost –"

"*We* almost made a mistake," Morgan corrected him. "But I'm pretty sure it wasn't your idea to drink all night and play strip poker."

"It's not your fault," Josh said. "It's no one's fault because nothing happened. Well, some stuff happened but not that."

"I'm not confused," Morgan told him. "Well, there are a few foggy bits, but I know we didn't sleep together."

"That's right, we didn't."

"We came really close though." Morgan picked up the comb again. Her hair didn't need this much attention, but she wanted to keep her hands busy. "And I don't think I was the one who came to my senses in time . . ."

Josh chewed on his lip and said nothing.

"Why did you stop?" she finally asked.

It was hard to see the expression on Josh's face in the faint light coming through the curtains, but she could tell he had looked away.

"We're not ready," was all he said.

Not ready? Part of it might have been the alcohol. But physically, she was ready. And she was pretty sure Josh was too.

"Not emotionally, no," Morgan said. "Obviously, we need to be more careful. And I'm sorry I drank so much. But otherwise, can we not make a big deal about this?"

"But it is a big deal," Josh said, turning back to her, "and it's something we should talk about."

"Absolutely. But not today. Next topic?"

"We'll let it go for now," he agreed. "How are you feeling?"

"I feel like I got run over by a semi," Morgan groaned. "You?"

"Not too bad. With a little coffee I'll be fine."

"Right. You didn't even have any beer after we got back, did you?"

"Not much. I guess I'm driving today, huh?"

"If you wouldn't mind. I might still be a bit drunk," Morgan said. "Sorry I'm kind of pulling a Shack move after all."

That got a laugh out of him. "Trust me, you're nothing like Shack."

"Good to know. Do we need to plan a route today?" Morgan asked.

"We can if you want, but we're basically going to be heading east on the Trans-Canada from now on."

"East it is." Morgan got up from the bed. "My headache thanks you. I'll go pay for the room. It's the least I can do."

"My wallet thanks you," Josh said with a chuckle. "Do you want some of the breakfast pizza?"

"No. You go ahead. My stomach is closed for business."

By the time Morgan got back to the room, it was just after nine and Josh was packed and ready to go.

"Thanks for cleaning up the mess," Morgan said, nodding to the beer cans and trash stacked neatly by the door.

"Anything for my Angel," he said.

"How about a kiss? I really don't want things to be weird between us."

Josh obliged. As soon as their lips connected, Morgan's remaining tension dissolved.

The sky was dark with clouds as they set out. Rain began to fall just as they left the city behind. Josh turned on the headlights and set the wipers on low.

"Eeps. This isn't a shower," Morgan said as a flash of lightning lit up the sky. "I guess we should have checked the weather last night."

"I was busy losing my shirt," Josh said as he turned Zinger's wipers on high. "Hopefully it clears up soon. At least it's four-lane here."

"Yeah, and it's the Prairies. What's that saying? They're so flat you can watch your dog run away for three days or something?"

"Not in this weather, but they got the flat part right."

Morgan's eyes kept drooping and popping open. Josh noticed.

"You can go ahead and sleep, you know," he said. "It helps pass the time."

"You know I can't. My head may be killing me, but every time I start to fall asleep in a moving car I feel like I'm falling out of bed and get startled awake." She waved a hand. "It doesn't make sense, I know. Just the way I'm built."

Josh looked like he was trying to keep a straight face.

"Joshua Hampton, if you're thinking of making fun of the way I'm built . . ."

"I'm not," he protested, holding up a hand like he was taking an oath, but the laugh broke free. "You walked into that one."

Morgan laughed too. "I'll admit I did."

Her drowsiness continued as they crossed into Ontario. She almost nodded off several times but jerked back awake every time.

Josh wasn't very talkative. Morgan figured he was more hungover than he wanted to admit. Unless he was just doing that brooding thing again.

Whatever the reason, they both perked up as the highway merged into two lanes and they drove into . . .

"Are we in the mountains?" Morgan asked, sitting up straight, her eyes wide.

"I think this is the Canadian Shield," Josh said.

Steep cliffs of jagged rock lined the roadside, some as tall as a hundred feet. The shoulders of the highway were narrow, and Morgan doubted any cars larger than Zinger would fit on them. Beyond, the terrain dropped almost straight down into groves of trees.

Josh fiddled with the wipers but they were already wiping as fast as they could. A bolt of lighting flashed across the sky.

"Deer!" Morgan squealed as an animal shot out in front of them onto the highway.

Josh pressed on the brakes while checking the rearview mirror. Morgan looked behind them and saw another car do the same just in time.

"*Merde.* Keep an eye out for more of those, Angel?" His voice was a little shaky.

"I will, but it's hard to see through the rain."

The road became increasingly twisty and it was impossible to see past the vehicles ahead, yet the highway was painted with passing lines. Josh squinted his eyes to see through the window the wipers were barely keeping clear.

"Why isn't this a solid line?" Morgan asked while keeping her eyes peeled for leaping critters.

"Hell if I know." Josh had come up to a vehicle traveling way under the speed limit. "I can't see to pass."

"This has got to end soon, doesn't it?"

"Depends on which way the weather is moving."

"I was talking about the road."

Morgan cringed as a semi came up fast behind them. It rode their bumper while pulling in and out in an attempt to pass them.

"Are they nuts?" She ducked down in her seat, not that it would do her any good in the horrific pileup that was bound to ensue.

The semi made its move and whipped past them, rocking the car.

"Must be nice to be able to see from up there," Josh muttered.

Morgan sat up again as she remembered she was supposed to be watching for –

"Deer!"

Josh swiveled his head and the car drifted slightly over the line into incoming traffic. "Where?"

"Not here. Sorry. Josh, cars!"

A horn sounded and Josh straightened Zinger out with only feet to spare. He wiped a free hand across his forehead. The other gripped the wheel tightly.

"Shit. I'm really sorry. The deer was down in the ditch." Morgan was close to tears.

"It's okay. We're okay," Josh assured her.

Another semi flew past and he muttered something under his breath. Morgan was willing to bet one of those words had to be *merde*.

In a blessedly straight stretch of road, they passed the slow-moving vehicle in front of them. Morgan shook her head at the tiny little man with gray hair who was driving. He could barely see over the steering wheel.

It seemed like forever before they came to the city of Kenora. Josh took the first exit and stopped at a gas station. No discussion required.

Morgan again offered to pay for the gas to make up for last night's spending. Inside, she spent a fair amount of time in the washroom composing herself. She also added a small item to her gas purchase and tucked it quickly into her wallet.

Her inclination was to flee as soon as she had paid, but she decided she was too old to be embarrassed about buying condoms. Instead, she asked the lady at the counter about the highway heading east.

"Oh, it gets better very soon. You've come through the hardest part. That mustn't have been pleasant, what with the rain today. Where are you off to?"

"We're going home to New Brunswick."

"Ooh. Long way from home yet. Is there anything else I can help you with?"

"Not unless you have a pair of ruby slippers behind the counter."

The woman just stared at her, obviously not getting the reference.

"You know, like in the Wizard of Oz," Morgan said. "Click them three times and . . . never mind. Thanks for your help."

Morgan waved and left the woman looking supremely confused. She dashed through the rain and threw herself into Zinger's passenger side. Josh had the map of Canada open and folded to their general area.

"The lady inside says the road gets better soon."

"Glad to hear that," he said, continuing to study the map.

"Josh?"

"Yeah?"

"What's wrong?"

He looked up. "Nothing. I'm just figuring out where we might stop for the night."

"I know you, remember? I can tell something's up. Are you still thinking about last night?"

Josh sighed. "No. Well, maybe a little bit. But I have some other things on my mind." He folded the map and placed it back in the glove compartment. "I think we should be able to make it to Thunder Bay tonight."

Morgan considered pursuing the topic of his thoughts but decided against it. She grabbed his arm that had crossed to her side and pulled him in for a kiss. "Do you want me to drive for a while? You look tired."

"No, it was just a stressful drive. If the road gets better, I'll be able to relax. But I won't lie, I'm looking forward to a hot shower and some extra sleep."

"Don't have to tell me. I'll be glad when we're parked somewhere for the night."

The road straightened before long and rocky cliffs gave way to tree-lined scenery. The rain continued, but not as intensely, until they stopped for lunch just outside of Dryden. Josh had some sort of greasy meal while Morgan picked at a plate of fries. She and her stomach were still not on speaking terms.

They were heading out to the car when Morgan's eye landed on a payphone at the exit.

"Shit."

"What's wrong?" Josh asked, looking around for their latest peril.

"I forgot to call home this morning. I'll meet you at the car?"

"Sure."

Morgan watched Josh walk out and couldn't shake the feeling something major was bothering him. His posture was slumped, the brim of his hat pulled low over his face.

She reminded herself again that whatever was up with him was either none of her business or he'd tell her when he was ready.

Morgan grabbed the phone off the hook and dialed her home number. She dumped in the required amount of change and was pleased when the answering machine came on. She left a short message saying they'd had a late start and promised to call again tomorrow.

The rain had stopped completely and Morgan was treated to the sight of a rainbow as she left the restaurant. Yes, things were looking up. She hoped the sun would brighten Josh's mood.

Chapter 9

In Which Brooding Happens
Sunday, August 27, 1995

When the sun broke through the clouds, Josh's spirits lifted somewhat, especially since it was shining behind them.

They drove on in silence and Morgan seemed content to let him brood. He felt bad because he knew it usually bothered her when he became withdrawn, and he wanted her to be happy.

That thought in and of itself was unsettling. He had seldom cared about, or felt responsible for, someone else's happiness in the past. But Morgan was different.

The events of last night drifted across his mind again, both happy and a bit terrifying.

Would he have completed the act if he'd had the protection handy? He was very afraid the answer was yes. His desire had almost taken complete control. At least he'd had the presence of mind to go looking for his wallet.

Would she have let him continue if he hadn't left? Again, Josh was very afraid the answer was yes.

Regardless of what happened or what might have happened, they had reached a higher level of intimacy and their relationship had significantly changed. They would need to talk about it. And soon.

But Morgan wasn't the only girl Josh would need to speak with. The last words he'd said to Trixie before he left Bathurst continued to play through his mind. *We can see what happens.*

Oh, there were other words as well, such as the all-important "if" and "no promises." But Josh was very afraid she hadn't heard the other words – only the ones that suggested he would be hers.

Josh could never be Trixie's. He was Morgan's. Something he could not have imagined on that Sunday he left for Seattle. Had it only been three weeks ago?

Yes, they had started out on the sixth, four days before Morgan's birthday. If he'd known her age at the time, none of this would have happened. There was no way he would have traveled across Canada and the States with a seventeen-year-old girl. They were well on their way by the time Josh had discovered the birthday she was about to celebrate would be her eighteenth.

Merde! Birthdays . . . Trixie's birthday was right after Labor Day. When he was buying gifts in Seattle, she hadn't even crossed his mind. Not that it mattered, because even though they'd be home by then, he wouldn't be celebrating it.

Returning home next week was something else he hadn't imagined three weeks ago. He'd expected to be in Marine Corps boot camp already. No chance of that now. He'd been disqualified from enlisting last week – possibly forever.

Merde! He had to get his mind off this disastrous path and onto something else.

Josh rolled down his window a crack for some air and turned the radio on. He waited as it scanned for a station. Nothing. They must be too far from civilization to pick one up.

"Morgan, you awake?"

She turned her attention from her window to him and stretched. "I'm in a moving car. What else would I be, Braniac?"

"I thought sleep might have finally won."

"As much as I would love that, it's not happening. Not in the car. I hope you don't want to go dancing tonight," she said and chuckled. "What's on your mind?"

"I'm not sure anymore. I'm tired of thinking. I'd rather talk."

"Sure, but I'm tired of sitting here doing nothing. Let's switch spots first."

Josh didn't argue. He pulled onto the gravel shoulder and got out. Morgan climbed over the console and slid into the driver's seat as he was getting in on the passenger side.

Josh thought he heard a faint squeaking sound as Morgan pulled onto the highway, but it disappeared when she rolled up the window.

"What would you like to talk about?" she asked.

Josh threw out a random non-Trixie topic. "What's your brother like?"

"Which one? I have two, remember?"

"The one at home. I don't expect to see the one in Seattle anytime soon."

"I'm surprised you didn't hear him when I called home yesterday," Morgan said.

"Was that the wailing I heard when I was in the bathroom? I thought Bathurst was testing its air raid siren."

"That was Matthew the Mouth. God, you don't know how good it's been to be away from that noise these last few weeks. But what do you want to know about him? It's not like he's old enough for you to be fishing buddies or anything."

"I imagine I'll see him from time to time when I come to your place," Josh said.

Morgan put on her turn signal and smoothly passed the first car they'd seen in almost half an hour.

"Yeah, but I don't see us spending a lot of time at my house. Besides, you don't have a vehicle."

"I'm part owner of Zinger."

"True, but not for long. I'm paying you back right after I pay my parents," she said.

"Don't worry, I won't pressure you to pay me back."

Morgan laughed. "I appreciate it, but it's too early in our relationship to be considering shared custody of Zinger."

"I'll probably have to get a beater until I can get Old Blue fixed. I don't want to be walking to Cal's this winter," Josh said, thinking out loud. The trip home with Morgan was an unplanned expense, but not one he regretted.

"You're still going to try fixing that old truck?"

"Hey, I'll have you know that 'old truck' was my first home away from home."

"Yes, the image of your mangy socks hanging out of its window will be forever seared into my mind," Morgan said.

They both chuckled.

"But we digress," Josh said. "How old is Matthew? You said he's just a baby."

"He's a year and a half."

"You know, if we were to have a kid in a couple of years, Uncle Matthew would be barely older than him," Josh said with a laugh.

"Or her." Morgan grimaced. "Why are we talking about having babies?"

"Just a stray thought," Josh said.

"Let's keep it that way," Morgan said. "Here's a better thought. When we stop tonight, we should go back to staying at someplace more affordable."

"Do you want to go back to getting two rooms?"

"No. What happened, happened. Or didn't happen. You know what I mean. My point is, we know where we went wrong. Okay?"

"I'm good with that for now, but I do want to talk more about it," Josh said.

Morgan risked a quick look his way. "We will, but when we do, we need to be completely sober and sitting face to face."

"I totally agree. This is neither the time nor the place."

Morgan frowned. "Have you noticed how rough this road got?"

Josh had. The slight vibration in the steering wheel had increased until her arms were shaking along with it.

"You should pull over," he said.

"Just wait. There's a car coming up behind me."

Sure enough, a pickup sped past them, and Morgan slowed down but continued to drive.

She looked in the rearview mirror again. "It's got to be this road. But why am I the only car kicking up dust? That truck ahead of us isn't –"

"Morgan! Pull over now!"

Morgan must have smelled burning rubber at the same time Josh did because her eyes widened. Still, she kept driving as the smoke she'd mistaken for dust began to fill the car.

A loud bang sounded from beneath the car as Zinger bucked and a chunk of rubber flew across the highway's other lane.

Josh didn't need to repeat his request. Morgan turned the wheel hard and Zinger limped onto the shoulder.

As soon as she put the car in park, Josh threw off his seatbelt and jumped out. He rushed over to Morgan's side, nearly stepping into the path of a passing truck.

Josh let loose a string of words he usually didn't say as he stood looking at the left front tire – what was left of it, anyway – that continued to smoke.

"*Merde*. We are so screwed." Josh looked up and realized Morgan was still sitting in the car.

She had her window rolled down and smiled sweetly at him when she said, "My tire fell off."

Josh stared at her, wondering if she'd gone mental. "Dammit. I should have known better than to try driving on a God-only-knows-how-old spare tire." He was angry, but angry at himself more than anything. He was supposed to be this damned great mechanic.

"Stop it, Josh. Listen to me. It's okay."

"It's okay? It's okay? Please tell me where you obtained this enlightenment that everything is good!" His anger now spilled over onto Morgan.

"Don't make me slap you again to get you to listen," she replied calmly from her seat in Zinger.

Josh took a cautionary step back. "Sorry I yelled at you. Tell me why it's okay."

"Because we have a spare," Morgan said.

"A spare? Did the beer affect your memory?"

Morgan flung open the door and got out of the car.

Josh stepped farther back. "Okay, okay, continue with your story."

“What I’ve been trying to say, lava lips, is that Randy replaced the spare while I was in Seattle. This isn’t even the same tire that went flat last time. We just need to change it and we can be on our way again.”

“He did? Why didn’t you tell me that?” Josh asked in a calmer tone of voice.

“I just did. It wasn’t important before. Now go set the brake and put the flashers on while I open the trunk.”

“Okay. I just hope the lug nuts are easier to get off this time.”

They did come off easier. Before they were done, Morgan and Josh were laughing as hard as when they’d had their first flat tire on the trip to Seattle.

“Sorry, Josh. I should have pulled over when you told me to.”

“It’s all right. We weren’t hurt and the tire wouldn’t have been any less flat. We must have run over something when we stopped to switch places. But since we’re apologizing, I’m sorry I lost my temper.”

“I’ll let it go. This time. Don’t make a habit out of it,” Morgan said. “You can drive again if you want.”

They wiped their hands clean on the towel Morgan had in the trunk and kissed before they got back on the road.

The sun set while they were still driving, the clear sky spreading out above them. Although they couldn’t see past the trees on either side, the stars were bright in the moonless night.

A meteor streaked across the sky heading east. Morgan clasped her hands and closed her eyes.

“What’re you doing, Angel?”

“Making a wish on a falling star.”

“What did you wish for?”

“You know better than that, silly boy. If I tell you, it won’t come true,” Morgan said.

“Look, there’s a glow on the horizon. We must be getting close to Thunder Bay.”

They both gave tired sighs of relief.

After stopping for gas and a quick fast-food dinner, they found a Comfort Inn near the airport. Josh hoped air traffic wouldn't be busy, but he was too tired to look for anyplace else.

After they checked in, Josh headed straight for the shower but didn't linger. He was drying his hair when he came out of the bathroom and said, "Morgan, I'm going to the soda machine. You want anything?"

"Yes, Mom, that's Josh," she said.

Puzzled, he looked at her. She was holding the phone and making a shush motion with her finger.

"He just stopped in to see if I wanted a soda." To Josh, she said, "Get me a lemon-lime, please."

Josh lifted his hand in acknowledgment, returned the towel to the bathroom, and left as quietly as he could.

He was weary from the day's drive, and knew Morgan was too; but he was determined to take a stab at having that conversation.

Alas, it would have to wait. Morgan was passed out cold by the time he returned with the sodas.

Chapter 10

In Which They Have the Talk
Monday, August 28, 1995

Morgan finished packing her bag and sat down at the small table in their room to wait for Josh.

He'd gone down the hall to pick up something from the continental breakfast so they could sit and enjoy eating before getting on the road.

Morgan just knew the talk was coming. Hopefully it would be quick and painless, but she had her doubts.

Their close call in Winnipeg was not something to be taken lightly, but Morgan didn't want to take something that was supposed to be romantic and beautiful and dissect it like a dead body.

She'd already had the sex talk with her mom and she'd taken sex-ed in school like everyone else.

Morgan shook her head and drummed her fingers on the table. Surely Josh wouldn't do that. Maybe he wanted to talk more about their feelings for each other than have some sort of clinical discussion.

The door clicked open and Josh pushed his way in using his back. His hands were busy balancing their breakfast tray. Morgan jumped up to help him and nearly burst out laughing when she saw the bananas. Yes, sex-ed had left its mark.

"What did I miss?" Josh asked.

"Nothing. I'm just in a good mood today," Morgan said, collecting herself. "Let me take the tray."

"Thanks." Josh handed it over and allowed the door to swing shut behind him. He took off his shoes and brought over the drinks that hadn't fit on the tray.

"Did you get one of everything?" Morgan asked as she plucked a hard-boiled egg from a bowl.

"Looks like it, doesn't it? They had so much food laid out this morning I couldn't resist."

"I'm not complaining. I'm actually starving this morning."

Josh sat across from her and opened a package of butter for his toast. "Sleep well last night?"

"Not bad. God, I really wish I hadn't agreed to call home every day. It's such a pain in the ass. I would have been better off asking Randy for a loan." Morgan finished her egg and took another.

"I'm really sorry your mom heard me last night. I thought you switched to making the calls in the morning."

"Yeah, but I was hoping to strike a deal. Maybe get her to agree to phone calls every other night or something. Needless to say, that idea has been scrapped."

"Maybe we should go back to getting our own rooms," Josh said as he bit into his toast.

"For what? It's not going to make any difference. We'd still have adjoining rooms and the door would be open. Don't you remember the first night in Seattle? If you feel like you can't keep it in your pants or you just don't trust me anymore, maybe we shouldn't even be staying in the same hotel." Morgan crossed her arms and sat back.

Josh finished chewing his toast and wiped his mouth with a napkin. "The reason I suggested it was so you wouldn't have to lie to your mom."

Well, shit. Morgan felt her cheeks flush with embarrassment and she looked down.

She heard Josh move his chair closer and he lifted her chin so she would have to meet his eyes. He was smiling, not laughing, so that was a good sign.

"Sorry," she said. "I haven't been looking forward to this conversation."

"I know."

"I didn't mean what I said. I know we got carried away in Winnipeg, but everything turned out all right. Why can't we just leave it like that?"

"Because I think our relationship is too important to sweep stuff like that under the rug," Josh replied.

"Okay." Morgan sighed. "What do we need to talk about then?"

Josh brushed a lock of hair behind her ear and leaned back in his chair. "Well, I think it's obvious we care about each other. It's also very clear how much we're attracted to each other."

He cleared his throat as Morgan sat waiting for the problem.

"Do you remember why we didn't go through with it?" he finally asked.

"You left for your own bed and then I fell asleep."

Josh shifted uncomfortably. "I didn't leave for my bed. I went to find my wallet."

Morgan's eyes widened as she realized what he meant. She had no idea he'd had protection available. "You were planning on coming back then?"

He nodded. "You were asleep by the time I found it."

Silence hung heavy in the air between them. The weight of this newly discovered responsibility threatened to crush Morgan. She'd believed that Josh, being the wise one, had known when to stop. Not so, apparently.

"But I thought you just didn't think we were ready."

"I don't," Josh said. "Do you?"

"I wasn't thinking about anything like that at the time. It just felt so good. But no, I don't truly believe we're ready to do that. I mean, clearly our bodies disagree, but I've never even had a boyfriend before."

"Do you think we should slow things down?"

"In the physical department, I guess. But didn't we already do that? Or am I missing something else?" Morgan threw up her hands in frustration. "Are you suggesting we shouldn't even kiss anymore?"

"No, no." Josh took her hands and held them tightly. "I'm just saying we need to be really careful. I think making love is the most intimate thing two people can physically do together and it should be saved for someone special. I'm not saying you're not special – you know what you mean to me –

but we don't want to ruin what we have. I don't want us to end up being friends with benefits or something. We deserve better than that."

Morgan couldn't help but wrinkle her nose at the term "making love." That's how her mother had referred to it. She dismissed the thought and asked, "Have you ever done it?"

"No. Not every guy is like Shack, even though there's a lot of peer pressure to become a man, as he says."

"I'm starting to think I'm really, really not going to like this guy when I meet him."

"Well lucky for you, you won't be meeting him anytime soon."

"Is there anything else we need to iron out or can we try finding our way back to where we were before that – almost – happened?"

"Just one thing," Josh said. "A small but potentially dangerous thing."

"Hormones?" Morgan offered with a laugh.

"Those aren't something we can get rid of." Josh chuckled. "But the alcohol is."

Morgan frowned. "Are you saying I can't drink anymore?"

"Of course not. I'm not your keeper. I'm just suggesting that if you do want to have a drink, I should stay sober."

"I can accept that." Morgan grinned. "Are we good now?"

"I think so."

"That wasn't that bad," she said, standing. "Now kiss me, please, so we can get out of here."

Josh stood and did so. Despite their discussion, Morgan didn't feel any fewer sparks or tingles. If anything, she felt more of them. They were both slightly out of breath when they parted.

"Good talk," Morgan said.

Josh chuckled and shook his head. "Maybe we should get some rope and hang a sheet between our beds at night."

Morgan swatted him and started clearing up the breakfast.

Once she was finished, they opened the map of Canada and took a quick look at their route for the day.

"It's hard to tell on such a large map, but it looks like the Trans-Canada splits here at Nipigon. I guess we'd want to take the southern route."

"No!" Morgan exclaimed. "We're not going anywhere near Sault Ste. Marie. Besides, it looks like a big old circle anyway. I say we stay on the northern route. It's not going to be any farther."

"As you wish." Josh began folding the map. "Would you like to drive first today?"

"Not unless you really want me to. I'm sick to death of driving. I just want to get it over with already."

Josh took the folded map and went to grab his gear. Morgan took her bag and checked the room to make sure they hadn't left anything behind. She pictured a sheet hanging between the two beds and suppressed a giggle. Then a more sobering thought took its place.

"It's going to be really weird when we're back home in our own houses in a few days. I mean yeah, we were apart for a bit in Seattle, but we had plenty of stuff to keep us occupied."

Josh stepped over and put his arm around her. "I know. I thought of that too. But we'll have lots of things to tend to when we get home. Besides, we still have a ways to go yet." He kissed the top of her head and they headed out to Zinger.

Once they were on the road, Morgan found a radio station they both enjoyed. The day was warm and sunny. However, Morgan's thoughts slowly but surely began turning sour.

Okay, they'd cleared up the awkward talking bit, but really . . .

Instead of being thankful for Josh's restraint – eventually – Morgan found herself getting hung up on the part where he oh-so-subtly called her "not special enough." How long was it going to take him to make up his damned mind?

And sure, he'd confessed to being a virgin, but she hadn't asked what other sort of things he might have done. He had an "almost girlfriend" at one point. In fact, right before they left. Had he had the same physical urges with Miss Trix-a-lot? Morgan shuddered, hating this girl she hoped never to meet.

Morgan had been slumped down in her seat with her feet on the dashboard, and now pushed herself upright with force. Her foot kicked up and hit the windshield.

"You all right?"

"No," she grumbled. "I'm cranky and I'm bored."

Josh pulled the car over to the side of the road.

"What are you doing?" she asked.

"I just remembered something."

He disappeared behind the car and popped the trunk. A moment later, he returned with a book.

"Here. I bought this for you in Silverdale and forgot all about it. I'm sorry those thieves stole your library books."

Morgan glared down at *Carrie* by Stephen King. Not Josh's fault he didn't know she didn't like horror. Not Josh's fault she was suddenly reminded of the library bill she would have to pay when she got back.

She managed a thank you as they got back on the road.

It wasn't the worst book in the world, but Morgan found her eyes drifting off the page, her thoughts leading back to anything and everything wretched she thought she'd locked up in the vault.

"I'm tired of sitting here. I want to drive," she announced.

"No problem. Do you want to stop for lunch in the next town? Then we can switch."

Morgan shrugged her agreement and silently reprimanded herself for once again being a bitch. She also made a mental note to stop giving Josh such a hard time about his brooding. Everyone needed some time alone with their thoughts. At least he had the decency to be civil while doing so.

The roadside diner they stopped at was both bright and cozy. It was mostly filled with elderly people, but they were a lively bunch. Morgan and Josh found seats at the counter. Morgan ordered a grilled cheese sandwich with freshly-made tomato soup. Josh went for an omelet and the soup.

Morgan swiveled around on her stool and swung her legs as they waited, simply enjoying being out of the car and with Josh.

"Sorry I've been such a grump this afternoon," she said, taking his hand and giving it a squeeze.

"I've seen worse," Josh said.

"I love Zinger, I love that we're traveling home together." She stopped herself short of saying she loved Josh. "I guess I'm just having a day."

"We all have our days."

Lunch was delicious. One can never go wrong with grilled cheese, and the homemade soup warmed Morgan's stomach and spirits.

Back on the road, Morgan rolled down the window and settled into a speed slightly over the limit. Josh took one of his customary naps and Morgan reveled in the warm sunlight on her face.

When her grumbling thoughts threatened to intrude, she turned on the radio. It refused to pick up a station and Morgan refused to succumb to moping. She shut the thing off and sang her own songs as she drove along.

When Josh woke up, he even tried singing a few with her. He was terrible at it, but they laughed and had fun. Morgan was determined to keep things on that fun note and decided on a whim where they should stop for the night.

Moonbeam, Ontario. Because who wouldn't want to stop there?

Chapter 11

In Which They Pay It Forward
Monday, August 28, 1995

As Morgan drove into the town of Moonbeam, Josh sat upright and swiveled his head. *Was that a flying saucer?*

It had the general shape of one.

"Did I just see a UFO?" he asked, turning his attention to Morgan, who was now searching for something.

"Probably. I was looking for a gas station."

"We just passed one," he said.

"It looked crappy," she said.

They passed through town and the area around them became farmland again.

"Well, shit. Does this town only have one gas station?" She pulled to the shoulder and, when a pickup truck passed, turned back toward town.

"Don't we have enough gas to make it to the next town?" Josh asked.

Morgan shrugged. "We're under a quarter of a tank and I don't want to chance it up here in the wild country. Besides, I want to stay here. The name of the town is cool and we can go see the flying saucer."

"So you did see the UFO," he said.

"Only out of the corner of my eye. But I've seen signs along the way."

On their way back through town, Josh examined the object more closely. It was spherical at the center, bisected with a disk and covered with windows. The whole thing stood on three legs.

They reached the two-pump gas station back on the west side of town and both got out of Zinger.

After a quick stretch, Morgan said, "I'll pump. Can you go pay and find out where the hotel is?"

"Sure, Angel." Josh rolled his shoulders and headed for the small building.

A young woman with blue hair and tattoos on her arms hopped off the stool and stepped to the counter. Her nametag identified her as Zora.

"How much you getting, dude?"

"We'll fill it. I'll pay when she's done."

"It's pretty rad letting your girlfriend pump the gas."

"It just happened to be her turn," Josh said. He wanted to change the subject before this woman asked if he let Morgan be on top. "Where is the nearest hotel in town?"

"The nearest hotel is back in Kapuskasing, but Ms. Anna has a bed and breakfast."

"Do you know if Ms. Anna has any rooms with two beds?"

"What, you guys like Ozzie and Harriet or something?" Zora asked.

Josh had no idea who those people were, but inferred she was asking if Morgan and he slept in separate beds. "Ah, we have to have a second bed for Zinger."

"Oh, I think all of Ms. Anna's rooms have a single bed. She doesn't allow no pets anyway."

Not wanting to drive back the way they came, Josh asked, "What about the next town east of here?"

Zora shrugged a bare shoulder. "Don't know, never been that way. I think it's kinda small like here. Never heard of a hotel there."

Josh excused himself and went to the washroom. When he came out, he saw Morgan was leaning against Zinger.

Josh paid for the gas and returned to the car, stealing a kiss when he arrived. "Bad news, Angel."

"What?" Her face turned from happy to concerned.

Josh pointed west. "Nearest hotel is back that way. There's a bed and breakfast here but Ms. Anna only has one bed per room."

"I guess we'll need to drive back. Sorry." She flashed him an endearing grin.

It melted what little annoyance he had. "Not your fault. We don't exactly have a tour book."

"Can we go get some pictures of the UFO before going to the hotel?" Morgan asked.

"Sure, we can do that."

"Great. I'm going to go use the washroom before we go."

"I'll be waiting. Don't let Zora interrogate you," Josh said.

Morgan laughed and headed inside.

Josh wondered if his sister would look like Zora in a few years but decided Rab was more Goth than Punk. She might get some tattoos though.

Morgan returned to the car with a puzzled look on her face. "What did you say to that poor girl? She asked what type of dog Zinger was. When I told her Zinger was the car, she looked confused."

Josh laughed. "She was getting a bit nosy about our sleeping arrangements, so I told her Zinger needed a separate bed."

Once they'd composed themselves and Morgan wiped the tears of laughter from her eyes, she drove to the flying saucer. She parked at the visitor center next to the attraction and they walked across the grass.

The central disk portion cleared their heads. Morgan and Josh explored around the sides and underneath it. They took turns snapping pictures of each other and managed to get a local to take a shot of them together. Before they left, they took one last peek through the lower windows.

"There's not much more room in there than there is in Zinger," Morgan observed. "Too bad we can't go inside."

"Riding across the country in Zinger is one thing. I can't imagine trying to fly across the universe with two or more people in that."

"Especially with no bathroom," Morgan agreed.

"Maybe aliens don't need to pee," Josh said and laughed.

"Lucky them. Come on, I think we've played tourist long enough and I'm getting hungry."

"Good call. Me too." He took her hand and they walked back to Zinger.

She took one more shot of the cut-out of a green alien on the porch of the visitor center before climbing back into the driver's seat.

On their way back to Kapuskasing, they came across a car on the side of the road. An older woman stood behind it, looking confused.

"Pull over," Josh said.

He got out of the car as soon as it stopped and crossed the road.

"Do you need help, ma'am?" he asked.

"I don't know, young man." The woman took a step back from him. "My car just stopped and I can't get it started again."

"I know a little bit about cars," Josh said. "Would you mind if I take a look?"

By then, Morgan had gotten out of Zinger and came to stand next to him. He hoped her presence would put the older woman at ease.

"If you wouldn't mind," the woman said.

Josh nodded to Morgan to suggest she wait with the lady while he checked the car.

He slid into the driver's seat, checked that the car was in park, and tried the key. Nothing.

"I tried that already, young man," the woman called from where she stood with Morgan.

"I'm sure you did, ma'am, but I needed to hear for myself if it was making any sounds," Josh replied.

He popped the hood and got out of the car.

"I found the problem," Josh said after a minute. "The cable to your alternator broke."

"Can you fix it?" the woman asked.

"Do you have any tools? I'm afraid mine are in my other vehicle."

"You can look in the trunk. I'm not sure what all Alfred kept in there. It's been so hard since he passed."

Josh took the keys out of the ignition and opened the trunk. There was a small tool bag with some rudimentary tools, but more importantly he found jumper cables.

"Bring Zinger around to the front of this car," he said to Morgan.

She gave him a thumbs up. "Would you like to sit in my car while Josh tries to fix yours?" Morgan asked the woman.

"That would be nice. Thank you, young lady."

Morgan led her across the road to Zinger.

By the time Morgan brought the car around, Josh had been able to use the tools he'd found to reconnect the cable to the alternator.

He returned the tools to the trunk and collected the jumper cables. Once he had them hooked up, he let the dead battery charge for a few minutes before turning the key again.

He was rewarded with a roar as the engine turned over.

Josh left the car running as he went to disconnect the cables. Morgan was already helping the woman out of the passenger seat.

The lady's eyes were moist as she reached her car and opened the door. "Thank you so much, young man. Can I give you anything for your help?"

"No, ma'am. We're paying it forward for someone who helped us out not long ago. I've fixed the cable for now, but you should get a full charge on your battery and get that cable replaced when you can. There's a gas station just a few miles away in Moonbeam. We'll follow you to make sure you get that far."

Morgan now stood next to Josh and laced her fingers with his, apparently not caring that they were slightly grubby from working under the hood.

The older woman touched each of them on the forearm. "Bless you. You're a beautiful couple. I wish more people were like you."

Josh and Morgan backed up and Morgan closed the door for her.

Ten minutes later the older woman had pulled off at the gas station. Morgan pulled in just long enough to turn around and wave goodbye as they headed off once again for Kapuskasing.

"Thank you for helping Mrs. Kramer," Morgan said.

"Was that her name?"

"Yes. We talked some while you were doing your mechanic thing."

"I'm glad it was something easy to fix," Josh said.

"Still, I know you wouldn't have left her there even if it wasn't," Morgan said.

"Of course not. I'd have sat in the back if we needed to drive her somewhere."

"You're making it too easy to fall for you, Josh."

"I thought you already had." He smiled and reached out to stroke her hair.

"I mean deeper. You know, the L-word."

"Yes deeper." He cleared his throat. "I can't help feeling a little sad for her though, having lost her husband and all."

"But they had a good life together and she has a family to care for her. Isn't that kinda what life's all about?" Morgan asked.

"Are you getting all philosophical on me now?"

"Sure. It'll pass the time until we get back to where we should have stopped for the night. Now pretend I'm my dad." She said in a deeper voice, "Tell me young man, what are your intentions toward my daughter?"

"*Merde*."

"Just answer the question." Morgan laughed.

Josh lifted his ball cap and ran a hand through his hair. "Well sir, while we were on the road . . . hmm, maybe I shouldn't start with that," Josh said.

"Maybe not. It might lead to more uncomfortable questions."

"How about this? Well sir, I knew your daughter in school, of course, but since graduating, I've had a chance to learn more about her and the more I learn about her, the more I like her."

"That's all well and good, young man, but can you provide for her?" Morgan asked in the deep voice.

"Well sir, I intend to continue my apprenticeship as a mechanic until I can earn my master mechanic certificate. A master mechanic makes pretty good money. She shouldn't have to work."

"Isn't that a bit old-fashioned?" Morgan asked in her normal voice.

"Maybe. But I'm an old-fashioned kind of guy. I think a woman should only have to work if she wants to."

"What if the woman is making enough money to support the family? Would you be willing to stay home with the children?"

"It would be tough. I think I'm conditioned to want to work," Josh admitted.

"And you don't think taking care of kids is work? Trust me, it's a hella lot of work."

"No, no. It's not that. I'm getting all confused and tongue tied. Can we talk about his later when I'm not hungry?"

Morgan laughed. "Okay, where do you want to eat?" she asked as they came into the city.

"Some place we can sit and eat. I don't want to take fast food back to the hotel," Josh said.

"I think I saw a bar and grill when we passed through earlier."

"That'll work. But remember, we're in Ontario now."

"Oh, don't worry, I'm not ready for another hangover just yet," Morgan said.

The evening was still nice, so they sat on the covered deck at the grill and had dinner by the river. Morgan ordered a burger and a basket of fries that she shared with Josh, who tried a milder flavor of wings.

They sat and talked about happy things until well after dark. Before they knew it, the grill was closing for the night.

Morgan leaned into Josh while they walked slowly back to Zinger. He wrapped an arm around her shoulder to protect her from the chill they hadn't noticed because of the patio's space heaters.

As luck would have it, they found a Super 8 nearby and checked into the last available room with double beds.

"Oh, look, there's a pool here. We should go swimming," Morgan said as they went up to their room.

"We've stopped at several places that have had pools. We haven't gone swimming yet. Why now?"

"I don't know. I just had the urge."

"Did your urge happen to consider the fact we don't have bathing suits?" Josh asked.

Morgan bit her lower lip and give Josh a coy look. "Do you think we'd get in trouble if we went down and skinny dipped after dark?"

"I really don't want to find out if the Kapuskasing jail offers more than a blanket to people who are arrested naked."

Morgan laughed. "Sometimes I'm glad you're a stick in the mud."

Josh opened the door and they entered their abode for the night.

Pulling his bag of dirty clothes out of his duffel, he said, "Toss me your laundry. I'll get it started while you make your phone call."

Morgan got her stuff together and he left the room with both bags.

When he discovered the hotel didn't have laundry services, he returned to the room. Josh paused at the door to see if Morgan was still on the phone. Not hearing anything, he entered.

She was sitting on the bed hugging a pillow.

"Things that bad?" Josh ventured to ask.

"About the same with Mom, but I still can't reach Mel. Clothes done already?"

"They don't have washing machines. I can soak them in the sink."

"I'm good for another day." Morgan patted the bed next to her. "Come sit with me for a bit?"

Josh hesitated.

"I just want to be held. No funny business." She smiled weakly.

"Not even a kiss or two?"

"I might allow you one."

He kicked off his shoes and sat next to her.

Morgan looked up and gave him a kiss before snuggling into his chest. Five minutes later she was sound asleep.

As gently as he could, Josh got out of bed. He took the blanket off his bed and covered her. He debated going out to the car and getting the blanket he'd dragged to Seattle and back for himself but was too tired. The thin sheet would have to do.

Chapter 12

In Which They Slow Down
Tuesday, August 29, 1995

Morgan and Josh were up early but neither was in a hurry to get going. It seemed the closer they got to home, the shorter their driving days became.

Morgan wasn't sure of Josh's reasoning, but she simply wanted to spend more time with him before they got back to Bathurst and everything that awaited them there.

Morgan took a shower while Josh went to raid the continental breakfast. That jinxy little name attempted to flit through her thoughts again but she swatted it away. Whoever the girl was, she was no longer an issue. Josh had said so.

Wait a minute. He'd also said his former not-quite-girlfriend was his sister's friend. How "out of their lives" was she really?

Morgan shut off the water and dressed quickly, yanking the comb through her hair. *Forget about her. You already had your insecure mental day,* she reminded herself.

Yet when she emerged from the bathroom to find Josh sitting at the table watching TV, the first question out of her mouth was, "Why do you call your sister Rab?"

Josh muted the television and gave her an odd look. "Her middle name is Rabeau. She doesn't like her first name, so she goes by Rab."

"What's her first name?" Morgan could hear the snappiness in her voice but found herself unable to control it.

"Mary. Why do I feel like I've done something wrong here?"

Morgan sighed. "Sorry. Just thinking about home." She looked at the breakfast Josh had brought and smiled. "You didn't rob the place blind this time."

He smiled in return. "I can go back for more if you want."

"No. This is fine. I love the eggs. Nice and simple." She sat down and they both helped themselves to eggs and toast. "Sorry I was a bit short with you."

"It's okay. We all have our moments."

"This is true," Morgan agreed. She noticed both quilts were still on her bed and it just occurred to her Josh must have slept with only a sheet. "Why did you give me both blankets?"

He shrugged. "You fell asleep on the one and I didn't want to wake you."

"Aw, you should have. You must have been cold."

"I was fine. The room was warmed by your presence."

Morgan blushed and focused on her egg. "Well, thanks. I'm so tired of making those calls home but it was the one to Mel that bugged me the most. She didn't really say anything, she just hung up again when she found out it was me, but it sounded like she was crying."

Josh frowned. "Is it normal for her to hold such a grudge?"

"Not at all. And that's the thing. I can't help but wonder if something else is going on. I'm starting to get worried."

"You said she moved recently. Have you tried calling her parents?"

"No, but that's a good idea. I think I'll wait until I get home though. Mel's mother wasn't exactly keen on talking to me last time either."

"Speaking of home, any thoughts on how long you want to drive for today?" Josh asked.

"Not really. Just not all day. I say we keep going until we find something interesting."

"You mean like the UFO last night?" Josh laughed.

"Yeah, my bad. I shouldn't have assumed they had a motel there. I told you, I'm an artistic soul." Morgan waved her hand in a dramatic fashion. "I follow my heart."

"Never stop doing that," Josh said and grabbed her hand to kiss it. "I was looking at the map. We could be home in a couple of days if we pushed hard, but I think we're in agreement that's not something we want to do."

"Absolutely not," Morgan agreed. "We'll get there soon enough."

Morgan finished her breakfast while Josh took a shower, and soon they were on the road again.

As far as Morgan-and-Josh drives went, this one was supremely uneventful. Morgan drove until they stopped for lunch. There were no flat tires, keys locked in the car, or throwdowns on the side of the road. They listened to the radio where they could find a station and held hands over the console more often than not.

Morgan had made decent progress in reading *Carrie,* the book that Josh had bought for her, and decided it wasn't so terrible after all. Before she knew it, they were coming up to North Bay. She spotted a sign on the sign of the road she thought might interest Josh.

"Did you see that? They have a Canadian Forces Museum here."

"I noticed it."

"We can stop there if you want. In fact, we could stop for the night. Treat ourselves to an evening in," Morgan suggested.

Josh looked pleasantly surprised. "You said in not out, right?"

"Yes." She laughed. "We can grab some junk food and watch a movie on TV."

"You have no idea how good that sounds to me."

"Sure I do. It was my idea." Morgan grinned.

"Well, you don't have to ask twice. Are you sure, though? I mean, it's only three o'clock."

"Wait. Is that right? Please tell me we didn't switch time zones again."

"Not since yesterday. I've been keeping our clocks set."

"Thanks," Morgan said. "You've been stealthy about it. I haven't even noticed most of the time."

"Anything for my Angel."

Josh drove into the city and found their favorite hotel, a Super 8. This one was fancied up on the outside with a castle-like stone entrance.

"Funny how they're all so different, hey?" Morgan commented as they walked inside to check in.

"I know. Hopefully this one has laundry facilities."

It did. But it didn't have a room with two beds available, only suites. Morgan grumbled on the way up about the added expense – it was equivalent to a two-night's stay at a much cheaper motel.

She stopped her grumbling when they entered the room.

Morgan threw down her bag with a squeal and dashed through the living room to the glass doors that led to the bedroom. "This is perfect! Dibs on the bedroom."

Josh laughed and lifted the cushion of the couch to examine the pullout bed. "Rats. You'd better make sure to lock that door in case I have one of my sleepwalking episodes."

Morgan turned from the bedroom. "You sleepwalk?"

"Not yet." He grinned and ducked as she threw a pillow at him.

Morgan walked over to the TV and found it came equipped with a VCR. The guest services book advised video rentals were available in the lobby.

At this news, Morgan and Josh rushed out to pick their movie for the night as excited as – well, as the teenagers they actually were.

The receptionist was kind enough to provide them with not only directions to the museum but also a complimentary map of North Bay. Morgan and Josh each picked a VHS tape. With their plans in place, they returned to their room to freshen up before heading out.

The Canadian Forces Museum wasn't actually in the city. It was a twenty-minute drive out to the base. When they got there, Morgan was shocked to see how small it was and considered leaving her camera in the car. The squat little building had her doubting her suggestion, but Josh was unfazed.

Inside, a woman in a military uniform offered to give them the tour, but Josh was content to wander on his own. Morgan found nothing of interest in the displays. She was more interested in studying Josh and his reactions as she followed along.

He breezed past most of the displays of uniforms but paused at a World War II getup. His face turned sad, and Morgan looped her arm through his, remembering their stop at the Quebec Vietnam Memorial. He seemed to have gotten over his obsession with the war and how he had once thought his father was a draft dodger. Still, she didn't want him to begin brooding today. Not when they were supposed to be having fun.

"You okay?" she asked.

"Mm hm. Just thinking," he replied.

"You're not getting back on that honor kick again, are you?"

"No. I've amended my views on honor. Honor is important but everyone has to find their own honor."

Morgan let the comment hang and was happy when Josh turned from the uniform and headed for the section dedicated to airplanes. He even climbed into the cockpit of the one fighter plane they had on display.

Finally, a use for the camera. Morgan had to call his name twice before he looked up from a possible brooding situation. If it had been one, he recovered quickly and flashed her a silly grin.

It wasn't long before they'd had enough of the museum. Morgan apologized for her lousy choice on the way out, but Josh assured her he'd found it interesting. He thanked her for her thoughtfulness with a kiss.

Morgan thanked him for the kiss by returning it threefold. She also bought the movie-night snacks when they stopped at a convenience store on the way back. They returned to their room with bags of potato chips, soda, gummy bears, and the all-important microwave popcorn.

Instead of going out to eat, they decided to order pizza in honor of a genuine night in.

While they waited for the pizza to arrive, Josh set out on his mission to wash laundry and Morgan jumped on the opportunity to get her nightly phone call out of the way.

She was peppered with question after question. Why were they taking so long? Was Morgan sure there was no hanky-panky going on? Why was Morgan in such a mood every time she called home?

"Because of this!" Morgan finally yelled just as Josh returned. He slunk over to the couch and sat quietly while she continued.

"How am I supposed to speak reasonably to you when all you do is nag?"

At that point, her mom started crying softly and Morgan felt like shit.

"Mom. Stop that. Please. I'm sorry I raised my voice. I'll be home soon, okay?"

"I'm sorry too. I'll just be happy when you're safely back here with us. It's not easy on a mom when her children are away."

"I'm not a child anymore, Mom. I can take care of myself."

"In my mind, I know that, but it's hard for a mother's heart to believe that. You'll understand when you have children."

After her mom's emotional flip, they exchanged farewells and Morgan hung up the phone before rolling her eyes to Josh.

"I swear to God she's gone mental. She was never this bad before. Maybe she's going through menopause. You get the laundry going?"

"Yep. I'll just have to run out and switch it to the dryer in a bit. They have a few machines and it doesn't look like anyone else is using them."

"Good. Pizza should be here soon. Which movie do you want to watch first?" Morgan asked.

"Let's go with the one you picked."

Morgan put the cassette into the machine.

"I think this one might be a bit sappy. If it sucks we can switch to yours. I'm not usually big on romance movies."

"A little romance never hurt anyone," Josh said.

Morgan picked up the movie Josh had chosen. Yeah, a movie about a boy and his dog sounded a lot more appealing.

Wanting to clear the serious stuff from her mind before the night began, Morgan blurted, "You're not thinking about enlisting in the Canadian Forces now, are you?"

Josh got up from the couch and gathered her in his arms, taking her back to sit with him. He stroked her hair as she leaned her head against his chest for a reply.

"Of course it's crossed my mind. My goals have changed since our first trip. I'm thankful you were with me for that." He paused and kissed her head. "Now, I have to focus on finding a means to support myself and maybe a family one day."

"Right, that workaholic wife." Morgan laughed.

"What about you? Didn't you say you and your dad were going to look at some school programs? I imagine most of them would take you from Bathurst."

She sat up and bit on her lip. "I know. I was so excited when we talked about that just a week ago, but now I'm not so sure. The closer we get to home, the more I'm concentrating on short term goals like finding a job I like for at least this year. I'm not in a hurry to flee Bathurst – and you – in pursuit of some silly dream."

"Your dreams are not silly," Josh said. "You'll figure out what you want to do. I might have to leave for school myself for a while, but I would return." He kissed her and added, "I'd always return to you, Angel."

Morgan smiled and kissed him back. "Thanks for saying that. I like to think that no matter what happens we'd make it work and always find our way back to each other."

Just then, the pizza arrived. All talk of future plans was banished by the cheesy goodness they devoured slice by slice.

Before starting the movie, Josh put the popcorn in the microwave and ran out to switch the laundry.

Morgan changed into her shorts and tank top and grabbed a blanket out of the closet. She'd given Josh permission to wander around in his boxers this evening because he had no other comfy clothes to choose from.

She'd also decided she didn't mind the look of them anymore.

Chapter 13

In Which They Try a Little Culture
Wednesday, August 30, 1995

After a very restful night in North Bay and another leisurely morning, Josh took the wheel as he and Morgan continued their journey home.

I could get used to this, he thought, risking a peek at Morgan who was engrossed in her book.

They'd agreed that morning to drive as far as Montreal before deciding whether they would push on for a few more hours or stop for the night.

Josh believed Morgan was leaning toward stopping. He was too, even if the hotels would be twice the price of most of the places they'd been staying. However, they'd earned a little luxury by sharing rooms along the way.

Josh didn't want to think about returning to Bathurst and sleeping in his sister's old room without Morgan nearby. Even his former room, which Rab had claimed when he left home, wouldn't be the same.

A strange place with Morgan was more of a home than a familiar place without her.

Yes, he definitely wanted to drag this trip out a bit longer.

"You know, Angel, Montreal is liable to have a nice art museum. Would you like to go?"

"Wouldn't a museum be in the middle of the city?" she asked.

"Probably. But if we stop for the night in Montreal or nearby, we wouldn't need to rush."

"Good point," Morgan said. "Yeah, I'd like to go. But we can still drive for a bit after. Montreal's probably really expensive."

When they reached the city two hours later, they stopped at the information center and learned that Montreal had not one, but no fewer than ten art museums and numerous galleries. Morgan chose the Montreal Museum of Fine Arts.

Josh was pleased to see the museum was close to the highway. Once they finished touring it, they could leave the city with ease.

"You might have to do most of the talking here," Morgan said when they got back in the car. "I don't know a lick of French."

"Didn't you take French in school?"

She grinned sheepishly. "I did, but I only studied enough to pass."

"*Merde.*"

"I know that word well enough by now." Morgan laughed.

"I hope I don't have to use it today. My French isn't the greatest. But we should be all right. Most signs will have English words too, just in smaller letters."

After finding the museum and parking the car, Morgan and Josh walked up the broad steps to the columned entrance of the classical structure. Josh paid for admission, and they skimmed the pamphlets the attendant handed them.

"Let's go to the modern art section," Morgan said. "That's what I'm mostly interested in."

"Sure. I had no idea it would be this huge."

Morgan snagged Josh's hand and gently tugged him along. "We'll start there and see what we have time for afterward."

"We can stay until it closes," Josh said, though he was feeling quite out of his element.

"I'm sure we'll get hungry before than happens. Wait, what time does it close?"

Josh checked the pamphlet. "Five o'clock."

"In that case, let's get going."

When they reached the modern art wing, Morgan's eyes lit up and she was immediately enraptured. She went from painting to painting, stepping back as far as possible to study the overall effect, then getting as close as allowed to examine it minutely.

Whose idea was this anyway? Josh thought as he trailed along behind her. *Oh right, mine. Merde, it's going to be a long afternoon.*

"What are you looking for?" he finally asked, hoping his impatience wasn't reflected in the tone of his voice.

"The brush strokes. You don't know anything about painting, do you?"

"I know how to mask off a window when painting a truck," Josh offered.

Morgan laughed so loudly several patrons turned her way. She covered her mouth and offered a quiet apology, but mirth still showed in her eyes.

"We don't have time to do a full lesson, but you can tell a lot about a painter by they way they apply the paint," she said. "Many forgeries are discovered because the forgers didn't do their homework and study the original painter's brush strokes."

"I'll remember to do my homework if I ever want to forge a painting," Josh said with a grin.

"The sad thing is forgers must get really good at their craft before they can forge a painting. If they just did their own paintings, they could make a decent living and not rip off other artists. Now hush and let me study these strokes."

Josh complied. After examining each picture for a moment, he decided to spend the rest of his time watching Morgan. Her appearance appealed to him far more than these modern paintings anyway. He couldn't imagine what the artist was attempting to express in most of them. Well, practically any of them.

Morgan stopped at one titled Woman Walking Down Steps. The work completely puzzled Josh.

He couldn't help himself. "How is this even a person? It looks like a jumbled bunch of boxes and bears no resemblance to a person, much less a woman."

"If you want to see realism, you can stroll through the rest of the gallery. I'm sure you'll find plenty of portraits to satisfy you. I'll be here when you're done," Morgan said somewhat impatiently.

"No, it's not that. It's just the title and what's on the canvas don't seem to match."

"Modern art, Josh. It goes beyond the pure visuals. Shall I explain this piece to you?"

"No, I'm good," he said. Then he smiled weakly and stepped back to let her study the painting in peace.

Josh followed along as Morgan went through the rest of the section in relative silence. Every once in a while, she would comment on a piece under her breath and Josh assumed she was thinking aloud.

The afternoon continued this way until the public address system announced the museum would be closing in fifteen minutes.

"Hey Angel, I'm going to go check out the gift shop. Meet you at the entrance?"

"I'll go with you. We should probably take advantage of the facilities before we go."

At the boutique, Josh searched until he found a sketch pad and some art pencils. He purchased those for Morgan while she was in the washroom.

When she arrived at the boutique, she immediately noticed the bag. "You actually found something you liked?"

"Just a little something for someone special."

"Anyone I know?" she asked with a coy smile.

"I'll show you later. They're about to lock the doors."

They left the museum and found themselves having to cross rush hour traffic to get to Zinger.

Before they got in the car, Morgan wrapped her arms around Josh's neck and gave him a soft kiss. "Thank you for bringing me here. I know it's not your thing, but I appreciate your patience."

"Maybe next summer we can plan a trip here and spend a couple of days taking in the whole museum."

Morgan's eyes lit up. "Oh, that would be amazing. Do you really think we could do that?"

"We can't say for sure, of course. That's why I said maybe." He climbed into the driver's seat.

Morgan got in as well. "I'm good with maybe, but I'll probably remind you about it from time to time."

"I would expect nothing less from my Angel." Josh passed the gift shop bag over to her. "I got these for you."

She gasped when she pulled the sketch pad out of the bag. "My God, I've been missing this so much. It's wonderful." Placing the pad in her lap, she reached for him again and they kissed over the console. "Thank you."

Josh put on his seatbelt and started the car. "There are pencils in there too."

Morgan quickly fastened her seatbelt and dug in the bag for the pencils.

"Oh, these are perfect," she said as she tore open the package. "How did you know which ones to get?"

Josh laughed and confessed, "They were the only pencils they had."

"A very difficult process of elimination then."

"Oh, absolutely. Speaking of decisions, what would you like for supper?"

After a brief discussion they chose to dine on pasta and found an Italian restaurant nearby.

Since they could drink legally in Quebec, Josh ordered each of them a glass of Wine O'clock pinot grigio, a Canadian white wine. Josh ordered the baked ziti and Morgan had shrimp alfredo.

Josh filled up on the complimentary salad and breadsticks and could only eat a few forkfuls of the entrée. Morgan wisely paced herself and finished her meal along with Josh's wine when he didn't want to drink any more.

Josh took the remains of his meal with him and Morgan slipped the leftover breadsticks into the bag.

"They'd only throw them out," she said when Josh gave her a look.

After settling the bill, they left the city on Highway 40 and drove as far as Charlemagne before they found a Super 8.

When they checked in, they were told the only room left with two beds had bunkbeds.

"Surely, Monsieur and Madame would be comfortable in one of our other rooms," the clerk suggested. "A king-sized bed is very roomy."

Josh turned to Morgan with a questioning expression.

Morgan said, "We'll take the bunk beds."

Josh nodded in agreement and started filling out the paperwork.

"I'll take the top bunk. I know how you are with heights," Morgan said with a wink.

"Bridges. Very high bridges. Regular heights I don't mind."

"Still, I called the top one."

Once they got their keys, they headed for their room, passing the swimming pool on the way.

"Wow, this is the nicest pool we've seen yet," Josh said.

"There's a department store right down the street," Morgan said. "Maybe we could get some bathing suits there."

"We could look, but isn't it end-of-season for swimwear?"

"Yes, but they'll have great discounts if they have any left," Morgan said with a grin.

When they arrived at their room, they found it was sized to match the bunkbeds. Neither cared as they shrugged and dropped off their bags. Josh put the leftovers in the tiny fridge, and they headed out to the store.

Morgan stretched out in Zinger's passenger seat, unconcerned about the traffic Josh fought as he drove. He recalled them driving through large cities on their first trip and smiled at the difference. She trusted him now. He vowed never to let her down.

Chapter 14

In Which Shadows Loom
Wednesday, August 30, 1995

Morgan dug through the clearance racks in the women's department, wondering if Josh was having better luck in the men's. There weren't many bathing suits to choose from, and the ones she did find were crushed willy-nilly between other garments. She supposed one couldn't be too choosy when shopping discount and trotted off to the changing rooms with a handful of choices.

The shiny blue one she'd liked best was clearly sized wrong. Small, her ass. She didn't have to put it all the way on to know it would hang like a muumuu on her slender form. The garish floral-patterned suit fit but it looked even worse on than it did crumpled in a ball on the floor, which is exactly where Morgan left it.

After finding a half decent off-white one-piece suit, Morgan decided it wasn't the staff's fault the flowery bathing suit was ugly. She took it along with the others and returned them to the unmanned changing station counter. Whoops. She was only allowed three items at a time. She'd taken six.

She noticed Josh leaning against the wall by the counter as she dumped her discarded choices on top of a pile of other garments.

"Is there no one working here?" she asked.

"Doesn't appear to be," Josh said. "Did you just let yourself in?"

"Yeah. Most of the rooms are unlocked. You find one?"

"It wasn't too hard," he said holding up a pair of beige trunks that looked suspiciously like his boxers with slightly thicker material. At least his boxers weren't that color.

"Our suits clash," Morgan said. "We'll have to keep our distance in the pool."

Josh looked at her strangely.

"I'm kidding." She took her bathing suit and Josh's arm and led him toward the checkouts. "You need to lighten up, Sunshine."

"Sunshine? Really?"

"Why not? I let you call me Angel. Besides, I liked it when you called me that in my birthday card."

"You don't like Angel?" he asked with a frown.

"I love it," she said and kissed him. "Now turn that frown upside down, Sunshine. Don't worry so much about everything."

Josh shrugged, but he did smile.

Back at the hotel, they changed into their new suits and headed straight for the pool.

Morgan trudged along in her socks. "Ugh, I wish I would've bought some sandals," she said. "I hate walking around strange pools in bare feet."

"I thought you worked as a lifeguard before?"

"Yes. But that wasn't a strange pool."

Josh laughed. "Just because you knew the pool doesn't mean you knew the feet that walked around it."

Morgan shook her head. "That's not the point." She stopped at the entrance to the pool and took off her socks, tucking them into the towel she'd brought. Peeking her head in, she saw the place to be clean and well kept. There were no other guests inside. "Actually, this might be all right."

They went in and decided to sit in the whirlpool first. Morgan eased into the hot water and heard Josh echo her sigh of contentment.

"We should have started doing this long ago," he said. "*Merde,* after all those long days in Zinger, we should be getting massages too."

"Hmm, that's an idea for later," Morgan said with a grin.

Josh's eyes popped open and it was her turn to laugh at him.

"I meant innocent massages, you goof. But we've definitely spent too much time in the car lately. I wouldn't be surprised if I've gained five pounds since leaving Bathurst."

"You could stand to gain some weight," Josh said.

Morgan shot him a dirty look. "I happen to like my body just fine."

"I didn't – I mean I was trying to say – I wasn't –"

"Just say you're not calling me fat," Morgan suggested coolly.

"Of course I'm not calling you fat! I was only –"

"And then stop talking."

Josh looked like he was going to keep sputtering but then they both broke out laughing.

"I'm going to do a few laps in the pool," Morgan said once they'd calmed down. "It looks like it was made more for kids but there's a bit of a deep end."

Josh stayed in the whirlpool while she dove in and delighted in the sensation of stretching her muscles as she propelled herself through the water. She knew Josh was watching her and she enjoyed that feeling as well.

When she'd had enough, she drifted over to the shallow end and relaxed on a shelf, leaning against the edge of the pool. Josh joined her.

"Brr. This is a bit chilly after getting out of the whirlpool," he said as he sat and dipped his feet into the water.

With a big sweep of her arm, Morgan splashed his torso and giggled.

Josh recovered from the shock and jumped in. It quickly became a contest of splashing and dunking. When they tired of it, they returned to the whirlpool to soak in its warmth again.

"So, where to tomorrow?" Morgan asked.

"Honestly, I don't know. If we really wanted to, we could push hard and get all the way home. It's probably only an eight-hour drive or so."

"That would please my mother," Morgan said and scrunched up her nose. "Plan B?"

"Actually, I wouldn't mind stopping in Yamachiche to see my grandparents," Josh said.

"Hey, I forgot about that. They don't live far from here, right? Do you think they would mind if you brought me along, though?"

"I think they would be interested in meeting whoever I'm interested in," he said.

"Well, we can't just drop in unannounced. Do you have their number?"

"I would have to call home to get it but if you're up for it . . ."

"If it means not getting home tomorrow, I'm definitely up for it," Morgan said.

A family with three screeching children entered the pool area. Morgan cringed and called an end to their relaxation time.

Back in their room, Morgan took her shower first. When she came out, Josh was still on the phone. She walked quietly to the fridge and eyed the leftovers from the restaurant.

"Get off the phone, Trixie. I was talking to Rab."

Morgan's spine stiffened and she turned ever so slowly to Josh. He didn't look up from the hotel notepad he was doodling on. Actually, doodling wasn't the word. He'd nearly scratched a hole through the thing as he worked viciously on an ink square.

"You're not my girlfriend," Josh growled.

Morgan shut the fridge, appetite gone, and took a seat at the small table to listen to the rest of his side of the conversation. She wondered if Josh even realized she'd come out of the bathroom.

"It only means you caught me by surprise. It won't happen again," he said after a long pause.

Morgan narrowed her eyes. She wasn't thrilled to find him speaking to that girl, but she understood why she might be at his house. Friends with his sister and all . . . the thought didn't comfort Morgan anymore than the first time she'd realized it, but Josh's tone certainly did.

"Give the phone back to Rab," he said firmly.

Morgan swore she saw him shiver as he waited for his request to be carried out.

Finally, he spoke again. "I didn't say anything I haven't told her before. Now please, give me the number."

Satisfied he was speaking to his sister again, Morgan's appetite returned and she went back to the fridge. She waited until Josh got the number and said goodbye before clearing her throat. He looked up at her with tired eyes.

"Problems at home?" she asked.

"No. It's just that . . . well, I'm sure you heard part of it."

Morgan took the leftovers from the fridge back to the table. Josh brought the phone and notepad over to sit with her.

"I'm proud of you," she said and gave him a kiss, not wanting to pursue the topic of the meddling girl. It sounded like he'd at least put her in her place.

He looked relieved and picked up the receiver. "I hope this next call goes better."

Morgan dug into the leftovers as he called his grandparents. After what must have been quite a few rings, Josh launched into a much cheerier conversation.

When he hung up, Morgan offered him the remaining pasta.

"No thanks. I'm good. We're set for tomorrow. *Grand-mère* is excited we're coming, although *Grand-père* will likely be at work."

"That's great news. I'll put the rest of this back in the fridge in case you want it for breakfast."

"Thanks, Angel. I'm going to take my shower."

Josh held her arm as they got up and pulled her in for a kiss. Morgan set the takeout back on the table and leaned into him. Good thing he was still full of chlorine-smell because she was quite tempted to suggest some not-so-innocent massages.

They broke apart, breathless, and Josh hurried off to the bathroom.

Morgan stuffed the food in the fridge and sat down to make her call home.

She couldn't keep the glee from her voice when she informed her mom they would still be another couple of days on the road. Morgan cut the call short, claiming they had yet to eat, before her mom could start with the hysterics. Yes, Morgan was certainly happy they would not be arriving home the next day.

She grabbed her new sketchpad and pencils and climbed up to her bunk where she found a handy little nightlight over the pillows. Perfect.

She stretched out and opened the pad, staring at the fresh blank page. Images flashed through her mind of pictures she'd drawn and lost from her last pad. They intermingled with the paintings she'd seen at the museum that day.

In the end, she decided to draw another sketch of Josh.

Morgan didn't even hear him come out of the bathroom. He'd poked his head up over the bunk by the time she noticed him.

"That didn't take long. I take it you'll be up for a while drawing?" he asked.

Morgan nodded, her attention focused on the page. "I've got a light. You can turn the other ones off," she said.

"Can I have a kiss goodnight?" Josh asked.

Morgan turned to him and smiled. "Sorry, I'm really into this. Of course you can."

They kissed and Josh left to turn off the lights.

Morgan took a good look at her drawing for the first time since she'd begun and was surprised at what she'd put down.

She'd started with an outline of Josh, and then began sketching in Zinger to have Josh leaning on the hood.

She didn't quite remember abandoning those tasks and filling in the sky with dark, heavy clouds.

She certainly didn't recall starting an outline of a girl's face peering through them, glowering down on Josh and Zinger with a look of malice.

Abstract art indeed.

Chapter 15

In Which Nostalgia Reigns
Thursday, August 31, 1995

Josh's first thought upon waking was how it might not have been such a good idea to take this room. He rolled out of bed, avoiding the ladder to the upper bunk, and stretched to loosen his muscles.

When he turned, he found Morgan was still asleep and wondered how late she'd stayed up drawing. He suspected he'd be driving most of the day, as he had done for the past several days.

The trip was wearing on them both. On the way to Seattle, they had the excitement of the unknown and the possibility that their lives would change.

And they did. Just not the way they'd expected.

Now, as they neared the end of the return trip, the unknown and life-changing possibilities still loomed, but neither of them seemed capable of mustering much excitement about them.

Josh smirked. If all had gone according to plan in Seattle, and he'd been accepted into the Corps, Morgan would have been making this trip home with her father instead of him. He believed they would have been home already. He also believed Morgan would have been miserable.

Morning urges broke Josh's rumination and, as he started to deal with them, his foot bumped something. He discovered it was Morgan's new drawing pad. He picked it up and opened it without thinking.

Only the first page had anything on it. He recognized himself and Zinger, but the face in the clouds wasn't Morgan's. He suspected who it might represent.

"Good morning, Sunshine. Getting nosy again?" Morgan's face peered down from the top bunk.

Josh flipped the cover shut. "I guess so. I found it on the floor and didn't think you would mind. You've shown me your work before."

She smiled from her lofty perch. "It's not finished. Trade you a kiss for the sketch book?"

How could he refuse such an enticing offer? With the exchange made, Josh trotted to the bathroom to complete his previously forgotten task.

When he was finished, he left the bathroom to retrieve his bag, figuring he could use a shave before visiting his grandmother.

Morgan was sitting in her bunk stretching. "You done in there?"

"I was going to shave but if you need to use it . . ."

"Yes, please," Morgan replied and hopped off the bunk without using the ladder. "Ouch."

Undeterred, she snatched her bag and dashed past him into the bathroom.

Josh snickered, reminding himself to never, ever get in the way of a girl and her water closet. He turned on the TV and flicked through the channels as she had her shower.

A few minutes later, Morgan called out, "I'm decent. You can come in now."

When Josh entered the bathroom, Morgan was dressed and using a towel to wipe the fog from the mirror.

She inspected her face for – Josh couldn't imagine – wrinkles? Blemishes?

He stepped up to the sink and nudged her with his butt to get her to move to the side. She picked up her comb, ran it through her hair, and finished the rest of her styling process with her fingers.

Josh turned on the tap and pulled off his T-shirt.

Instead of leaving, Morgan went to sit on the edge of the tub, trailing her finger across his bare back as she did.

"Is everything okay?" Josh asked.

"Sure. I just thought I'd like to watch you shave."

"You want to talk about something, don't you?"

"Well, since you mentioned it, I'd like to ask that you not look at my art until it's ready. I'm not angry, it's just I don't like people looking at my work when it's incomplete. I guess I don't want to be judged based on something unfinished, or something I may never want to finish."

As she spoke, Josh lathered his face. He took a new disposable razor from the pack he'd bought on the trip. In his hurry to leave home, he'd forgotten to take his regular razor – a reliable double-headed one with real blades.

"So, I can't even offer my opinion on it?" he asked.

Morgan laughed. "Boy, if I want your opinion on my art, I'll beat it outta you."

Josh held up his hands in surrender. "Say no more."

"Next topic. What's your grandmother like?"

"*Grand-mère* is my maternal grandmother, born and raised in Yamachiche. When Rab and I were younger, *Maman* would drive us over a couple times a year to visit her and *Grand-père*."

"Your father didn't go with you?" Morgan asked.

"He doesn't get along with *la mémé*. I suspect that if *Maman* had listened to *Grand-mère*, she wouldn't have married my father. I'm pretty sure the two of them haven't seen each other since Rab was born and my grandparents came out to see their newest grandbaby. Next topic."

"Whoa. Okay, um, we don't plan to push on to Bathurst after our visit today, do we?"

"Nope." Josh lifted his head to shave under his chin.

"Do you think we could go as far as Edmundston and stay at the Happy Inn again?" she asked.

"I think I can remember how to get to it. You really want to stay at that place again?"

"It was our first stop together. I think it would be a good place for our last stop too."

"I'm not sure we'd get the same rooms," Josh said and rinsed his razor.

"We want a single room anyway." Morgan stood and came up behind him as he cleared the last of the shaving cream off his face. "You missed a spot." She wiped a patch behind his ear with her finger.

"Thanks," Josh said.

Morgan wrapped her arms around him and rested her face on his back. "You have a nice chest."

"You . . ." Josh started to return the compliment but thought better of it.

"I what?"

He turned to face her and completed the embrace. "You don't know how glad I am you agreed to let me go with you to Seattle."

Morgan smiled and kissed him in reply, pressing into him so hard he leaned backwards over the sink. When she broke the kiss, lips barely apart, she said, "Maybe I should have let you brush your teeth first."

He gave her a peck as she laughed and broke away.

It was ten o'clock by the time they got on the road. *Grand-mère* had suggested they stop by for lunch. Yamachiche was only an hour and a half away.

Accordingly, they arrived in Yamachiche a little before eleven-thirty. Compared to the bustle of Montreal, the city felt as sleepy as the St. Lawrence River flowing along its south edge.

Josh stopped at a gas station so they could fill up Zinger and refresh themselves before going to meet his grandmother. As he paid for the gas, he asked the clerk to confirm the directions to the street she lived on. It had indeed been a while since he'd visited.

It wasn't long before they pulled into the driveway of a blue cottage. The name on the mailbox said Rabeau.

Josh parked the car, and they entered the yard surrounded by a white picket fence. Large purple flowers were in bloom in boxes attached to the porch rail.

"Ooh, chrysanthemums," Morgan said as she scurried over to smell them.

Josh smiled and followed her at a more leisurely pace.

The wind chimes on the door sang and the screen door squeaked as Josh's grandmother made her appearance. "Joshua Évariste, come let me get a good look at you. You must have grown a foot since I last saw you."

Josh stepped forward and let her embrace him. "It hasn't been that long, *Grand-mère*, I don't think I've grown very much." He stepped back and said, "Let me introduce you to my girlfriend, Morgan Parker. Morgan, this is my *grand-mère*."

Morgan beamed when Josh said the word girlfriend. "It's a pleasure to meet you, Mrs. Rabeau. I can certainly see where Josh got his striking blue eyes from."

"Thank you, dear. No need to be so formal. You can call me Mary, or *Grand-mère* if you wish. Now come on in, I have lunch almost ready," she said.

"Thank you, Mary," Morgan said.

"We've been looking forward to this all morning," Josh added.

As they entered the house, the yeasty aroma of fresh baked bread filled the air. The scent brought back memories of lazy summer days spent here.

"You're in for a treat," Josh said, grinning at Morgan.

"I'm suddenly hungrier than I thought I was."

A tortoiseshell cat jumped off a rocking chair to rub against Morgan's legs.

"Well, Creo likes you," Josh said, reaching down to scritch the cat behind the ears. "She doesn't rub on just anybody."

His grandmother glanced at the cat. "Oh, that's Lady Sif, Creo's daughter. The only way you can tell them apart is Lady Sif has the white boots on her rear legs. If you need to wash up, Josh can show you where the bathroom is. Otherwise, go on into the dining room and sit while I put the last touches on lunch."

Josh took the not-so-subtle hint and led Morgan down the hall where they washed their hands together.

When they finished, they went to the dining room and Josh pulled out a chair for Morgan.

She eyed him as she sat and looked like she was about to say something but didn't.

Josh assumed it would have been something along the lines of, "I can get my own damned chair," so he left her to push it in by herself.

The table was set with a tablecloth, placemats, and blue willow patterned dishes. A lazy Susan covered with condiments and bowls of lettuce, tomatoes, and onions sat in the middle. A pitcher of ice-cold lemonade gathered condensation beside it.

Josh filled the glasses with lemonade and sat next to Morgan while his grandmother brought in a tray with a sliced loaf of French bread, cold cuts, and cheeses. After she sat down and asked blessings on the food, they all dug in, each designing their own sandwich.

As they ate, they talked about the weather, plans for the coming fall, and *Grand-mère* told Morgan embarrassing stories of Josh's childhood.

"Thank you for speaking English, Mary. I would have had a hard time following in French," Morgan said.

"I prefer to speak to others in their primary language. Other members of the family have different opinions."

"I'm really sorry I didn't get a chance to see *Grand-père* today," Josh said.

"He felt terrible he couldn't be here, but he simply couldn't get off work. I'll be glad once he can officially retire."

"Why is he still working? I thought he was supposed to retire years ago."

"Economy," she replied with a shrug and turned to Morgan. "Did you graduate with Joshua?"

"Yes, just this past spring," Morgan said.

"I understand that you and Joshua have been out to the west coast. How was your trip?"

Morgan and Josh spent the next hour talking and laughing about their trip. They shared the good times, such as taking the ferry from Seattle to Bremerton and visiting the Space Needle, but left out the bad times.

"Well, you kids probably want to get going. I don't want to keep you. Thanks for stopping and visiting."

"Thank you for a wonderful time and a delicious lunch. I may not need to eat supper now," Morgan said and hugged Josh's grandmother.

"You're very welcome, dear."

Josh hugged his grandmother as well. "It was good to see you again. Thank you."

"Listen to me, Joshua, you take good care of this young lady. She's a keeper."

"I plan to do my best," Josh said and smiled at Morgan, who was blushing.

After another round of goodbyes, they climbed into Zinger and waved as they drove away. *Grand-mère* remained on the porch, waving back, two cats sitting at her feet.

"Your grandmother is really sweet," Morgan said.

"I've always enjoyed my visits here. I still wish you could have met my *grand-père*. When I visited as a boy, he had a boat and would take us out on the river. I loved watching all the big ships going back and forth. Once, we even saw a submarine sailing upriver."

"It's sad he has to work at his age. But as your grandmother said, I guess that's the economy nowadays. Hey, wait. Why would a submarine be on the river?" Morgan asked.

"It was probably going to make a port call somewhere. It was flying an American flag."

"If you had joined the Marines, might you have been on a sub?"

"Oh, God no. I can't begin to imagine being enclosed in a 400-foot-long sewer pipe underwater for days at a time." Josh shivered.

"Smart boy," Morgan said.

"Mind if I ask a question?"

"You just asked a question," she said and laughed.

"Okay, point. I was just wondering . . . does the woman in the clouds represent who I think it does? It sure doesn't look like you."

Morgan became quiet and sat for a minute.

"Morgan?"

"See, this is why I don't like people looking at my art before I'm finished," Morgan said. "It was just a conceptual sketch for a piece I'm thinking about painting."

"It looked really good for a sketch. I mean, I could tell that was me and Zinger."

"Let's say the dark woman represents the uncertain future. When I finish the piece, it could be something else entirely – maybe a dog with a bone hanging out of her mouth."

"So you're saying the future's a bitch?" Josh asked.

Morgan laughed. "Yeah, you could say that."

"I hope to see the completed piece one day. Maybe it'll be brighter than you think."

"We can hope," Morgan muttered, though she continued to smile.

The drive to Edmundston passed quickly. Morgan finished her book and declared it wasn't *utter* trash. Josh decided to stop buying her books.

"We should find a place to eat before checking into the motel," Morgan suggested.

"Good idea. If I remember correctly, there wasn't much to choose from near the motel."

They found a fried chicken place and chose to eat inside.

Morgan gave him her order and handed him her purse. "I'll pay, but I really need to use the washroom. I drank way too much lemonade."

Josh placed the order and as he went to pay, he was surprised to find a condom in her wallet. *Weird.* Before he had time to dwell on it too much, the cashier cleared her throat. He handed over the money and zipped the purse shut.

Morgan returned and took his place to wait for their order as he dashed off to the washroom. By time he came out, she had already found a table and devoured a piece of chicken.

They took their time eating and laughing as they threatened to rub their greasy hands on each other's faces.

Their meal finished, and hands thoroughly cleansed from the abundance of grease, Josh drove the remaining distance to the motel.

When they stopped to check in, the parking area was nearly full.

"I hope they have a room for us," Josh said.

"We're not driving home tonight. I don't care if we have to sleep in Zinger."

"I'm sure we can find a room somewhere."

"What's with all the traffic everywhere today, anyway?" Morgan asked.

"Labor Day weekend?" Josh guessed.

"It's only Thursday. Whatever, I'm sure they'll have a room. It's the Happy Inn for crying out loud. I can't imagine too many people wanting to stay here."

"You want to stay here," Josh said.

"Sentimental reasons," she replied.

Inside, the clerk informed them they were in luck. They had one room available and it had double beds.

"Told you they'd have a room for us," Morgan said as they walked out to Zinger.

"What do you want me to say, you were right?" Josh asked.

"Couldn't hurt." She grinned.

"Fine. You were right and I'm lucky to have you," he said and kissed her.

Her grin grew wider and remained in place as Josh drove around to their assigned spot.

Once Zinger was parked, they grabbed their things and went to their room.

As Josh opened the door, Morgan's perma-smile disappeared and her mouth dropped open.

There was only one bed.

Josh tried to hold in his laughter but some escaped.

Morgan narrowed her eyes and reattached her grin. “I’m still right. They had a room. Nothing we can’t handle.”

Chapter 16

In Which All Good Things Must Come to an End
Friday, September 1, 1995

The last time Morgan had woken up in the Happy Inn, she'd done so in a panic as she realized where she was and what she'd done. What had she been thinking, running away from home with a virtual stranger?

This time was a lot different. She and Josh had been up most of the night talking, unable to sleep. Yet for her the panic remained, although its source was different.

Today's the day. End of the road. Time to face the music. No more stalling.

"What're you thinking about, Angel?" Josh asked.

"Same thing you are, probably," Morgan answered while continuing to stare at the ceiling. "What time is it?"

"Just after seven."

She heard Josh's grunt as he rolled over onto the ironing board and couldn't resist a giggle. He'd been doing that all night.

"Ugh, can we get rid of this thing now?" He pushed at the board and poked his head over it.

"Nuh uh. Not until we're both fully clothed. Can't be too careful," she teased.

After being presented with the one-bed dilemma the night before, Morgan had remembered Josh telling her of an Amish custom used to prevent scandalous behavior between courting couples – they placed a bundling board between them in bed. Morgan still wasn't sure what exactly a bundling board was, but she'd made her own version of one by plopping an ironing board on their bed.

Josh gave her a strange look before returning his head to his pillow.

"What's wrong with you?" she asked, sitting up. "Neither of us got much sleep and I heard you smash into the board quite a bit last night, but it wasn't that bad, was it?"

"Not the greatest," he replied. "There's just something I wanted to ask you."

"So ask it."

He seemed to be struggling to find the words. "Well, when I opened your wallet last night – after you told me to," he clarified, "I saw you had a condom in there."

"Oh." Morgan sank back down on her side of the bed.

"I was just wondering when you got it. You said your purse was empty except for your license when it was returned."

"It was."

Josh sat up and looked at her with more questions in his eyes. Morgan wanted to sink into the ground and disappear.

"You had one in *your* wallet," she muttered.

"Right. You know why it was there."

Morgan sat up with an exasperated sigh. "Fine. I bought it after the night in Winnipeg. Just in case. I didn't know you had one then, remember?"

"I remember. I'm just wondering why you bought one."

"Just in case," she repeated, enunciating each word.

Josh held up his hands in surrender as she got out of bed.

"I'm going to shower unless you need to get in there first," she announced.

"Go ahead," he said.

Morgan took her bag into the bathroom and cranked on the water. How awkward. Why couldn't he have just pretended not to see it? And what was the big deal anyway? She only bought it in case . . .

In case what?

By the time Morgan had showered and cleared her head some, she'd come up with the answer to her own question. Josh's question too, really. Not that she felt like sharing the information with him.

She'd bought it in case the opportunity presented itself again.

Not to be super safe and responsible. Not because she expected to get wasted and find herself swept away beyond all reason again.

She'd bought it because she had wanted to use it.

But then they'd had the talk about special people and intimate acts and, well, it was clear he didn't feel the same way. They weren't ready, he'd said. And she'd agreed.

Morgan was finished in the bathroom but was still too embarrassed to face Josh. Nevertheless, she couldn't sit there all day.

Josh was dressed and putting the ironing board back in its place when she came out.

"I'll give it to you," he said. "The board was a brilliant idea."

Morgan laughed as he grimaced, feigning pain in his side, and was thankful he seemed to be willing to let the issue of the wallet-find slide.

"You're the one who told me about bundling boards," she said. "I never would have thought of it otherwise."

"Nonsense. You would have come up with something. The best I would have come up with would have been me sleeping on the floor or in a chair. You're definitely the creative soul you claim to be. Hey, since we're on the nostalgia train, what do you think of going home the same way we came?"

"You mean up through Campbellton?" Morgan sat on the bed. "Nah, I think we've dragged our feet enough. Today's the day," she said, echoing her morning thought.

Josh came over to join her. "It was bound to happen."

"I guess the bright side is my dad will still be at work when I get home. I'll just have to deal with my rabid mom and screaming brother to begin with."

"Hey, at least your family's happy you're coming home," Josh said with a hint of sadness in his voice.

Morgan put her arm around him. "Come on now. Your mom will be happy to see you, won't she? And surely your sister . . ." Green eyes flared greener as she thought of who might be lurking around that sister.

Josh got up and tugged her hand. "You're right. There are good and bad things waiting for us in Bathurst, but we're going back together."

He pulled her up and kissed her. She reciprocated, never wanting it to end.

But sadly, all good things do end.

"I'll drive," she said.

Morgan and Josh dragged themselves out to Zinger. Morgan drove around front and waited in the car while he checked out.

So strange to think this was the last time their morning rituals would consist of waking up next to each other, planning their day together, and spending nearly every minute with each other.

By the time Josh came out and got back in the car, Morgan had been struck with another hysterical thought.

"What am I supposed to do when we get there? Just drop you off in front of your house and drive away?"

Josh stared at the tears falling down her cheeks that she didn't bother brushing away. "That's the general idea to start with," he said, looking confused.

"But I don't know where you live. I don't even know your damned phone number!"

And that was it. Josh held her best he could over the console while she wept.

Morgan felt like she'd lived an entire life with this guy since that day long ago when she'd thrown caution to the wind and set out on the open road with him. She loved him. She couldn't imagine not being with him.

And she didn't even know his phone number.

Morgan allowed herself to cry until she had no more tears and then looked up at Josh. He'd somehow managed to wrangle a pen with one hand and write his number on the corner of one of the many maps littering Zinger.

He smiled and handed her the map.

Morgan sat up and wiped her face. Josh continued to sit patiently. He looked so confident, so calm.

"You're my rock." She sniffled. "What am I going to do without you?"

"Nothing. I'll always be with you. I might be sleeping in my house across town or maybe I'll screw up and be living in Old Blue," he said. "But wherever I am, you'll be here in my heart." He took her hand and placed it on his chest.

Morgan took a deep breath, allowing his words to comfort her. "Thanks. Oh, shit – your truck keys. They were stolen with my bag!"

"Don't worry, Cal has a spare set."

"Josh, I'm trying my best here, but why do I suddenly feel totally unprepared? It's not like we didn't know where we were going for the last ten days."

"Nonsense," Josh said. "We're a lot more prepared than when we left for Seattle. But you're not the only one struggling today."

"You're holding up a lot better than me."

"I'm being manly. You're sure you want to drive?"

That got a genuine laugh out of her. "Yep. I'm really sorry about all that. I'm just – well, you know. End of an era."

"It feels like it, doesn't it? But it's also the beginning of a new one. Let's look forward to building a future – together."

Morgan nodded and started the car with shaky hands. The day was warm and sunny as they set out on the final stretch. After they'd left the city behind, Josh found a radio station playing the top hits and cranked up the volume for her.

Morgan smiled her appreciation and finally allowed herself to relax. Might as well appreciate the last few carefree hours they had. The music, the sunshine, the open road, and Josh's presence were all she needed.

They stopped for their final tank of gas in Saint Leonard and had breakfast at a donut shop. Morgan's stomach wouldn't allow anything more than coffee, but Josh managed to get a couple of donuts into his.

Back on the road, their talk turned to memories of their initial trip and Morgan found herself excited to start an artistic chronicling of their journey. Once she got the disposable cameras developed, she intended to lay the photos out in scrapbook form and add her own sketches and eventually paintings.

She was telling Josh about her idea when the sign for Bathurst appeared.

They were home.

Morgan trailed off midsentence and placed her hand on the console for Josh to hold. He did.

"I guess it's time to give me those directions to your house," she said.

"I guess so."

They continued to hold hands as they drove and the only words spoken were from Josh, telling her where to go.

It felt so surreal, driving through the streets of Bathurst as if she were a stranger. Not exactly a stranger, but someone who'd gone back in time. What had that one clerk said? You can't go home again.

Josh lived across the river from Morgan's place. The houses in his neighborhood were closer together and the trees were more abundant. Children were out playing in their yards or riding bikes on thc streets as they enjoyed the last days of summer vacation.

By the time Morgan pulled into the driveway of Josh's house, she was trembling. "This is so weird."

She stopped between two vehicles parked there. Josh's face darkened for just a second. "I know," he said. "Come help me get my bag out of the trunk?"

"You have your own – oh."

Morgan got out of the car and met Josh at the back of Zinger. He opened the trunk with his key and grabbed his bag and blanket, then closed it and turned to her.

His gear ended up in a heap at their feet as their farewell kiss turned steamy. Morgan wanted nothing more than to hop back in the car with him and flee once again.

They broke apart, breathless, and Morgan laughed. "Well, at least that'll give you something to remember me by until I see you again."

A frown flitted across Josh's face before he smiled at her. "I love you, Angel, and am so damned glad we made this trip together."

Morgan's heart skipped a beat and she found herself at a loss for words.

"You . . . you love me?"

"I do," he said. "Don't feel you have to say –"

"But I love you," Morgan whispered. "I've known for a while."

Josh blinked. "Then I guess we really have nothing to worry about. I'll call you tonight, okay?"

Morgan nodded and forced herself to get back in the car without further ado. She waved from the street as she drove off, watching him in the rearview mirror until she turned the corner.

Chapter 17

In Which the Welcome Was as Expected
Friday, September 1, 1995

Josh watched from the front steps until Morgan and Zinger were out of sight.

It wasn't the first time she'd driven off without him. But at least this time they had parted on good terms – the best by far.

Well, as Morgan would say, it's time to face the music.

Josh faced the door and tried the doorknob. Locked. He dug in his pocket for his house key, but then remembered tossing it on the table the day he'd been kicked out of the house. The only key he possessed now was the key to Morgan's car – the one she'd just left in.

Josh wondered why his father's car was parked in the driveway. His father should be at work and he was the last person Josh wanted to see. Well, maybe next to last. Trixie's Honda was parked there too. Rab might have borrowed it, but Josh wouldn't bet on it.

He sighed heavily and knocked on the door. No one responded.

He knocked again and someone turned the deadbolt. The door opened and Rab greeted him with crossed arms and a smirk.

"Well, the prodigal son has returned. Quick! Slay the fatted calf. Whoops, too late, she just drove off. By the way, you're not getting your room back."

"Hello to you too, sis," Josh said.

"Keep your voice down. Dad's sleeping."

Josh pushed his way past his sister, who hadn't moved, and dropped his gear in the kitchen. "Why is Father sleeping? Is he sick? Why wouldn't you have told me?"

Rab closed the front door. "As seldom as you called, it's amazing you even knew we still lived here. Did your hussy keep you that busy?"

"Let's get one thing straight right now. Morgan," he emphasized the name, "is neither fat nor a hussy. She is my girlfriend, and you will stop insulting her."

"Or what?"

"Or I'll inform *Maman* about how you got puking dog drunk at the party."

"She already knows and grounded me for two weeks. I made sure you got the blame, though," Rab said and made an ugly face.

"Okay, then, I'll kick you out and take my old bedroom back."

"You can't do that."

"I'm the oldest, it's mine by right, especially when I start paying rent. I only let you use it because I didn't expect to be living here again," Josh said.

Rab eyed him, considering the threat. "Okay, okay, I'll try not to insult your friend."

"Morgan."

"Okay, okay, okay, Morgan. Are you happy now?" Rab asked.

"Back to my previous question, why is Father sleeping?"

"Because, he-who-can't-be-bothered-to-call-home, Dad now works the graveyard shift."

"When did this happen?" Josh asked.

"Obviously, while you were away. Or did you want a specific date and time?"

"That'll do," Josh said. "Any other surprises you want to toss at me while you're at it?"

"I have a boyfriend. Or had. He wasn't happy with me getting grounded and hasn't called in a few days," Rab said with a shrug.

"Am I going to have to punch his lights out?"

"I'll tell you if he ever needs it, but don't give me the third degree about David. He's a decent guy." Rab narrowed her eyes and added, "Enough chatter, there's someone here waiting to see you."

Josh frowned, scanning the house from the kitchen. “So Trixie *is* here. I’m surprised she didn’t glom onto me when I stepped in the door.”

“She’s waiting for you in her room.”

“Her room? Since when did she start living here? Never mind, I know – while I was gallivanting across the country.”

“Got it in one. She’s not really living here. She’s just been spending a lot of nights in my old room since you abandoned her,” Rab said and crossed her arms again.

“I didn’t . . .” *Careful what you say, Josh.* “I left to join the Marines. You were there when I told her not to wait for me.”

“Yeah, and she kissed you. Hard. But the kiss you laid on Morgan? I’m surprised the car didn’t melt.” Rab put one hand over her heart and fanned herself with the other.

“Why were you watching?”

“We wanted to see who drove up and you two were standing in plain view. The whole neighborhood will be talking for weeks,” Rab said.

“Well, that has nothing to do with Trixie. I’m not going to talk to her in your old room or any bedroom in this house,” Josh said. “To be honest, I’d rather not talk to her at all. I said everything I needed to say the other night.”

“And she cried all night afterward. Do you think she’s going to let you get away with a telephone breakup?”

“She was never my girlfriend. She might have thought she was, but I never asked her to be my girlfriend. I never claimed she was my girlfriend,” Josh said, loud enough for Trixie to hear. He was sure she was listening to their every word.

The uncertain future came storming out of the bedroom and stopped directly in front of him.

“How can you say that, Joshua Hampton? How can you say that after all the times we went out on dates? And those private times we shared? Didn’t they mean anything to you?”

"It meant we were two young, kinda lonely people who enjoyed each other's company. That's it. Nothing more," Josh said, shrugging.

Rub backed away and sat at the kitchen table to watch the show.

"So you spend a couple of days joyriding with that blond slip of a girl and all of a sudden she's your girlfriend?" Trixie asked, her face growing redder by the second.

"It was more than a couple of days, we weren't joyriding, and yes, she is my girlfriend."

"She *looks* like a tramp. Tell me, how did her tonsils taste?"

"There's no need to be crude," Josh said.

"God, I knew I shouldn't have let you go with her. I should have delayed you until she left without you."

Trixie had clearly lost her mind. Yet Josh continued trying to reason with her. "She wouldn't have left without me. She needed my help to make the trip."

"But if you hadn't been there to meet her, she would've waited a little while and gone home, madder than a hornet, thinking you were the biggest jerk in the universe. Which you are, by the way." Trixie was practically screaming now.

"Only from your point of view. And it wouldn't have worked. I would've called her and sorted things out. You would only have delayed the inevitable," Josh said, trying hard to keep his voice even.

"Maybe. Or maybe she never would have spoken to you again. And who would have been here waiting for you? Good old me." Her eyes shone with a delusional sort of triumph.

"Trixie, it didn't happen," Josh said warily. "I was leaving to join the Marines anyway."

"Oh, that worked really well for you, didn't it, Josh? They rejected you. Now here you are, dragging your ass back home. Forget Morg. I'll help you get back on your feet."

Trixie held her arms out to Josh, but he stepped back, keeping his arms crossed.

"Nothing has changed since we spoke on the phone."

"So I'm nothing? Is that what you think of me? Was I just a plaything you used for a while and discarded when you grew tired of me?" Trixie shrieked. Hot, angry tears streaked down her face.

A door opened down the hall. "What in the Blue Blazes is going on out here? I'm trying to sleep."

"Shit. Now we're in for it," Rab said and slid down in her chair.

Heavy steps came down the hall and Josh's father appeared at the kitchen door in a bathrobe.

"I was trying to be civil, but this girl can't accept the fact that she's not my girlfriend," Josh said.

"I'm sorry I disturbed you, Mr. Hampton." Trixie sniffled. "It's just that I love your son and I'm trying to get him to understand that."

"I think it's time for you to go home, young lady," Josh's father said. He waited as Trixie wiped her eyes and trotted down the hall before addressing Rab. "If this is going to happen every time she's here, then she can't come over. Go help her on her way."

Rab got up and left the kitchen with her chin on her chest. "Yes, Dad," she said as she passed him.

Only Josh and his father remained. Neither spoke, but they stood gauging one another.

Josh watched Trixie and his sister slip quietly past his father without turning their way.

After the front door opened and closed, Josh's father asked, "Did you sister leave too?"

Josh peered through the kitchen window. "She's getting in the car with her."

"Just as well. Sit down," his father said and lowered himself into a chair.

"Can I get you some coffee or something, Father?"

"No. We're going to talk and then I'm going back to bed. I trust there will be no more outbursts." He looked pointedly at Josh.

"I tried to keep my voice down, but when she started yelling it was hard not to yell back."

"Try harder."

"I'll try to avoid her," Josh said.

His father stared at him for a long quiet moment.

"Your mother talked to you about paying rent." It was a statement not a question.

Josh nodded.

His father turned toward the calendar on the fridge. "Today's the first, so rent is already due. You will pay before the fifth or you can find someplace else to live. Is that clear?"

"I'm a little low on funds, Father."

He shrugged. "It's not my fault you wanted to run across the country to be a hero. Didn't work so well, did it?"

"Why didn't you tell me you couldn't enlist because of asthma?"

"Because you were a pig-headed little snot who wouldn't have listened. I simply spared myself the hassle."

Josh took a breath and let the comment slide. "The point is, my funds are low," he said, lifting his hands in a plea.

"Well, you need to cough up four hundred dollars by the fifth or get out."

"Four hundred for rent? That's highway robbery. It's almost as much as the mortgage."

"You probably spent at least that much on hotels."

"But this isn't a hotel," Josh argued.

"Do you enjoy electricity? Running water? Food on the table? Clean clothes? Living expenses are more than just rent. You're welcome to find out for yourself."

"I'll do my best to get it to you," Josh said, frowning.

"By the fifth."

"Yes, by the fifth."

Satisfied, Josh's father leaned back in his chair. "Now what's this I hear about that girl you ran off with? She's your girlfriend now?"

"You heard correctly. Morgan is my girlfriend."

"It takes more than a couple of weeks to develop a lasting relationship."

"It was an intense couple of weeks. We were together during the highs and the lows and helped each other through them," Josh said.

"For better or worse, eh? Are you already engaged?"

"No. We both know we need to learn more about each other."

"Well, you've got a little sense then. Are you sleeping with her?" his father asked.

"I'm not going to discuss that with you," Josh said.

"It doesn't matter to me as long as you're using protection. Don't make babies until you're ready for them."

Josh kept his mouth shut. He wanted to spend at least one night at home.

"Is there anything else we need to discuss?" Josh asked, hoping to put an end to the conversation.

His father stood. "Nah, I think we covered the important parts. Will you be here for supper?"

"Is it still at six?"

"No, at eight. Your mother prepares it later so I can eat and then get ready for work."

"Congratulations on your new position," Josh offered.

"It has its advantages, but I'm still trying to adjust to sleeping during the day," his father said and shuffled back toward the bedroom.

"Welcome home, Josh," he said to himself.

Because no one else had.

Chapter 18

In Which Things Go Suspiciously Well
Friday, September 1, 1995

Morgan slammed the car door harder than she'd intended and sat back in Zinger's seat, grateful to be out of the bank.

What was that woman's problem? If she disliked her job so much, maybe she should think about retiring.

With the long weekend coming up, Morgan had stopped to get a replacement bank card before going home. She also wanted to withdraw the money she owed her parents so she could pay them back straightaway.

What should have been two simple requests ended up taking over an hour, as the cranky black-haired woman dragged out the process and lectured Morgan for failing to report her card missing when she'd lost it weeks ago in North Dakota. She even had the gall to question why Morgan was taking out so much cash.

Morgan tossed her purse and a pamphlet she'd grabbed on the way out onto the passenger seat and muttered, "Good luck with the customer feedback survey, Margaret." She absolutely intended to fill that out later.

It was early afternoon when Morgan parked her car in front of her house, but she was ready for bed. Her mother's car was in the driveway. True to her word, she'd taken the day off to be home when Morgan arrived.

Morgan would rather have been welcomed back by Clarissa, the babysitter.

She honestly didn't know what to expect as she gathered her things and walked up to the house. She paused at the front door, feeling like she should knock. Weird.

Morgan shook her head and swung the door open. The first thing she heard was Matthew's laughter coming from the living room just around the corner of the entry. At least he wasn't crying today. It smelled like her mom was baking cookies, too. She set her bag down and took off her shoes.

"Morgan, is that you?" her mom called out.

Morgan stepped around the corner and just stood there with her best apologetic smile on.

Matthew was up in his walker and screamed at the sight of her. Morgan's mom dropped an armload of toys and ran over to hug her.

"Honey, we missed you so much. Welcome home."

Morgan hugged her back just as hard and was surprised when tears sprang to her eyes. She really had missed her mom.

"Thanks, Mom." She wiped the errant tear that escaped as her mom released her and chuckled. "So, what did I miss?"

"Oh, my girl. I don't know where to begin."

Matthew, who was not about to be left out of the reunion, had made his way over and rammed his walker into Morgan's legs.

"Hey, kiddo." She patted him on the head and he squealed with delight.

"Oh, listen to this." Morgan's mom leaned down and spoke to Matthew. "Now who's here? Who's your sister? Can you say . . ."

Matthew hollered and waved his arms in the air, spinning the walker in circles.

After a lot of prompting and calming on their mom's part, Matthew finally managed to address his sister as "Morg!"

Morgan frowned at the distasteful nickname but quickly recovered. She congratulated Matthew on his achievement, and she and her mom went into the kitchen to make a pot of coffee.

Morgan noticed the stack of birthday presents waiting for her on the table and peeked in the oven where she saw not cookies, but a cake baking. A pang of guilt shot through her when she realized they were probably planning on celebrating her belated eighteenth birthday today.

"So, should I save the apologizing for when Dad gets home or start now?" Morgan asked.

Her mom brushed a strand of blond hair out of her eye as she considered Morgan.

"I think we all have apologies to make, and I think I should go first."

Morgan's eyebrows shot up in surprise. "I ran away from home, remember?"

It was hard to tell if her mom was laughing or crying. A bit of both, it seemed. She looked as if she'd aged over the past few weeks. Her brown eyes were lackluster, the wrinkle lines around them more prominent.

"I do remember," her mom finally said. "You have no idea how scared I was. But I understand why you did it. Sort of. Promise me you won't take off like that again."

"I promise," Morgan said.

"I hope you can forgive me – us – for keeping the secret of your dad's family from you for all these years. It's what he wanted."

"I can't say I wasn't angry when I found out, but I've had a lot of time to think about it on the trip home. Like you said, it's what he wanted." Morgan shrugged.

"Let's take this into the living room."

Morgan's mom poured the coffee and they returned to sit with Matthew. He rushed over to Morgan and she fiddled with the blocks on his table to keep him entertained.

"I haven't seen Randy since, well, since you were born," her mom said, staring down into her coffee. "Was he good to you?"

"He was fine. He wasn't what I was expecting, obviously, but I'm glad I met him. His wife's nice too, and their son is cute," Morgan added before her mom could ask.

She nodded and looked up. "Now tell me about this Joshua person," she said with a smile.

Morgan grinned. "You're going to love him, Mom. He's so nice and he's definitely respectful. He's . . . he's my boyfriend."

"Well, when do we get to meet him?"

"I don't know. Soon, hopefully."

Morgan couldn't believe how well-behaved her mom was being. After all those hysterical phone calls and all the grief she'd given her, Morgan was still waiting for the other shoe to drop.

As the afternoon wore on, she allowed herself to relax and just enjoy being home. When her mom went to put Matthew down for his nap, Morgan took her bag to her room. It wasn't hard to tell someone had searched it. Probably looking for clues as to where she'd gone. But really, what could she expect?

She sighed and tossed her bag onto her bed. On the way out, Morgan noticed the door to her dad's home office was open and a computer sat on his desk.

"When did you get this?" Morgan asked as her mom came out of Matthew's room.

"Last week. Your dad's really excited to show it to you. It connects to the internet and everything."

"That's cool. You want help with supper?"

"Sure. I'm making lasagna. You can work on the salad if you like."

Morgan and her mom chatted happily as they prepared the meal. Morgan did most of the talking, and most of it was about Josh.

A while later, Morgan heard the front door open and ran from the kitchen to greet her dad.

She threw herself into his arms and mumbled, "Welcome home, Dad."

Just like her mom, if there were any hard feelings present, they were buried deep as he hugged her back. "Welcome home, my girl."

He was full of smiles and eager to show her the new computer. They played around on the internet for a while and her dad showed her some of the school programs she could enroll in, based on what she'd told him she was interested in. She didn't have the heart to tell him she was reconsidering leaving Bathurst to go to school. However, she didn't need to right away. Some of the courses were even offered online.

The future was looking bright indeed as they left his office for dinner. Morgan could only hope Josh's homecoming was going as well. She couldn't wait to talk to him tonight.

The mouth-watering aromas of home-cooked food that had been tantalizing Morgan for hours did not disappoint. By the time she'd polished off her Caesar salad and two large pieces of lasagna, she didn't think she could eat another bite.

Morgan leaned back in her chair and watched as her mother lit the candles on her birthday cake. Devil's food cake. She'd make room.

Her parents sang Happy Birthday as Matthew screeched along and Morgan felt another pang of guilt. She didn't deserve this.

"Thanks, you guys," she said after blowing out the candles. "I'm really sorry I wasn't here for my actual birthday."

"You're here now," her dad said.

Morgan nodded her gratitude and began cutting the cake.

After the cake was consumed, Morgan and her mom did the dishes while her dad kept Matthew entertained until it was time to open presents. She chatted on about bits of her trip that were parent-appropriate, and her dad was also eager to meet her boyfriend Josh.

After they settled back at the table for presents, Morgan squealed with delight as she opened the camera she'd known she was getting. "This is so great. Thank you!"

She continued to open packages and stick the bows on Matthew's head, receiving the usual gifts she got each year. Art supplies, CDs she'd asked for, and of course her card had a generous offering of cash in it.

"Thanks," she said again. "But I believe I owe you some money. I have it in my room; let me go get it."

Morgan's dad placed a hand on her arm as she went to get up. "No. You keep it. Happy birthday."

"No. I can't. I told you I'd pay you back and I will."

"We insist," her mom added.

Morgan sat back down, not sure what to think. It was nice of them and all, but something else was going on here.

Yes. Studying them more closely, Morgan saw what she'd been trying to put her finger on all day. Matthew was cluelessly gnawing on a bow, but her parents looked nervous.

"We have one last gift for you," her dad said, pulling a rectangular package from under the table.

Morgan regarded them suspiciously as she opened it. "A cell phone?" She tried to sound more excited than she was. The walkie-talkie shaped contraption had to be expensive, but she really, really hated phones.

"Yes. It's the newest model, better than the ones we have at work," her dad said. "You have sixty minutes a month on this plan and it's paid up for the year. After that we'll expect you to take over the contract on your own."

"Sure. Uh, thanks. Again." Morgan stared at the thing, wondering who'd she'd ever need to call besides Josh and maybe Mel, once she started speaking to her again. "Well, you've certainly spoiled me. That's got to be all, right?"

Her mom and dad looked at each other and her dad nodded. Her mom's eyes filled with tears, but she was smiling.

A nervous smile.

"That's all the birthday gifts." Her dad chuckled.

Morgan sat and waited. That shoe was coming.

"We do have some news," her mom said.

Morgan continued to sit.

Her dad cleared his throat. "Morgan, you're going to have another little brother or sister!"

As if on cue, Matthew grunted and filled his diaper.

The smell was the perfect punctuation for that moment.

Morgan couldn't remember what she said, if anything, as she got up and left the table. She only recalled thinking, *Well, it's settled. I'm moving out.*

No way was she living in a daycare center.

Chapter 19

In Which Josh Attempts Plan B
Saturday, September 2, 1995

Josh rolled over to check the time, only to find his alarm clock wasn't on the white and gold nightstand next to the bed. He hadn't attempted to sort through the hodgepodge of boxes before flopping into bed the night before.

When claiming Josh's old room, Rab had randomly filled boxes and unceremoniously dumped them into hers. With another eviction pending in three days, Josh wasn't in a hurry to unpack.

Even though he'd stripped the sheets and pillowcase off the bed, the room still smelled of patchouli, Trixie's favorite perfume. Josh hadn't bothered to remake the bed, but instead tossed a quilt over the mattress and slept on top of it with his trusty green woolen blanket.

Josh heard the front door close and sat up to grab his wristwatch. It was seven o'clock. Since it was Saturday, his mother wouldn't be heading to work, so his father must have just arrived home.

Low conversation coming from the kitchen and the sound of a frying pan being set on the stove confirmed this. Josh was in no hurry to get up. Although he and his father were on better terms than before he left, Josh wasn't quite ready to be all chummy with the man yet.

He flopped back on the pillow and stared at the pastel blue ceiling. A flying pink unicorn stared back at him from between fluffy white clouds.

The walls were no better. Faded strips of cheery sunflower wallpaper marked the few places where posters had not festooned the walls. Here and there bits of cellophane tape remained with a fragment of poster left behind.

Josh sighed, recalling how his mother had completed his lackluster homecoming the night before. She'd arrived home in a bad mood and, after a perfunctory hug, told him to wash up and help her get supper going since he'd driven his sister off.

He decided to focus on the best part of yesterday – his phone call to Morgan. At least Rab had left a phone in her old room for him. The welcome home Morgan had received from her family had gone better than his. However, she'd been quite upset about the prospect of another infant in the house. Josh had spoken to her with soothing words, assuring her things would be all right, and hadn't troubled her with his own problems.

By the time their conversation finished, sometime around midnight, Morgan had sounded happier and told him again that she loved him – first. Josh had replied in kind and his heart was lifted to know her earlier declaration of affection hadn't been spurious or simply spontaneous. Whatever the future held, he could get through it with Morgan by his side.

When Josh heard the door to his parents' room close, he checked his watch again – seven-thirty. He got up and went down the hall to the bathroom to get ready for the day. The door to Rab's room was shut and he hoped she was sleeping.

His sister had glared at him throughout the meal after she arrived home – thankfully without Trixie – the night before. The only time she'd spoken to him was to tell him not to tie up the phone all night. He had summarily ignored her demand.

Once Josh was dressed, he went to the kitchen. He would have to endure whatever his mother had to say to him this morning because he needed to borrow her car.

She was reading the paper when he entered. "Breakfast is at seven Tuesday through Saturday," his mother said in French.

"I'll get my own breakfast, *Maman*," Josh replied in the same language.

"I understand your father spoke to you on the matter of rent." She laid the newspaper on the table and folded her hands on it.

"Yes, but I'm concerned about my ability to pay. I don't suppose I can get a loan?" Josh asked. He got a box of Fruity Rings out of the cupboard, and, because his mother was there, a bowl.

"I may work for a bank, but I am not a bank. Furthermore, the bank won't give a loan to an unemployed person."

"So I've been set up for failure?" Josh stopped with his hand on the refrigerator handle.

"If anyone set you up for failure, son, it was yourself. You knew we would expect rent if you returned, but you insisted on spending most of your savings on a trip to the other side of the continent. And for what? To fall flat on your face."

"The trip helped me figure out a lot of things. At least I no longer hold Father's actions against him," Josh said and took the milk from the fridge. He grabbed a spoon before sitting down.

"You should have just flown home and saved yourself a lot of money."

Josh poured cereal into the bowl. "I couldn't let Morgan drive back by herself."

"As I understand it, her father was going to fly to Seattle and drive her back. She would not have been alone, or did you have a hidden agenda?" his mother asked, folding her arms across her chest.

"We became fond of each other on the drive to Seattle. We wanted to see if there was really something there on the drive back."

"You could have done that after she arrived back here with her father."

Josh swallowed a mouthful of fruit-flavored, sugar-coated, oaty-goodness. "I guess it didn't occur to me."

"I'm afraid you let your hormones think for you. Am I going to have to worry about a rushed wedding and a teenaged mother?"

"No, Morgan isn't pregnant," Josh said.

"Well, thank God for that. I'm not sure this Parker girl is right for you, son."

"How would you know? I doubt you've ever met her."

"I'm sure I've seen her at least once, but her parents and I spoke several times while you were joyriding across the provinces. She seems to be ungrounded and very irresponsible. She didn't even bother to report a lost debit card until weeks after it went missing."

"While she didn't leave on the best of conditions, she worked it out with her parents from Seattle. And, as you've pointed out, they let her return with me rather than sending her father to accompany her," Josh said, punctuating the point with an empty spoon.

"That wasn't the best decision on their part. They don't know you from Adam. If it had been your sister, your father would have flown out to get her, no matter how much she protested."

"That's got nothing to do with Morgan and me," Josh said.

"Well, you've danced the dance; now it's time to pay the piper, son. I hope you have a plan."

Josh stood and took his dishes to the sink. "I plan to go talk to Cal today so I can start working again."

"That will help you in the future but not for this month's rent," his mother said.

Josh shrugged. "I'll think of something and if I don't, as you said, it's on me. It would help if I could borrow your car."

"You can use it this morning, but I expect you to have it back by noon with a full gas tank. I have places to go this afternoon."

Josh cringed inwardly. "Yes, *Maman*."

"You know where my keys are. Remember, noon."

"May I have my house key back?" Josh asked.

"When you pay the first month's rent, you may."

Unreal. Josh washed his dishes in silence and returned to his room.

Remembering it was Labor Day weekend, he decided to call to see if Cal's was even open today.

Josh spoke to Cal's youngest daughter, Robin, who was happy to hear from him and surprised he was back in town. She confirmed they were open until noon.

Well, there's no time like the present. Josh made sure he had his wallet and collected his mother's keys before heading out the door.

Driving her car made him painfully aware he would soon need his own means of transportation. He'd gotten used to driving Zinger almost every day in August.

At least they would still have Morgan's car when they went somewhere together, as they would tonight. However, if they were using Zinger, Josh would prefer it was their choice and not his need. She would have thought that old-fashioned, but that's the way he was.

When Josh turned onto the dirt road where Cal's was located and his pickup truck Old Blue came into view, he had mixed feelings. He was glad to see his labor of love again, but sad to know he wouldn't be able to drive it until he replaced that engine.

Josh parked next to the truck. He got out of the car and paused in front of his vehicle to put a hand on the hood. "Hey old girl, bet you didn't expect to see me this soon. We'll get you up and running again. I promise."

Cal came out of the garage, wiping his hands on a rag.

Josh was glad to see him and hurried over to shake his hand.

"Welcome back, Josh," Cal said. "I wasn't expecting to see you for a few months yet."

Josh shrugged. "Me neither, but the Marines didn't accept me and it seemed best to come back here."

"I'm sorry to hear that you couldn't enlist. I know how much you were looking forward to joining."

"I was, but that ship has sailed," Josh said. "The reason I came by today was to ask when I could start working again."

Cal grimaced. "That's kind of a problem. You see, you weren't planning on coming back and I needed help around the shop, so I hired another kid. You might know him; name's Brian Dunn."

Disappointment crushed Josh. What was he going to do now?

Cal stood quietly waiting for him to answer.

"Yeah, I know Brian," Josh finally managed.

"I'm sorry I don't have a position for you, Josh. My budget only allows for one part-time assistant. It would be wrong to let him go just because you came back."

"I understand," Josh said, but it was only partially true. "Well, I'm going to need some transportation until I get Old Blue up and running. Do you know anyone who has a beater they'd be willing to part with?"

"Robin's driving a Chevy Vega that's almost as old as your truck," Cal said.

"I remember her car, but won't she still need it?" Josh asked.

"She's been saving up to get a newer car. Once she's done with the Vega, I don't have any more kids to pass it down to. I'd rather sell it to you than park it out back of my house."

"It still runs? Weren't the engines in those things notorious for warping their aluminum blocks?"

"They were," Cal said, "so I jerked this one out, modified the engine compartment, and put a Honda engine in it. Runs like a champ."

"What do you want for it?" Josh asked, wondering how comfortable it would be to sleep in.

"Two hundred dollars and it's yours."

Josh grimaced again. "The trip pretty much wiped my savings out. Can we work out some kind of payment?"

"I'll tell you what we can do. I have some odd jobs around the garage I want to get done. How about I hire you for seven an hour until you get the car paid off? By then Robin should have her new car," Cal offered.

"That's about thirty hours," Josh said. "Do you have that much work?"

"I have plenty of odd jobs I need done. And after you finish paying off the car, you can continue to help around the place on an as-needed basis."

"Thanks, Cal," Josh said, and they shook on it.

"So what are you going to do about that truck of yours?" Cal asked, nodding at Old Blue. "I've had someone make an offer on it, more than I'm selling the Vega for."

"Did the person know it doesn't run?"

"Yep. Didn't faze him a bit. I could connect you two if you're interested."

Josh considered the offer. That kind of money would almost cover the rent, but it probably wouldn't happen soon enough. And did he really want to give up his truck for a single month's rent?

"I'd rather keep my truck here if you're still okay with that," Josh said after his brief deliberation. "I'm still planning to get her fixed up."

"Okay, I thought I would just pass that on to you. If you're free Tuesday, stop on by and I'll set you to work."

"Sounds like a plan."

Josh waved goodbye and returned to his mother's car.

It was officially the worst homecoming ever. Time to come up with Plan C.

Chapter 20

In Which There Are More Babies to Come
Saturday, September 2, 1995

Morgan took her paintbrush and flung a huge blob of black onto the canvas.

"Whoops."

She'd used more force than intended. Checking around the plastic tarp that sat under the easel, Morgan saw she hadn't gotten any on the rug. Good enough.

She took the brush and continued to swirl mindless patterns into the glob. Not completely mindless; her thoughts were running full steam ahead as she added the strokes.

"Welcome home, Morgan," she muttered and stabbed the middle of the blackness, creating a circular impression.

She should have known the way her parents acted yesterday was too good to be true. All was forgiven for leaving a note and running off with a strange boy? Birthday presents and cake standing by? No need to pay back the money they'd lent her?

Oh, by the way, Morgan, things are about to get smellier and noisier around here.

A vicious slice appeared across the bottom of her painting.

The night before, Morgan had returned to the kitchen and choked out a congratulations to her parents. She didn't mean it in the slightest. She only wanted to remain on good enough terms with them until she found a new place to live. She'd snatched the newspaper on her way back to her room and dug right into the want ads.

The want ads were utterly useless. She was neither interested in nor qualified for any of the jobs listed. Which was fine. She'd made her own list of places she was intending to inquire at and had circled a few last-resort options in the paper.

But job hunting wouldn't begin until Tuesday, after the long weekend. In the meantime, Morgan intended to stay busy and in her room as much as possible, with the exception of seeing Josh.

She was working on the edges of her black splotch, fashioning them into a wavy border, when Matthew's shriek rang through the house. The brush jerked up and to the right, leaving a lightning-like impression in its wake. Morgan set the brush down with a sigh and looked at her painting.

Seemed about right. Darkness, chaos, disorder.

She was absolutely finished with them all.

Morgan picked up her brush and heard Matthew come tearing down the hall, banging into the walls with his walker and hollering gibberish at the top of his lungs. She calmly traced an X through the circle.

Another baby. Another bout of sleepless nights for everyone. Good lord, more teething. At least she wouldn't be around for it.

Morgan left the black paint to dry and placed the brush in its rinsing cup. She'd wait to clean the plastic until her brother was done smashing around out there.

A knock on her door was followed by her mom's voice. "Morgan, we're having lunch if you're interested."

Her stomach growled. "Traitor," she told it. Her mom sounded like she was wrangling Matthew just outside the door. "I'll be out shortly," she called back.

By the time Morgan made her way to the table, her parents were already seated and Matthew was in his high chair. How her mom found the time to cook was beyond her. The table was covered with assorted sandwiches and pastries. A pot of homemade soup sat simmering on the stove.

They really wasted a lot of food around here. Morgan had never actually considered it before. But now that she was faced with the possibility of having a food bill of her own, never mind rent and utilities . . . no, not the possibility, the reality . . .

"Have a seat, dear," her mom said as she got up to fill Morgan's bowl with soup.

"Thanks," she muttered as she browsed the variety of sandwiches, settling on roast beef and Swiss cheese.

"Coffee or soda?" her mom asked as she set the steaming bowl of soup on the table.

"Coffee. But I'll get it. You should sit down," Morgan said.

Her mom sat down and let out a sigh. "Yes, I guess I'll have to get used to taking it easier around here now."

Morgan was referring to the fact she shouldn't be waiting on her and her dad hand and foot when they were perfectly capable of getting things on their own, not her condition; but whatever. She poured her coffee and returned to the table.

Morgan's dad cleared his throat in a way that always meant he was about to lay something on her. He'd taken off his glasses and focused his gray eyes, which matched his graying hair, intently on her.

"We have a proposition for you, Morgan," he said.

Morgan choked on her coffee. The last time he'd said that things hadn't gone well. But again, her time here was almost up. She managed to recover and ask, "What you got?"

"Well, with our new arrival coming in April, we'll need to do some rearranging around here."

"You want me to move out?" Morgan asked with a grin.

"No, no, of course not. You won't be going off to school until at least next year now," he said.

That again. She couldn't be bothered to argue with him today. "What's the deal then?"

"It's not a deal. We were simply wondering if you'd like your own room in the basement," he said.

"The basement?" Morgan wrinkled her nose. "It's not finished."

"Exactly. We're doing up the new floorplan this week. Since we've run out of rooms upstairs, we thought you might like a bit more privacy. Depending on how long you're planning on staying at home, we can make your new room as large as you like."

"And you could have your own bathroom," her mom added enthusiastically.

Perhaps a bit too enthusiastically. Morgan eyed her parents and saw they both looked a bit nervous. They probably felt bad for basically kicking her out of her room. Which might work to her advantage . . .

"I'll let you know this week," Morgan said. "But I'll probably only need a small room. Can't live here forever, you know."

Morgan's mom teared up for reasons known only to her. Morgan took the opportunity to get up and pat her on the shoulder as she took her dishes to the sink.

"I'm going out with Josh tonight, so don't wait up," she said as she turned to leave for her room.

"Hang on a minute," her father said.

She stopped and faced him. "The 'don't wait up part' was a joke."

"I understand that, but when do we get to meet this young man?"

"After I've been back for longer than a day," Morgan answered.

Luckily, for Morgan, Matthew tipped his bowl of oatmeal onto the floor and she was able to slip away during the distraction.

Back in her room, she checked on her painting. Still wet. It wouldn't be ready for the next layer of color today.

Morgan dug through her drawers until she found what she was looking for. Her high school yearbook. She took it to her bed but didn't open it.

A room in the basement might not be so bad. Just in case she couldn't save up enough money to move out right away. Really, she had no idea what living on her own would actually cost. At least a room downstairs would be quieter. She would hardly have to see her brother and the new baby at all.

Feeling better about her living situation, Morgan considered the yearbook in her lap. Hopefully, this would make her feel better too. Josh hadn't mentioned his ex-not-technical-girlfriend since they'd been home, but she couldn't help being curious.

Against her better judgment, Morgan opened the book to last year's Juniors section, scanning for the name Trixie. Nothing. She went back another year to the Sophomores. Really, she wasn't even sure either Trixie or Josh's sister went to the same school as they had. Maybe they went to the French one.

Nope. Not his sister at least. Morgan spotted Mary "Rab" Hampton's name and looked closely at the picture. She was kind of pretty, but Morgan couldn't remember ever seeing her in the halls.

She continued her search in the same grade until she landed on Jasmine "Trixie" Beaumont. Morgan immediately felt better about herself, but kind of wondered what Josh had ever been thinking.

The girl was not at all attractive. The black eyeshadow and lack of a smile probably didn't help, but Morgan nearly laughed out loud when she saw her hobbies and interests. There were none. She'd taken the time to make sure they got the atrocious nickname in her bio but the rest of it was blank.

Morgan shut the book and decided she had better things to do until it was time to pick Josh up for their date.

Maybe she should give Mel another try. Surely she couldn't still be angry.

Morgan retrieved the number from her wallet and dialed Mel's apartment in Saint John.

Wrong number. This one was disconnected.

She dialed again, reading the digits aloud as she did so. Same result.

Morgan chewed on her fingernail before deciding to call Mel's parents. Mel's mother answered after a few rings.

"Hello?"

"Hi, it's Morgan. I tried calling Mel, but it says her number was disconnected . . ."

She wasn't sure what to say next. The last time she'd called, Mel's mother had been as angry as Mel herself after finding out Morgan had run away.

After a long pause, the woman sighed deeply. "Melanie is back home. But I don't think she's up for visitors yet."

"Back home? For good? What happened? Is she okay?"

"Morgan, she'll tell you herself eventually, but I really don't think –"

"I'm coming over."

Morgan hung up and jumped to her feet. She should have known Mel wouldn't have stayed mad for so long. She was going to get to the bottom of this.

Morgan grabbed her wallet and keys and dashed out of the house, calling out a "later" to her parents. Had she worn her fingernails long, she would have lost one or two as she grabbed Zinger's door handle. Cursing and sucking on her bruised hand, she unlocked the door and got in.

Mel only lived a couple of blocks away but Morgan did not have the patience to walk. She barely had the patience to throw the car in park in front of her house and shut it off.

Seconds later, she was pounding on the door of the house.

Mel's mother stood there looking heartbroken. Goddamn. This was it. She was about to find out Mel was ill. Desperately ill. She was going to lose her just like she lost Kendra all those years ago.

Morgan was practically in tears as she begged to see her friend.

Mel's mother simply sighed again and stood aside to allow her in.

Morgan took off her shoes and dashed down the hall to her friend's old room. She didn't bother knocking.

It was dark inside, so she didn't see Mel right away.

"I knew you'd show up here eventually."

Morgan squinted through the darkness in the direction of Mel's voice and saw her curled up in bed. She swallowed hard as she walked over to turn on the bedside lamp.

Mel looked horrible. Her short brown hair fell over her face, covering most of it, but it looked like she'd been crying for days.

"What's wrong?" Morgan asked, dreading the answer.

Mel laughed a crazy laugh and sat up, throwing off the covers. "What does it look like?"

Morgan frowned. "You're sick?"

Mel's laughter turned to tears. "I wish!" she wailed. She pressed down on the nightgown over her stomach. "I'm knocked up!"

Morgan couldn't see anything different about her friend's stomach but stopped trying as the words reached her brain.

"You're pregnant?"

Mel collapsed back onto her side and sobbed.

"Shit." Morgan sat beside her and patted her shoulder awkwardly. "Mel, I'm so sorry."

Mel continued to cry and Morgan continued to sit at a loss for words. Finally, Mel stopped and turned to her, her eyes dry and blank.

"It happened over the summer. I only found out after you left."

"So that's why you kept hanging up on me? I thought you were mad because I got you into trouble."

Mel laughed again for so long Morgan seriously considered fleeing. However, this was her friend. She couldn't leave her this way.

"Sure, I was mad. I got grounded for keeping your secret when you took off. Grounded until I left home to go to university." Mel's words tumbled out one over the other as she continued with her insane giggling. "To think that was the biggest of my problems at the time, being grounded."

Morgan just stared at her, wondering if she would ever stop laughing. "Whose is it? I mean, what are you going to do?"

Mel stopped laughing but skipped over the first question. "I'm giving it up for adoption."

"What about school?"

Mel shrugged. "Try it again another time," she said despondently.

"But what about the father?"

"Doesn't matter. He's not around anymore." She held up her hand when Morgan opened her mouth to press the issue. "Please stop asking."

Morgan closed her mouth and nodded with a frown. They would have plenty of time to discuss it later once she'd calmed down a bit.

They talked a while longer, with Mel alternating between fits of weeping and laughter. Apparently, she was due in April, the same time as Morgan's mom. *Ew.* When Morgan mentioned she was dating Josh, Mel did one of her emotional flips and squealed, thrilled that she'd predicted them falling in love. Then she promptly gave her a stern lecture, warning her not to sleep with him without using a condom. Morgan assured her she would not. Boy, she certainly would not.

Morgan finally left after Mel had cried herself out yet again until she was half asleep.

The drive to Josh's house went by in a blur. Morgan got turned around more than once as her muddled thoughts continued to plague her. She'd only been gone for a few weeks. What in the hell had happened to everyone?

The answer was actually simple. Hormones. At least in the case of her mom and Mel.

Josh was waiting outside his house when she pulled into the driveway. Morgan felt like she hadn't seen him in years. He hurried over to Zinger and jumped in.

They shared a quick kiss and Morgan asked, "Where do you want to go?"

"Anywhere but here," was his answer.

Morgan could tell something was bugging him, but she was calmed by his presence nonetheless. The sun was setting as she drove out of town until she found a side road that led to a thicket of trees and parked.

"I don't feel like being around anyone else," she said before he had a chance to question her choice of locale.

"Have I ever told you how much I love you?" Josh chuckled.

"Exactly twice," she said, grinning. "You would not believe the day I had."

Josh smiled weakly and leaned his head back on the seat.

"Actually, you look like you've had a day yourself," Morgan said, reaching out to take his hand. "You didn't tell me much about what happened yesterday. You go first."

"Long story short? My father wants his rent and he wants it now. My job at Cal's is no longer there and I'll be pounding the pavement come Tuesday."

"What?!" Okay, his homecoming was definitely worse than hers. "What are you going to do?"

Josh shrugged. "I'll find a way. So long as I've got my Angel by my side." He leaned over to kiss her.

Morgan cut the kiss short and grabbed her wallet. She pulled out the wad of bills she'd taken from her account to pay back her parents and shoved them at him with a smile. "Will this help?"

"Whoa!" Josh pushed the money back to her. "I'm not taking your money."

"It's not my money," she said, "it's yours. There's five hundred dollars here. I'm paying you back for Zinger and all the other stuff from when I lost my wallet."

Josh frowned. "I told you there was no rush."

"I don't like to owe people. And don't worry, you can use Zinger from time to time until you get your truck fixed." She pushed the money at Josh again and he at least held onto it.

"Actually, I might have a car of my own soon. It's just a beater and it's the most God-awful orange you could imagine, but –"

"I love orange," Morgan said. "It's one of my favorite colors. I can't wait until you get it and pick me up in it."

Josh laughed. "So what happened today that I won't believe?"

Morgan's smiled faltered. "Remember my friend Mel?"

"Sure. Is she still mad?"

"Not at me. She's pregnant."

"What?"

"Yeah," Morgan said. "She's back in town living with her parents. But you know what? I don't feel like talking about crappy stuff anymore today." She took off her seatbelt and climbed over the console with a wicked grin.

"What are you doing?" Josh asked as she climbed into his lap.

"I am kissing the man I love," she answered.

It wasn't long before the money found itself on the dashboard beneath Zinger's thoroughly fogged windshield.

Chapter 21

In Which Details Are Explained
Wednesday, September 6, 1995

Bathurst Automotive wasn't Josh's first choice for employment. It was, however, close enough to home that he could walk. He didn't want to be tied to his mother's work schedule until he could get the Joshmobile.

Of course, it was only a temporary name for the beater, and far too reminiscent of the Shackmobile. Josh's navy-blue coveralls also had a temporary name tag. If he survived at Bathurst Automotive for ninety days, he would receive iron-on patches with his name on them and, more importantly, a pay raise.

Morgan promised to help him come up with a better name for his car once she met it. Josh was looking forward to seeing where Morgan lived and finally being able to pick her up in a vehicle of his own. He was not, however, looking forward to the inevitable meeting of her parents.

While he understood and appreciated the necessity of such a ritual, he was sure they blamed him for conniving their daughter to drive out to Seattle and then seducing her into bringing him back.

Josh wondered if Morgan would make him ask her dad for her hand in marriage – when the time came. He believed Morgan would not. Quite frankly, he was surprised they hadn't eloped yet.

Josh gave his head a shake. He was getting ahead of himself – way ahead – and should be concentrating on work instead of daydreaming.

Not to be deemed a time waster, he busied himself preparing for the day's task until Peter arrived to continue the indoctrination. Really, though, how long did they think it would take him to learn to wash and detail a car?

Minutes later, Peter drove the day's first vehicle into the wash bay. It was an old Chevy pickup the company had received as a trade. Josh was reasonably sure the former owner didn't get much in trade for it. He marveled that it was running but remembered Old Blue's appearance when he and Cal had hauled it out of that barn.

Their first task would be to remove years of accumulated dirt, pollen, and other debris from the surface. Then, mechanics would evaluate the vehicle to see if it would be sold on the lot or to a junkyard.

"Good morning, Josh. How was your night?" Peter asked as he climbed out of the truck.

"It was good. We went to a movie and had coffee afterwards."

"What movie?"

"We went and watched Babe," Josh said.

"Babe? That's a kid's movie."

"It was that or Babysitter's Club, and Morgan flat-out refused to go to that. Anyhow, it wasn't terrible."

"Well," Peter said and slapped the hood of the pick-up, "this one might take us most of the day. You get started on cleaning the tires and wheel wells. I've got to help Fred pull a transmission."

"I'm on it."

Peter wandered off and Josh picked up the hose and bucket. Positioning himself by the right front tire, he sat on the mechanic stool and began to clean the truck.

The scuff of a shoe on grit alerted Josh that someone was outside the wash bay. A quick glance revealed a lack of coveralls, indicating it was a customer.

"The service bays are for employees only," Josh said, reciting the standard spiel. "Please return to the waiting area."

"Oh, how the mighty have fallen. The master mechanic has been reduced to washing tires."

Trixie. It couldn't be. Josh turned slowly to verify his suspicion.

"Aren't you supposed to be in class?" he asked her.

"School doesn't start until tomorrow. I thought I'd come by and remind you it's my birthday."

"Rab made sure I didn't forget," Josh said, trying to keep the irritation out of his voice. "I gather you're not here to get your car serviced."

"Maybe. How much is a car wash?" Trixie asked and crossed her arms.

Josh shrugged. "Go to the service desk and ask. This bay is for washing dealership vehicles."

Trixie sighed and uncrossed her arms. "Okay, the real reason I came here was to apologize for my behavior the other day. I was upset and I shouldn't have yelled."

"I'm sorry I yelled back, but it doesn't change the fact you're not my girlfriend," Josh said.

"But we were good friends once. We did a *lot* of things together," she said pointedly.

"Things have changed, Trixie."

"Can't we still be friends?" Trixie asked, stepping into the bay to the back of the truck.

Josh stood and moved the stool, bucket, and hose to the other front tire. There was no way he was going to get closer to her.

"I have no problem being your friend as long as there are no strings."

"No strings, I promise."

Josh nodded curtly. "Please step out of the bay. I don't want to get into trouble."

Trixie obliged and backed up to just outside the door. "Okay, friend, will you come to my birthday party tonight?"

"Who's going to be there?" Josh asked.

"Rab and a few other people. Your mom wouldn't allow too many, not that I have many friends to begin with."

"My *maman*? You mean to say the party's at my house?"

"You've seen where I live. No room there for a party." Trixie tucked her hands in her back pockets, looking slightly uncomfortable.

"I'll come to the party, but I'm bringing Morgan with me. If that's a deal breaker, then I won't come."

"You can bring Morgan, but don't expect me to greet her with open arms," Trixie said without much enthusiasm.

"I expect you to be courteous," Josh said.

"I can be courteous."

"I think you should go now. You're really not supposed to be back here," Josh said, focusing on the tire.

Trixie smiled and bent over so her head was about the level of Josh's. "Okay, then. See you tonight?"

"Yes, with Morgan." He didn't look back as her footsteps faded away.

Josh was wondering how his mother would juggle a party and still have supper ready for his father when Peter entered the bay.

"Was that Morgan?"

"No, that's Trixie. She just came to tell me something."

"She's not bad looking for a goth girl."

"I didn't notice," Josh said, picking up a brush to scrub the tire.

"I saw the way she was looking at you, man. She's got a thing for you."

"The feeling isn't mutual."

Peter shrugged. "She shouldn't be back in the service area," he said as he turned and left.

"Agreed," Josh muttered.

Josh worked on cleaning the pickup until his morning break. He purchased a candy bar from the vending machine and used the payphone in the waiting area to call Morgan. The babysitter told him she was out, so Josh called her cell phone.

The phone rang until a recorded message came on. Twice. Morgan finally picked up the third time he called.

"Hello?"

"Hey Angel, it's me. Why weren't you answering?"

"Sorry. I'm still getting used to having this thing. Mel and I just finished our interviews. We start training at the coffee shop tomorrow."

"Congratulations," Josh said.

Morgan laughed. "Not my first pick of jobs but it'll do for now. So, did you call to tell me what a beautiful girl I am and how much you love me?"

"You are a beautiful girl and I do love you bunches, but that's not why I called."

"What's up?"

"Trixie dropped by for a visit at work this morning."

"What did she want?" Morgan asked, icy words replaced her previous mirth.

"She wanted to apologize for her rant the other night and to invite me to her birthday party."

"You didn't accept, did you?"

"I told her I wouldn't come unless you were with me. She agreed to that."

"I'm not sure why we'd want to go."

"The thing is, the party is at my house, so . . . I figured we could make peace with Rab and you could meet my *maman*." Josh was sweating just a bit.

"I'm good with the second part, but why at a party?" Morgan asked.

"Well, I figure we could stay for presents and cake and then get out of there. That way you can meet my mother when she won't have the chance to bug you with a lot of questions. My father will probably be sleeping and that's fine. His big concern is that I don't get you pregnant, and we all agree on that."

"I hesitate to ask, but did you get a birthday present?"

"No. Until she came by this morning, I wasn't planning on going to the party. *Merde*, I wasn't even invited."

"How about this? I have some time this afternoon, so I can pick up a card and a present from both of us," Morgan said.

"Would you? Thank you. Just one more reason to love you," Josh said.

"You better believe it. I'll pick you up after work."

"I'll need to shower," Josh said.

"I've had your stinky butt in Zinger before. Why don't we go to the pool for a bit before the party? You can grab some clothes from your house, we'll have a swim, and you can shower at the pool. Then we can arrive at the party fashionably late."

"Fashionably late sounds fine," Josh agreed, picturing Morgan in her bathing suit.

They made kissy noises over the phone and Josh returned to work.

The work was dirty, but not difficult. The main benefit was that he was now employed full time – for the first time in his life. He didn't need to worry about rent. The money Morgan had given him covered the first month's rent and then some.

He figured he could continue to live at home for now, save for the future, and still have money to take Morgan out. Dates with Morgan weren't likely to be expensive. They were happy just to be with each other. When they were driving around in Zinger, it was almost like they were back on the road again.

Josh and Peter spent the entire morning going through the pickup truck. Once Peter was satisfied Josh had mastered the fine art of detailing, Josh was assigned to the regular washing of other vehicles for the afternoon.

At the end of his workday, the only car Josh wanted to see was Zinger. Morgan sitting in it brightened his day when he emerged from the building.

Morgan waited while he dashed into his house to grab a change of clothes, miraculously managing to avoid speaking to anyone.

Josh found the swim to be relaxing, and by the time they had finished at the pool it was almost seven. Morgan let Josh drive Zinger to his home where several cars were already parked in the yard.

Before they went in, Morgan handed him a box wrapped in white paper with pink ribbon and bows. A card was tucked into the side. Josh smirked at the irony and wondered if

Morgan had ever seen Trixie. Well, she would in a few minutes.

When he entered the house, his mother called from the kitchen in French, "Josh, is that you?"

"Yes, *Maman*, I have Morgan with me," he responded in English.

His mother came into the hall and stopped. "Good evening, Miss Parker."

Morgan stared at his mother for a moment and finally said, "Good evening, Mrs. Hampton, it's so nice to meet you. Again."

"You two have met before?" Josh asked, perplexed.

"Briefly, at the bank," Morgan said with a wave of her hand.

"The party is in the living room," his mother said. Facing Morgan, she said, "But do stop by the kitchen before you leave so we can get to know each other better. I want to learn more about the girl that has enchanted my son."

The women flashed each other strained smiles before his mother returned to the kitchen.

Josh didn't have time to question Morgan as they went to the living room. He passed the gift back to her. "It'll be better if you give it to Trixie."

Rab jumped off the couch where she'd been sitting next to a boy, whom Josh assumed was David.

"Josh, I'm glad you decided to come," Rab said. "You too, Morgan."

Trixie had been speaking with someone else but turned at Rab's greeting. "Josh, Morgan, thanks for coming."

Morgan held out the pink-bowed gift. "This is from *us*. Happy birthday."

The birthday girl gave each of them a hug, starting with Morgan. She hugged Josh a little longer than he thought necessary, but he wished her a happy birthday too.

The patchouli aroma lingered as Trixie released him. She was wearing less makeup than usual, but her shirt was unbuttoned as far as she dared in the Hampton house, offering a glimpse of cleavage. Josh pulled his eyes away.

He led Morgan to the table of beverages where they got lemonade, then circulated among the guests.

When they reached the sofa, the young man who'd been sitting with Josh's sister stood up and offered his hand. "You must be Rab's brother. I'm David."

"I'm Josh. Nice to meet you, David."

They chatted for a few minutes and Josh decided that David was okay. He certainly was polite enough and didn't have any obvious piercings.

About that time, Rab, who seemed to be playing Mistress of Ceremonies, called out, "Okay everyone, time for prezzies. Trix, sit right here."

Trixie sat in a folding chair next to the coffee table piled with presents. She picked up the one from Josh and Morgan first.

She opened the card, which had a scruffy cat on the front. Trixie read the card out loud. "Happy birthday. Party like there's no tomorrow." She smiled sweetly and looked at Morgan. "You're going to need to learn to forge Josh's signature better than that, sweetie."

Josh gawked at Trixie and wondered how often she had forged his signature.

The room fell silent as everyone stared at Trixie and Morgan.

Morgan returned the sickly-sweet smile and said, "He was at work and it was short notice. I knew he wouldn't mind."

Trixie gingerly picked up the package like it might explode or burn her fingers. She untied the ribbon and opened the top of the box. "Ooh, Charlie Blue. This is sure to be my new favorite perfume. Thanks, you two."

"You're welcome," Josh and Morgan said in unison, then grinned at each other.

Trixie continued to open presents, commenting on each and thanking the gift-givers in turn.

Rab scurried around collecting paper and ribbon, folding them nicely and placing them in a large gift bag that David held for her.

After the presents had been opened and packed away, the guests sang Happy Birthday as Trixie blew out the candles on the chocolate frosted cake.

Josh sure hoped her wish didn't involve him or Morgan, not that he really believed wishes came true. Dreams, perhaps, but not wishes.

After having a small slice of cake, Josh and Morgan said their farewells and headed for the door as someone started playing music.

Josh's mother stepped into the hall from the kitchen, blocking their path.

Morgan's hand tightened around Josh's, but her voice remained even as she said, "I'm sorry, Mrs. Hampton, I'm afraid we got off to a bad start."

"Do you understand a word I am saying, Mademoiselle Parker?" Josh's mother asked in French.

"I'm sorry, Mrs. Hampton, I understand very little French."

"I thought so," his mother said, switching to English. "Where do you attend Mass?"

"I don't go to church," Morgan said with a slight frown.

"I will be quite honest, Miss Parker. You are not the sort of girl I had in mind to marry my son."

"I'll be quite honest, Margaret, that's Josh's choice, not yours. Besides, we're not engaged."

"I will thank you to address me as Mrs. Hampton."

"Only if you call me Morgan."

"I will agree to that, Morgan. I bid you good evening."

"Good night." Morgan turned to leave but stopped and added, "For the record, I love your son."

Josh escorted Morgan out of the house before his mother could respond.

He was glad he'd gotten his key back because he was sure he would find the door locked when he returned home.

Chapter 22

In Which Dreams of Stardom Are Born
Thursday, September 7, 1995

"What is wrong with this thing?" Morgan yelled as she received yet another faceful of steam from the machine.

"Nothing's wrong with it," Mel said, coming over and pushing Morgan aside. "Quit sticking your face in it."

"I was trying to see if it was on or not."

Mel rolled her eyes and took the cup from the espresso machine. "You press the button, it hisses, it's on. I'll take this out."

"Thanks." Morgan wiped her face with her apron.

Who would have thought working in a coffee house would be so difficult? Morgan had a fairly high IQ, but she was doubting those test results right about now. She'd originally thought it silly when their first few days of work had been designated as training days. She knew how to make coffee.

Kind of, apparently. The industrial coffee makers were not at all like the coffee machine at home. The espresso maker was a whole other contraption entirely. Then there was the weird little warming oven for sandwiches and muffins. Not a microwave; more of a toaster oven on steroids. The morning had seen many a tasty treat tossed into the trash as Morgan continued to scorch the crap out of them. At least none had burst into flames – yet.

Mel, however, seemed to be thriving. Morgan watched from behind the counter as her friend filled a tray with used dishes and wiped the table while holding the stacked tray in the other hand. Morgan had yet to successfully balance more than one beverage on a tray without everything rattling as she delivered them.

Morgan sighed and returned to the nasty little oven where she inserted a sandwich that was supposed to have gone out with the last espresso.

The Classic Café was not Morgan's first choice of jobs. She'd set out on Tuesday morning, expecting to easily secure her old lifeguard position at the pool. Wrong. The full-time and part-time positions had been filled for the year. At least they still allowed her free admission to use the facilities.

Plan B was one Morgan was quite excited about. She'd walked right into the local newspaper office and announced she wanted to work for The Northern Light. She'd fetch coffee if she needed to and work her way to the top. After a few strange looks and a bunch of waiting, she did get to speak to someone in charge. She left with a hardy handshake and encouragement in pursuing a career in journalism once she got her degree. How embarrassing.

The want ads were full of jobs for truckers and farmers and masters of technical-whatever degrees. The rest of them were retail and food service positions.

Morgan had flat-out refused to even consider the fast-food places and this was where she ended up. On the bright side, Mel had come along with her on her job-hunting day, and at the very last minute decided to apply as well. Because in her words, what was she going to do, lie around the house all day until she popped?

"Morgan . . ."

"Shit." Morgan yanked the door to the toaster contraption open and went to snatch the tray out. A gentle hand on her arm stopped her.

Laura, the owner, reached past and used an oven mitt to remove the metal tray with the burnt sandwich on it.

"Try another one?" Laura suggested and headed for the trash can.

Another bright side. Their boss was super nice. Actually, the café was too . . . just on the other side of the counter. Half the seating area consisted of tables and chairs, but the other side held couches and stools facing a tiny stage. The stage was used for Karaoke nights and offered to local talent if they wanted to play for tips.

Laura returned with the tray and Morgan shoved the new sandwich in. She didn't move, she didn't blink, she didn't allow herself to think a single thought until it was perfectly browned.

Absurdly proud of herself, Morgan plated the sandwich with only a small burn on her finger from forgetting about the oven mitt and delivered it to the customer.

"You girls are angels," Laura said when they met at the counter. "You showed up just in the nick of time. Are you sure you can handle the lunch hour while I go pick up Teresa?"

"Absolutely," Mel said.

Morgan did her best to smile confidently. She was pretty sure it wasn't working.

Laura chuckled. "I won't be long. It's just her first day of school and since you're here, I thought I'd go get her myself."

"Don't worry about a thing," Mel assured her. "We've got this."

Laura thanked them and left to pick up her daughter, who had just started morning Kindergarten classes. She'd been in dire straits indeed until Morgan and Mel showed up to apply for the job. She'd just lost her two summer employees and was running the place on her own. She was a single mother and business owner and her daughter basically lived here at the café when she wasn't in school. She simply couldn't afford to hire more help.

Really, she could hardly afford to hire Morgan and Mel. The pay was – well, it was sad. It wasn't even minimum wage because their tips were supposed to make up the rest of their salary.

And the hours were – well, evenings and weekends after these first few days because Laura took most of the weekday shifts on her own.

Morgan couldn't imagine being in her shoes. She also couldn't imagine how she was ever going to save up enough money to move out by working here.

Mel had cleared another table while Morgan stood daydreaming and returned with a five-dollar tip. "Now we're making the big bucks," she declared, putting it in the tip jar.

"You should keep that," Morgan said. "I've done nothing to earn a tip yet today."

"Fair's fair. We split them. Besides, you got that one sandwich out."

Morgan laughed. "I suck so bad at this!"

"You just have to learn," Mel assured her.

"You're not struggling, and you've never worked at a place like this before," Morgan pointed out.

"Maybe I'm naturally gifted. Lucky me. I found my calling right out of the gate."

"You forgot the eyeroll," Morgan said.

Mel obliged.

The lunch hour came and went, and Morgan managed to get through it without burning her face or hands at all. The same couldn't be said for all the food, but she'd take it.

Laura returned with Teresa, who she set up in the backroom, and told the girls to take a lunch break of their own. They both got coffee and muffins and took a seat on one of the couches.

"Free food's a bonus," Mel commented.

"I get free food at home," Morgan grumbled.

"What's with you today? Do you really hate the job that much?"

Morgan put down the muffin she'd been fiddling with. "No. I like it here. I've got a lot of learning to do, but that's not what's bugging me."

"Things going okay with you and Josh?"

"Sort of. I mean, yes. I love him and he loves me. No doubt . . ."

"But?" Mel prompted.

"Do you know Trixie? . . . I can't remember her last name. She would have been in Grade 10 last year. Big boobs, dresses in black."

"I think I know who you mean. What about her?"

"Ugh." Morgan pushed her muffin over to Mel, who happily started eating it. "She's friends with Josh's sister and he used to kind of have a thing with her."

Mel's mouth was full but she raised a brow.

"Anyhow, I'm not worried he'd cheat on me or anything, but she seems a bit crazy and it's obvious she's not over him."

"You think she might try to break you two up?"

"I'm positive she'll meddle as much as she can, but like I said, I trust Josh. She's just an annoyance more than anything."

"What else?" Mel asked.

Morgan laughed at how well her friend knew her. "It's his mother. She's . . . not nice. On my first day back from our trip, I went to the bank to get a replacement debit card. I didn't know it was her at the time, but she was the woman who served me. God, she was rude. I only met her as Josh's mother last night and . . . just wow."

"She was still rude?" Mel guessed.

"She asked me something like which church I went to and then literally told me she didn't want me marrying her son."

"Are you serious?"

"Yes," Morgan said. "I mean it was almost funny. Like, why in the world was she talking about marriage?"

"What did Josh say?" Mel asked.

"Nothing at all. Well, he apologized some after we left to go get coffee, but he didn't seem eager to talk about it. Neither was I, to be fair. But enough of that. I can handle her."

"Well, good luck." Mel's face took on a greenish tinge.

"You okay?" Morgan asked.

"Yeah, yeah. Probably shouldn't have had that second muffin."

"You're eating for two though," Morgan pointed out.

Mel let out a crazy laugh. "Who would have thought we'd end up here? It wasn't even a month ago when we had our little goodbye celebration before running off to start our new lives."

"Weird, isn't it?" Morgan agreed. "I had no idea what I was doing at the time, but a coffee house is not where I thought I'd land next."

"At least you still have options. You can go off to any school you like at any time."

"You can do that too, eventually. But I'm not sure I want to go anywhere."

"Because of Josh?" Mel asked.

"Partly. But I also don't want to pick a career out of thin air, which is what I basically did when I told my dad I might want to look into journalism. Now he won't let the subject go. He keeps pestering me to at least take some online classes, but he's just annoying me already."

"Honestly, I was just going to university to get the hell out of here," Mel said sadly. "I didn't care what I was majoring in."

"Well, my goals have become more short term than long. I want to save up enough money to get out of that house before baby number two comes along." Morgan glanced at the mostly-empty tip jar sitting on the counter. "Doesn't look like this is going to cut it."

"Are you thinking of getting a second job?"

"Sorta." Morgan chewed on her thumbnail. "I could always go back to babysitting Matthew during the week. It sucks but it wouldn't be forever."

Morgan returned Laura's friendly wave and then realized she wasn't just waving to be nice. It was her oh-so-polite way of telling them break time was over.

The rest of the afternoon passed quickly. Morgan felt she was getting slightly better at dealing with dishes and machines, and most of the customers were pleasant enough. Still, at the end of their first eight-hour day, both girls' feet were aching.

It was only four o'clock, so Morgan stayed at the café when Mel left. She had a bit of time to kill before picking Josh up. Their plans for the evening were vague. They were going to grab a bite to eat and probably drive around or go for a walk together. Still, it was the highlight of Morgan's day. Time with Josh was the best sort of time.

Morgan hadn't known what to expect on her first day of work, so she'd brought along her carry bag and sketchpad in case they had downtime. Of course, they hadn't, but it came in handy now.

She thought of the painting she was working on at home and how she'd like to show it to Josh even though it wasn't finished. She was on the third layer of colors and had come to a point where the work in progress was no longer progressing. A second set of eyes – beautiful ice blue eyes – might just be in order.

But that would involve Josh meeting her parents. Morgan had no doubt it would go better than meeting his mother the night before, but honestly both her mom and dad were simply on her last nerve.

Morgan looked up from her doodles and recognized the guy who came in with a guitar slung over his shoulder. He was tall and thin, dressed in denim and a black T-shirt. He wore his shoulder-length brown hair in a loose ponytail and had a familiar black wristband on his arm. They'd been in a lot of the same classes at school and Morgan had to admit she'd had a crush on him at one point. The time for crushing had passed but she'd always enjoyed chatting with him, one creative soul to another.

"Tyler!" she called out and waved.

He beamed a smile and headed for Morgan's table.

"Long time no see," he said. "I thought you left the country."

"Ugh. Did everyone hear about that?"

"I remember the party, so kind of. What are you doing back?" He pulled out a chair and sat down, resting his guitar on the floor.

"It didn't work out. My plans, I mean. I work here now," she said, sweeping her arm around the café. She just wanted to get the shame over with.

"That's terrific," Tyler said, his smile growing. "It's a great place and Laura is wonderful. Are you working tonight?"

"No. I just finished my first day of training. Wait." Her eyes went to the guitar and her brain connected the dots. "Do you play here?"

"Yep. I get paid nothing except for tips, but it's all about the music, you know?"

Morgan nodded enthusiastically. "I took guitar for a while last year, but I kinda gave it up."

"I remember hearing you sing in high school. You have an amazing voice."

Morgan blushed. "I can't believe you remember that."

"Impossible to forget. I'm here a few evenings a week and I come by on the weekends. Maybe we could make some music together." Tyler wiggled a brow.

"I have a boyfriend, but I sure would love to do something like that. Real music, I mean. I remember your talent from school as well, and evenings and weekends are my shifts after this week."

"That's great! I'm sure Laura won't have a problem with you doing it while you're working. Like I said, she's fantastic."

"Trust me, I know. Waitressing is not exactly my strong suit," Morgan said.

"Ah, you're destined for stardom. You'll see. Well, this just brightened the hell out of my day. I had to fire someone for stealing and, well, that's never fun."

"Where do you work?"

"Shop and Save. Sad, I know. But they offered me a supervisory position after graduation and it pays well enough for now. One day, I'm going to be known for this." He patted the guitar next to his chair.

"How?" Morgan asked, genuinely curious. "Don't you have to get discovered or something? My dad, well, my biological father, used to be in a band, but I don't think it worked out at all for them."

"It depends on how you go about it," Tyler said. "The indie industry is a bigger thing now than it used to be. I write my own songs and I've got enough material for more than just one album. I have a bud out in Le Goulet who's part owner of the recording studio there. I won't be able to use it for free, but he'll give me a bit of slack on the price. It's just a matter of saving up now."

"That sounds awesome," Morgan said.

"You and I should work on something original together."

"Are you serious?"

"Very. We can start next week, just doing some covers or something to see how it goes."

Morgan blinked the stars from her eyes. "Count me in."

"I really think this is the start of something incredible," Tyler said, then checked his watch. "I should get set up. Can't disappoint my fans." He laughed and got up, gesturing to the mostly empty café. "See you soon?"

"Yes." Morgan watched as he walked over to the little stage and her mind raced with possibilities. This job had just gotten a lot more interesting.

She checked her watch, wondering if she had enough time to – "Shit."

Morgan shoved her things into her carry bag and ran for the door. Josh had gotten off work fifteen minutes ago.

Chapter 23

In Which Josh Takes a Ride
Saturday, September 16, 1995

Josh had a bit of a walk ahead of him, but it wouldn't be the first time he'd walked to Cal's garage. He really didn't mind, since leaving the house early allowed him to escape his mother's endless negative comments about "that Parker girl" and his father's – well, just his father.

Josh picked up his pace, remembering he'd told Morgan he would be at Cal's this morning but hadn't specified a time. He hoped she would stop by to visit because they hadn't seen each other much the past week.

Monday night, Morgan had picked up an extra shift at the café. He didn't begrudge her the work. *Merde*, he was taking a second job – third job if he counted the side work at Cal's – stocking shelves at Bag N' Go during the night.

He wondered briefly if the extra job was worth it – it would impinge on his time with Morgan, and on his sleep – but the meager paycheck he'd received from Bathurst Automotive yesterday reinforced his decision.

On Tuesday, Morgan's folks had gone out and she had to babysit. Then she was back to work at the café for Thursday and Friday, so Wednesday was the only day they'd spent time together.

And on Wednesday Morgan had been late.

She'd apologized, saying she stopped to talk with Tyler about some song ideas and lost track of the time but . . .

Tyler, Tyler, Tyler. What was it about that guy? He knew he shouldn't compare, but the dude was taller, darker, and not just a little better looking than Josh. Morgan assured Josh Tyler was only a friend, but it didn't silence the nagging in the corner of his heart.

A horn sounded and Josh jumped to the side of the road. Trixie's Honda pulled to a stop. *Merde*.

Rab stuck her head out the passenger side window. "Want a ride?"

"Nah, I'm good walking."

"Don't be stubborn. It's on the way."

Josh considered. With Rab as chaperone, it should be okay.

"Hurry up and make up your mind, we've got to get to work too," Rab said.

Josh trotted to the Honda and jumped into the back seat. Both girls wore a Burger Barn uniform.

"Good morning, scrub boy," Trixie greeted him as she got back on the road. "Going to Cal's this morning?"

"Yes, Cal's. Don't call me scrub boy."

"It's what they call you at the dealership, isn't it?"

"No, it's not, I'm not at work, and being condescending isn't winning you any points," Josh said.

"Oh, so you're giving out points now? How many do I have and how many do I need to get you back?"

Josh sighed. "It was just an expression."

He was considering getting a dig in about how flinging burgers wasn't much better than washing cars when Rab surprised him by adding, "Give it a rest, Trix."

Since when was she on his and Morgan's side?

As they neared the dirt road that led to Cal's, Josh saw Zinger turning onto it ahead of them.

"*Merde*," Josh swore softly. "You can let me out at the corner, okay Trixie? Thanks for the ride."

"Oh, no. I'll take you all the way, *friend*."

Josh slunk down in the back seat and shook his head. Trixie's huge grin beamed at him in the rearview mirror.

Trixie parked her car right behind Zinger as Morgan was stepping out. She wore a gray hoodie with a white ball cap covering most of her blond curls. She eyed the Honda with confusion until Josh stepped out of the back, then her face clouded over.

Josh grinned sheepishly. "Good morning, Angel."

"What's going on here?" Morgan asked.

Before he could answer, Trixie stuck her head out the window and said, "Bye, honey. Any time you need a ride, call me."

Josh swiveled his head between the two women, his mouth flopping like a fish gasping for air.

Trixie blew him a kiss, put the car in gear, and drove off.

Morgan scowled at him. "You could have told me you needed a ride."

"Sorry, Angel. I didn't ask for one. My sister and Trixie saw me walking and practically ran me over. Since Rab was with her, I figured it would be okay."

"Well, you know my number too," Morgan said icily, "if you find yourself in a pinch for transportation."

"I should be good," Josh replied, desperate to steer the topic away from Trixie. "Cal told me Robin's new car was delivered yesterday. I guess she got a good deal during the Labor Day sale, so she'll be bringing mine by today."

Morgan narrowed her eyes. "It's time you came completely clean with me, Josh. What's with you and that girl?"

"She was a friend is all."

"I thought she was Rab's friend," Morgan said, taking a step back.

"She is, but I told you we used to be closer." Josh sighed when Morgan continued to stand and glare at him. She wasn't going to let it go. "I was young and angry. We were both outcasts and we were lonely. Spending time together gave us a feeling of belonging."

"She acts as though you still belong to her."

"I never did," Josh said. "She's just having a hard time accepting that you and I are together."

"Why should that matter? What is with this hold she has over you? She's been nothing but disrespectful to me and all you do is make excuses for her."

"I'll talk to her about it," Josh said.

"I'd rather you didn't talk to her at all," Morgan muttered.

Josh was becoming more irritated than repentant. “How would you feel if I asked you to stop talking to Tyler?”

“Don’t even start with that. Tyler isn’t an old boyfriend, and he doesn’t slobber all over me like a dog.”

She had a point. “Okay, but it’ll be hard to avoid Trixie,” Josh said, throwing his arms in air. “She’s at my house nearly every day.”

“That’s another thing,” Morgan narrowed her eyes. “That girl sees you more than I do. Shit, I see *her* more than I see *you*. She and Rab are regulars at the café, as I’m sure you know. Rab’s actually nice to me but Trixie’s a bitch.”

“Look, I’m sorry about today. But I can’t stop them from going to the café. And I can’t banish Trixie from my parents’ house either.”

“Then maybe it’s time you started thinking about moving out. God knows I am.” Morgan tugged on her hair in frustration.

“Trust me, I consider it every day, especially when the rent is due. Stop pulling out your hair.” Josh took her hand in his and smiled. “Can you forgive me for this morning?”

“Of course I’ll forgive you. Just please don’t let her manipulate you anymore.” Morgan kissed him on the forehead then reached into her car. “I brought you some coffee.”

“Thanks,” Josh said, accepting the Tim Hortons cup. “It’ll keep me from having to drink Cal’s brew.”

As if summoned by the mere mention of his name, Cal drove up in his tow truck. He jumped out and called for Josh to come over.

Josh gave Morgan a quick peck. “Thanks for the coffee. I’ll pick you up after work in my new old car.”

“Can’t wait to see it. Oh, my parents will be happy. They’ve been dying to meet you.” Morgan rolled her eyes.

The mention of parents caused ice to form in Josh’s belly. “Okay. Love you.”

Morgan had already driven off by the time he’d found the words.

He gave his head a shake and made his way over to Cal.

"Open up and keep an eye on things," Cal said, handing him the keys. "I've got to go pull a car out of the ditch."

"Where are Robin and Brian?"

"Robin's cleaning up the car; she'll bring it in for you around noon. Brian starts at nine. Tell him to get Mrs. Gareth's Buick into the bay and change its oil."

"Okay, Cal. I've got you covered," Josh said, giving him a thumbs up.

Cal clapped him on the shoulder. "I always could depend on you."

As the older man drove off, Josh opened the shop for the day. He busied himself with tidying up the office and put the car in the bay for Brian. When Cal returned with the tow truck, he set Josh to clearing some brush until quitting time at noon.

As promised, Robin showed up with the car, and they signed the paperwork to make it official even though he had yet to finish paying it off. Josh thought the headlights and grill of Old Blue gave him a look of disapproval, but he reminded himself the car was only temporary.

Feeling about as ready as he ever would for the inevitable, he hurried home to shower and change before heading to Morgan's to meet the parents.

It was easy enough to find her house, but when Josh pulled into the driveway of the Parker residence, he was overcome with a sudden feeling of inadequacy. His car was entirely out of place in the upscale neighborhood. Even Zinger blended in better with all the newer luxury vehicles around him.

He wondered if he was a pretender, a young woman's whim who might quickly be discarded when she realized they were not in the same class. Well, dammit, he would sure fight for her heart. Wasn't that what he was running himself ragged for – to provide a livelihood for Morgan and himself?

Morgan came bursting out the front door and ran to the car.

"Oh my God, Josh, it's beautiful and hideous at the same time. It's like a big orange bug. Yes, we'll call it Bob for short."

Josh laughed. "I knew you'd give it a suitable name. Bob it is. Are you ready to go?"

"Oh, no. You're going to come in, especially since you got all dressed up. Might as well get it over with."

A drop of cold sweat hit his side. He suddenly wished he'd worn a T-shirt and perhaps used more anti-perspirant. Well, there was nothing to do but get it over with, as Morgan said.

"Morgan!" A woman called from the steps. "You can't leave the front door open when your brother is in the walker."

"Sorry, Mom," Morgan called. She laced her fingers with Josh's. "Come on."

"Up the thirteen steps to the gallows walked the condemned man . . ." Josh intoned.

"Oh hush, you. If I can endure your mom, you can at least say hello."

They climbed the front steps to the porch where her mother waited. "You must be Joshua," she said.

Not sure whether to offer his hand, he tipped his ball cap and said, "It's a pleasure meeting you, Mrs. Parker. You have a very lovely daughter."

She smiled and said, "Yes, but my son is hell on wheels."

On cue, Matthew ran his walker into the back of his mother's legs, and she moved aside to let them in.

Josh looked down at the boy. "Hello, Matthew, I'm Josh. I promise I'll treat your sister right."

The boy laughed and said, "Jos."

Morgan and her mother stared at each other and then down at Matthew.

Josh asked, "Is it okay if I pick him up?"

Morgan shrugged. "Yeah, but be warned. He gets fussy when anyone but Mom holds him."

"Oh, let him try," Mrs. Parker said. "If Matthew acts up, he can hand him to me."

Josh bent over and lifted the boy out of the walker. “Oh, my, you’re a big boy.”

The boy waved the rattle he was holding. “Jos,” he said and bonked him on the head.

Morgan and her mother laughed. “Come on in,” Mrs. Parker said.

Still carrying the child, Josh slipped his shoes off and Morgan closed the door behind them.

“By the way, congratulations on . . . on . . .” Josh stammered. How could he politely say this?

Morgan smirked at his discomfort.

“My pregnancy? Thank you.” Mrs. Parker grinned. “Gary and I are excited to be expanding our family, although honestly we should have done this years ago. The doctors are watching me like a hawk. Mid-life pregnancies can be difficult.”

“I wish you good health then,” Josh said, feeling idiotic.

He followed the women into the kitchen. Morgan’s mom took Matthew from him as Morgan’s dad stood up from the table and offered his hand. “It’s a pleasure to meet you, Mr. Hampton.”

His firm grip practically crushed Josh’s hand and he stared up into those killer steel gray eyes. How tall was this man? Much taller than him to be sure. He could grab Josh’s throat and lift him up the way Darth Vader did in Star Wars.

“It’s a pleasure to meet you too, sir,” Josh croaked out.

Sounds of construction seeped up through the floor.

“Please excuse the noise,” Mr. Parker said. “Would you like to go down and see how the new basement’s coming along? The contractors are working on the game room today.”

“Perhaps another time, sir. Morgan and I wish to spend some time together before her shift,” Josh said. He wasn’t sure the words came out right. His mouth was suddenly so damned dry.

“Actually, I want to show Josh the painting in my room,” Morgan said.

“Okay, but leave the door open,” Mrs. Parker said.

"Yes, Mom. Come on, Josh."

Josh waved awkwardly to Morgan's parents and followed her to her room. He had visions of an unmarked shallow grave down by the river. Every year Morgan would come and place a single sunflower on it to mark the day they left for Seattle.

Morgan entered her room and rolled her eyes as she made a point of swinging the door open as far as it would go. Josh had the craziest urge to make moaning noises to freak her parents out, but he'd seen the size of their yard. Forget about the river; they were sure to have a shovel on the property somewhere.

Morgan turned on the light over the easel. "Well, here it is."

Josh wasn't sure what to say, so he asked, "Does it have a name?"

"Right now, I'm calling it Looming Future. I'm ready to add another color. What do you think it should be?"

Josh studied the painting. Good thing she'd asked about colors and not for his general opinion. Because his general opinion was that she should start with a fresh canvas and paint something recognizable. Abstract art clearly wasn't to his taste.

"Maybe you should add a red swirl down in this corner to represent the anger and frustration people feel when facing the future," he offered.

"Hmm. Maybe. Is that how you feel about the future?" Morgan asked.

"Not so much anger anymore, but a lot of frustration."

"I know what you mean. I kinda feel that too, but I'm not sure red expresses it. Anyway, wait outside while I change my shirt and then we can go."

Josh lifted his arms to display his drenched underarms. "Can I borrow a T-shirt too? I can change in the car – once we're away from here."

Morgan grinned, grabbed a black T-shirt out of her drawer, and tossed it at him.

"Where do you want to go, by the way?" Josh asked.

"Anywhere they don't serve coffee," Morgan said and shooed him out to the hall so she could change.

As they passed the dining room on their way out, Mr. Parker called, "Mr. Hampton?"

"Yes, sir?"

"I look forward to you visiting again so we can discuss your prospects."

"I look forward to it too, sir," Josh said, trying to remember the penance for lying.

"So close," Morgan muttered under her breath with a chuckle.

Chapter 24

In Which Things Surely Must Get Better
Sunday, September 17, 1995

Morgan sat staring at her painting, paintbrush in hand. No, red was not the right color.

She jumped as the floor vibrated beneath her. It sounded like a wall collapsed. Damned contractors. They were almost as bad as Matthew.

Almost. When push came to shove, she'd choose construction work over screaming kids any day.

Morgan put down the brush, got up, and walked away from the painting. She hadn't touched it for days. That was the problem with the Looming Future. It was impossible to predict. Instead of attempting to do so, she decided to tackle the Annoying Present. No, it wasn't a piece of art. It was the newspaper. The want ads, to be precise.

Morgan enjoyed her job at the café most days. Although she rarely saw her boss, Laura was a great lady who Morgan had come to respect and admire. She'd built a successful business all on her own, worked hard, and had a beautiful daughter who meant the world to her.

Still, Morgan had no intentions of becoming like her. She'd learned the ropes well enough to open and close the shop on her own. In fact, she'd be doing so today as the café was only open from noon until five.

But she wasn't looking forward to her shift. She'd be working alone, as usual. How silly she and Mel had been, assuming they'd get to hang out together after their training week. They rarely crossed paths at the café now.

Tyler wasn't even going to be there today because he'd gone out of town for the weekend. And when Morgan calculated her wage and approximate tips she would make for her five-hour shift . . .

Well, that's why she was combing the want ads. Morgan circled everything that she was remotely qualified for – not including food service – and vowed to inquire at each and every place tomorrow.

Babysitting Matthew was not working out. He'd gotten even more annoying since she'd taken her trip to Seattle and her parents, much like the café, didn't even pay minimum wage. The absolute worst part was that Josh wasn't allowed to come over when she was babysitting. Her dad would not budge on that rule.

Morgan continued to circle boring prospect after boring prospect until the light bulb appeared over her head. She dropped the paper on her bed and left the room. Her dad was in his home office, and she knocked on the doorframe to get his attention.

"Hello, darling," he said. "Did you want to use the computer for something?"

"No. I was wondering about that job you mentioned before I left on my trip. The one at your office?"

"Oh, that's been filled."

Dammit. "Okay, thanks." She turned to leave.

"But while you're here, why don't we talk about Joshua?"

Morgan turned back but didn't step into the room. "What about him?"

"Well, he didn't have much to say when we met him yesterday. And he ran off in a hurry. Perhaps you could enlighten me as to what his future ambitions are."

"You're not serious."

"Of course I am. He's courting you. We don't know anything about him except for who his parents are and the sort of neighborhood he grew up in . . ."

Don't you dare say what I think you're going to say.

"Your mother and I just want to make sure he intends to do better for himself and perhaps one day, you."

He said it.

"Did you just hear yourself?" Morgan asked. "How dare you judge him when, as you just said, you know nothing about him?"

"Now there's no need to snap," her dad said.

"Oh, I beg to differ. You know what you are? You're a snob. There's absolutely nothing wrong with where Josh lives. Not everyone thinks having a marble countertop on their basement bar is the epitome of success."

"Morgan!"

"Seriously, get over yourself. And by the way, Josh may be my boyfriend but that doesn't mean I'm going to end up as some dishrag of a wife having his babies and depending on him to put food on the table."

Morgan heard the startled sob and didn't have to turn around to know her mom had overheard her rant. *Shit.*

Her dad got up from his office chair and pushed past Morgan.

Morgan held up her hands. "I wasn't talking about Mom!"

And she wasn't talking to anyone because she'd been left standing alone in the hall.

Morgan sighed and returned to her room to get ready for work. Just before leaving, the stack of envelopes containing the pictures she'd printed of the Seattle trip caught her eye. She'd forgotten all about them and her idea to make a scrapbook/artistic collaboration of the journey.

She flipped through a couple of the envelopes but instead of brightening her spirits, the images only depressed her further. Those were the good old days. She and Josh waking up every day together, getting into Zinger, and moving on to the next location. And always – well, almost always – he would be there at the end of the day when it was time for bed.

It seemed like years had passed since then. Not only did they hardly get to see each other now, they had absolutely zero privacy. Some days Morgan had to wonder why they were even bothering to date.

Whoa, give your head a shake, girl. Things will get better.

Morgan shoved the pictures back in the envelope and left for work. She was pleased not to run into her parents on her way out, hoping her mom would have gotten over her comment by the time she saw her again. This day was bad enough already.

By the time Morgan turned on all the machines and opened the café, there was a small crowd waiting to enter. At least tips should be decent.

No, no. That was not the case. Out of the five tables she served over the lunch hour, she ended up with a handful of coins that wouldn't have impressed a beggar on the street. Maybe she needed to start stuffing her bra.

Morgan eyed the group of teens sitting on one of the couches and wondered if it was even worth offering to refresh their beverages. They were weekend regulars and notorious for lounging around for hours without ordering anything other than drinks. Guaranteed non-tippers, too.

At times like this Morgan wondered if waitresses really did spit in people's cups. Disgusting? Absolutely. Slightly tempting? Most definitely.

Morgan finished cleaning off the last vacated table and felt a fleeting moment of pride over how many dishes she'd managed to balance on her tray.

Fleeting, because of course she dropped the damned thing right before she got back to the counter. She ignored the applause and cheers from the group of teens and went to get the broom.

"How much worse can this day get?"

Famous last words. When she emerged from the back with the broom, Josh's sister and Trixie entered the café and took their regular stools on the lounge side.

Morgan felt Trixie's eyes burning a hole through her as she swept up the broken dishes before walking over to take their orders.

"You guys having any luck getting served around here?" Trixie loudly asked the group of teens as Morgan approached.

The other kids laughed and held up their mugs and glasses. Morgan nodded at them and turned to the dastardly duo. "What can I get you?"

"My usual," Trixie said, nose in the air.

Rab frowned at Trixie and gave Morgan an apologetic smile. "She'll have regular coffee today. Same for me, please."

Morgan hesitated before returning Rab's smile and thanking her. Trixie didn't have a usual order. The look on her face told Morgan she was a bit pissed with Rab for putting a halt to what was surely going to be a game ending in an insult to Morgan's intelligence.

Morgan got their coffees and tended to the other patrons while wondering why Josh's sister would choose to hang out with such a person. Morgan hadn't had the opportunity to spend any time with Rab on her own, but she didn't seem bad. In fact, Morgan suspected she and Rab would have a decent chance at getting along if given the chance.

The afternoon continued with crappy tips and crappy thoughts. The little rain cloud hovering over Morgan's head lightened a touch when both the group of non-tippers and Trixie and Rab departed around three o'clock. As it turned out, Rab had been the most generous tipper of the day.

Yes, there was more to her than met the eye.

The rest of the day dragged on and the restaurant emptied at around quarter to five. Morgan risked it and started shutting the machines down. Of course, the bell over the door dinged when someone came in just as she'd turned them all off. She should have locked it.

"Tyler!"

"Whoa, happy to see me?" he asked with one of his infamous broad grins.

"Yes. Lock the door behind you. I just turned everything off."

"No problem." He laughed and turned the deadbolt.

Morgan finished turning out the lights in the back of the shop. "What are you doing here? I didn't expect to see you until next week."

"Got back early and I just had to stop by to see if you were working. I visited my friend in Le Goulet and took a tour of the recording studio."

"That's awesome! What was it like?"

"Just what you said, awesome! I took loads of pictures and I'll tell you all about it . . . are you free tonight?" he asked.

"Ye – no. I'm going out with Josh."

"No problem. He doesn't come around here much, does he? I've only met him once."

"I know," Morgan said. "He doesn't like to bother me when I'm working and he's really busy himself. In fact, he's taking on yet another job soon."

Tyler shrugged. "Sounds like a responsible young man. On a different note, when do you think you'll have time to catch up with a very irresponsible rascal?"

Morgan laughed. "I'm working Tuesday if you're around."

"I'll be here Tuesday, but I was wondering if you'd like to come over to my place sometime."

"Your place?" Morgan hesitated. "For what?"

"To work on those lyrics you came up with. It's too distracting to do it here. Properly, anyway. I really think we can make something great out of them. Plus, I know you'll be super jazzed when I tell you all about the recording studio. It's getting real, Morgan. And I think you can be a big part of it."

"Those were just silly musings I gave you. No way could they end up in an album."

"You underestimate yourself. They're terrific. And with your voice . . . you can't tell me you're not intrigued."

"You've only heard me sing a couple of times," Morgan said.

"Yes, and I'd like to hear more. What happened to the list of songs you were supposed to come up with? You know, the covers we might perform here to give it a try?"

"Oh! I forgot." Morgan dug through her bag and came up with a sheet of paper. "They're in order of preference, but I'm still not sure about performing here."

"Why not?" Tyler took the list and looked at it. "You know you're good enough."

"Yeah, but it's different than doing a school recital or drunken Karaoke at a night club." Morgan waved a hand at his raised brow. "Long story. My point is, I work here, and the atmosphere is so . . . intimate."

"You don't seem like the type of girl to let a little stage fright stop her. We all get it."

"We'll see," Morgan said.

"We can practice first if it makes you more comfortable. Just tell me what night you're free and you can come over to my place. I have some decent equipment and soundproof walls there."

"Where do you live?" Morgan asked suspiciously.

Tyler leaned forward and lowered his voice to a whisper even though they were alone. "It's a secret, so you've got to promise not to tell anyone."

Okay, she was getting slightly creeped out.

"I live in my parents' basement," Tyler finished dramatically.

"Oh, my God." Morgan swatted him on the arm. "You had me freaked out."

"What?" Tyler sat back and raised his hands in defense, keeping his grin in place. "Can't let my adoring fans know I don't have an ultra-cool penthouse in the sky. Yet."

"I'll come over one night. Just give me your number."

They exchanged phone numbers and Tyler left Morgan to shut off the rest of the lights and lock up.

Which she did in a hurry. It was way after five and Josh would be waiting.

Sure enough, Josh was sitting in Bob in front of her house by the time she arrived. Morgan parked Zinger and ran over to him.

"Just give me ten minutes to freshen up?" she asked. "I promise I won't make you come in."

"No problem," Josh said.

They kissed through the window and Morgan dashed into the house.

"Are you staying for dinner?" her mom asked as she passed the kitchen.

Morgan was going to call out her no but skidded to a halt as she remembered the hurt feelings from earlier.

She walked into the kitchen where her mom was preparing the meal alone. "Mom, I'm sorry about what I said earlier. I wasn't talking about you, you know."

Her mom smiled. "I know. You, Matthew, and . . ." she gestured to her stomach, "whoever this is, are the best things I've ever done in my life." Her smile turned a bit sad. "But you're right, what you said. I can't help wanting more for you."

"I told you I didn't mean –"

"No. You shouldn't have to depend on someone for your happiness. You should have a life of your own and do something you love."

"I've yet to figure out what that thing is," Morgan said.

"You will. Give yourself time. I know your dad pressures you, but he does mean well."

"So did you like Josh?"

Her mom's smile returned. "Very much. And while I don't think you should have to be dependent on anyone, it doesn't hurt to have someone you love to share your life with."

"I agree." Morgan grinned shyly before admitting, "and I do love him."

Morgan's mom hugged her tightly and kissed the top of her head. "Now go get ready. That poor boy's been sitting out there for half an hour already."

Morgan laughed and took off to her room. Minutes later she was running back out the front door, looking forward to her time with Josh.

He looked like he'd fallen asleep when she jumped into the passenger side of Bob.

"Sorry to keep you waiting," she said.

Josh straightened up and leaned over to kiss her. Oh, those lips. She could never get enough of them.

"Where do you want to go?" she asked when they parted, hoping more than anything he'd just say back to Seattle.

"I thought we'd stop for some pizza and then we could catch a movie."

"Again?" Morgan couldn't keep the disappointment out of her voice.

"Unless there's something you'd rather do," Josh said.

She could think of many, many other things she'd rather do but none of them were all that feasible or affordable.

"No, that'll be all right."

Josh kissed her again before starting the engine.

Morgan's thoughts drifted back to the movie night they'd had in Montreal as he drove to the pizza place.

Just the two of them. Alone. In comfy clothes under a blanket.

No noisy, crowded restaurant. No boring movie at a boring movie theater. And at the end of the night, no getting dropped off to sleep alone.

As far as Morgan was concerned, this night out was really just a waste of money. Sure, she got to spend time with Josh, but it certainly wasn't quality time.

However, she'd have to take what she could get for now.

Things had to get better eventually.

Chapter 25

In Which There Is a Calm
Sunday, November 26, 1995

"Josh, I'm ready." A female voice filtered into his brain.

"Give me another minute, Morgan."

"Josh, wake up!" That was not Morgan.

He opened his eyes and lifted his head from the table. Then reality set back in.

"Right. I must have dozed off. Let me go warm up the car."

"You should have done that already, sleepyhead," Rab said. "We need to go now, or I'll be late for work."

Josh stood and put his largely uneaten bowl of Fruity Rings in the sink before leaving the kitchen. He'd probably get chewed out, in French, for not wiping off the table, but at least he'd made some effort. Besides, he hadn't drooled on it.

Rab waited by the door as he pulled on his parka, then followed him out of the house.

He was thankful the car started right away. No new snow had fallen overnight, so Josh hoped the roads would be reasonably clear.

"How long has Morgan been waking you up in the morning?" Rab asked as she wrapped her arms around herself for warmth.

"She hasn't. It was just a dream."

"Must have been some dream. Sorry we didn't have time for you to take a cold shower."

"It's cold enough out here as it is," Josh said and checked to see if the heater had warmed enough to turn the fan up. "Where's your regular ride this morning?"

"You asked me that when I asked you for a ride."

"Pretend I forgot."

"I don't have to pretend too hard," Rab said. "Anyway, we've had a big turnover lately, so management had to split the most experienced workers up to make sure things run smoothly. I asked for the morning shift."

"That had to be some turnover if you and Trixie are the most experienced workers. You just started in September, didn't you?"

"August, when you and Morgan were on your grand adventure. She's told me a lot more about it than your postcards did."

"Oh, did she? Like what?" Josh asked.

"Nuh uh, sisters don't tell their secrets."

"Well, I appreciate that you're being nice to Morgan."

"It's not hard. She's a nice person. When we're at the café she's always courteous. And she doesn't treat me like I'm some dumb kid," Rab said.

"How are you getting home?"

"Were you asleep when we talked last night? David will get me if I don't work a double shift. Which I probably won't because with school, homework, and our jobs, he and I don't get to see much of each other."

They arrived at Burger Barn, but the morning shift manager wasn't there yet, so they sat in the car to keep warm.

"That's half the reason I'm moving out," Josh said, frustration coming through in his tone. "Whenever *Maman* is home, Morgan isn't comfortable at our house. Over at her house, her dad usually comes down to play pool with us and rattles on about schools and the future. We can't get a moment to ourselves. No place in town we can afford to go offers any real privacy."

"And the other half is Trix?" Rab guessed.

"Her and *Maman*. It's almost like they're double teaming me to convince me to dump Morgan. I appreciate that you're at least neutral on the matter."

"When you first got home, all I could see was Trix's side. But then I started to see how good Morgan was for you and, as I got to know her, what a nice person she was," Rab said.

"I'm sorry you're taking a lot of flak from Trixie because of us. I hope it doesn't cost you your friendship."

"It won't because she needs that friendship. When we first connected, we were both depressed, but we worked through that together. Don't forget, you were a part of it."

"I had my own problems, but yeah," Josh admitted. He'd said as much to Morgan.

"She saw you as the key to a stable future and took a pretty bad hit when she lost you."

"I never promised anything like that," Josh said.

"I know, I know. Still, maybe you think it's foolish, but I'm afraid if she loses me too, she'll fall back into depression. I can't let her do that," Rab said, folding her hands in her lap.

"Don't let her use that to manipulate you."

"She hasn't and I won't let her. She's getting better. We're even easing out of the goth thing." Rab pulled off a mitten to show him fingernails free of nail polish. No trace of black remained.

"I'm impressed," Josh said. "Sorry I hadn't noticed."

Rab laughed. "David says I should let my natural hair color grow out. He seemed disappointed when I told him this is my natural color."

"He'll get over it and probably start writing poems about your raven locks."

"You're going house hunting with Morgan today, aren't you?" Rab shook her head. "I'm going to miss you, and I'll have to deal with Mom all on my own."

"At least she's not set on trying to break you and David up."

"It doesn't hurt that he's a Francophone and attends Mass with us."

"He seems like a nice guy. I hope things work out for you two," Josh said.

"We have no illusions it's a permanent thing. It's just nice to have someone stable and not get caught up in all that teenage dating angst."

The morning manager arrived and opened the door.

Rab climbed out and leaned over to say, "Thanks, Josh. Tell Morgan I said hi. Be smart and listen to her instinct when it comes to a place?"

"I see she's already got you on her side." Josh quirked a brow.

Rab laughed and shut the door.

Josh drove off to Cal's, his first job of the day, where Morgan would meet him at noon to go house hunting.

***

Morgan was late. Again.

Josh would have been irritated with her, but the sun was out and it was warm enough that he could pull another part out of Old Blue's dead engine. A wrecked pickup sat next to his truck. Really, they were both his trucks, but the second one was only good for parts. It had been sideswiped and the frame was beyond saving, but the engine was intact.

Whenever Josh had time, he would pull parts out of the engines and decide which one would go back in when the new engine was moved over to Old Blue.

It was almost twelve-thirty when Morgan pulled up in Zinger and rolled down the window. "Did you forget we're going to look at places today?"

Josh closed the hood of Old Blue. "I thought you were going to be here at noon. I was just working on this while I waited."

"Sorry. I had to drop something off at the café."

"Give me a second to put my tools away and we can go," Josh said and opened the trunk of his car to drop his tool bag in.

After he climbed into Zinger and gave Morgan a kiss, she pulled a newspaper from the back seat and plopped it on his lap. "Today's want ads. Buckle up and start searching."

"Can we get a bite to eat first?"

"As long as it's not at the café," Morgan said. "I'd never get out of there a second time."

They went to a burger place that served breakfast late on Sundays and ordered pancakes and coffee.

"Have you found any places to look at?" Morgan asked.

"I've found a few. Can I borrow your phone?"

"Sure. It still has almost a full month's worth of minutes on it."

Josh cringed. He caught the implication that he didn't call enough. "I'll try to do better next month."

Morgan frowned. "Do better at what? I was talking about my cell phone." She slid it across the table. "It's a racket. It wouldn't be as bad if the minutes rolled over from month to month, but they just disappear if you don't use them."

Relieved his overtired brain had misunderstood her meaning, Josh began calling places he'd circled that had numbers.

Several had already been rented. One person told him to call again on Monday, and two others didn't answer. After twenty minutes, Josh had one appointment to see a house and several apartment complexes to check out.

It was already after one, so they headed off to the first place. Morgan reached into the glove compartment and placed a map of Bathurst on his lap. "Navigator, set a course."

"Cross the bridge to East Bathurst and get on Bridge Street. When did you get this map?"

"You got the map last week. You're really losing it, Josh. Tell me, what's my name?"

"You're Morgan, my Angel. I wouldn't forget that."

"Sometimes I wonder," she mumbled.

Josh barely registered her words. His eyelids drooped as he gazed out the window.

"Address, Josh," Morgan reminded him in a louder voice.

He snapped out of his half-doze and directed her to the apartment complex.

At the office, a woman told them where the empty apartment was and handed Josh a key.

"I can't wait until I save up enough to move out too," Morgan said as they walked through the snow to the apartment complex. "The basement bedroom's a bit better but I'm sick and tired of playing Morgan Day Care."

"I thought you agreed to it because you needed the money," Josh said.

"Yeah, but fingers crossed I'll be retiring soon."

Morgan gave him an annoyed look as he tried make sense of what she was saying.

"My second interview at the law firm is tomorrow," she said pointedly. "Wish me luck?"

"This is the first I've heard of it."

"I told you on Friday."

"You couldn't have," Josh said. "We haven't talked since Wednesday unless you count making these plans yesterday."

"Sorry, I thought I told you." Morgan frowned.

Josh shrugged. "Well, good luck tomorrow."

They reached the complex and found the apartment.

"There's no furniture at all in here," Josh said. "I wonder how much it would cost to rent a bed."

"If you do the math, renting furniture is far more expensive than buying it," Morgan said.

"I have my blanket. I guess that will have to do for starters."

"You mean your parents won't even let you take your bedroom stuff?"

Josh laughed dryly. "Not a chance."

Morgan had walked over to the window. "This is a nice place, and has a view of the ocean, but I'm afraid it'll be out of our price range."

"*Our* price range?" Josh said.

"Did I say our? I meant your price range."

"I guess you're as tired as I am," Josh said, but inwardly smiled.

They looked around a bit more before locking up and returning to the office.

It took Josh a lot of willpower to keep his mouth from falling open when they were informed the rent was six hundred dollars a month.

Back in the car, Morgan said, "Next!"

The next two apartments were equally expensive, and Josh's heart sank lower and lower.

Morgan let out a crazy sort of laugh as they drove along.

"What's so funny?" Josh asked.

"If I were writing country songs, this would be perfect. 'My Pickup's Dead and I Can't Afford the Rent.'"

"Since when do you write songs?"

She took her eyes off the road just long enough to glare at him. "Since months ago. I told you then and your only response was 'cool.' If you're not going to listen, why am I bothering to even tell you anything?"

"Sorry, Angel. Things will be better when I move out," Josh said, rubbing his tired face. "I'm hoping it'll be next weekend. I've arranged with Cal to take the day off on the second if I can find a place."

When they reached the next address Morgan stopped the car and turned to Josh.

"Next place?" she offered.

"Next place," Josh agreed with an exaggerated nod. To put it nicely, the neighborhood had seen better days. He refrained from telling Morgan that Trixie and her mom lived in the area – if they hadn't moved again.

The house they viewed was closer to what Josh was looking for, but still threatened to break the bank. He told the agent he would call back tomorrow. As he and Morgan drove off, they passed an elderly man putting a "For Rent" sign at the edge of his property.

"Stop the car!" Josh said.

Morgan hit the brakes and Josh jumped out to talk with the man.

"Good afternoon, sir," Josh said. "Have you advertised this rental in the paper?"

"Not yet, young man. The previous renters just moved out yesterday."

"I've been searching all day for a place. Do you mind if I have a look?" Josh asked as Morgan joined him and took his hand.

"Are you in school still?" the landlord asked.

"Graduated last spring."

"You gainfully employed?"

"I work at Bathurst Automotive," Josh said. "Full time."

The gentleman gave Josh a skewed look.

Josh held up his free hand. "As a mechanic, not a salesman."

The landlord relaxed his expression and nodded. "The former tenants left kind of a mess and banged it up some, but I'll get that taken care of."

"I'll keep that in mind." Josh held Morgan's hand as they followed the man around back.

"It isn't very big," he said, "but it has its own kitchen and bath. After the last of the kids moved out, me and the wife didn't need all that space, so we converted part of the house into a rental."

He unlocked the door and handed Josh the key. "I'll let you take a look. Just come around to my side when you're done."

"Thank you, sir," Josh said and went inside with Morgan.

After they closed the door, she lifted her eyebrows and curled her nose. "He wasn't lying about the mess."

There were stains on the walls and spots on the carpet. Someone had punched a hole in the drywall. A musty smell pervaded the air.

"Some people." Josh shook his head, feeling sorry for the landlord.

It didn't take long to see all there was to see. There were two bedrooms, one smaller than the other, and the bathroom only had a shower, no tub. The kitchen appliances looked like antiques. Other than the appliances, and a bit of trash lying around, it was unfurnished.

"It has potential," Josh said.

"I can't imagine the rent would be very much," Morgan said.

"It can't hurt to ask."

"I've seen enough if you have."

Josh agreed. They locked up and walked around to the front.

The gentleman let them into his part of the house. "Well, what do you think?"

"How soon do you think you could have it ready?" Josh asked.

"Don't want it sitting empty," he said. "Would the first be soon enough for you?"

"It would be perfect. How much is rent?"

"Two hundred a month, due by the fifth, with one month's rent down."

Josh looked at Morgan, but he didn't have to ask what she thought. "I'll take it," he said. "Do you want the down payment now?"

"You can give it to me on the first when you pick up the keys and sign the rental agreement. Just leave me your name and number."

Josh gave him the information and they shook hands.

When he and Morgan got back into the car, Josh's eyes were wide and alert.

"Are you really okay with this place?" he asked. "I mean, it'll be a bit cleaner by the time I get it . . ."

"Absolutely! I'm so happy you found something today. I guess you're officially an adult now."

They laughed and drove off back to Cal's.

Chapter 26

In Which the Lines Are Blurred
Monday, November 27, 1995

"Tyler! I got the job!"

Morgan threw her tray onto the counter and ran over before the door had even closed behind him. She stopped herself short of throwing herself in his arms – what was she thinking? – and instead did a little happy dance in front of him.

"Congratulations! I knew you'd get it."

"I don't know why I'm so excited. It's going to be *so* boring, but the pay is more than worth it."

"And goodbye to babysitting, right?"

"Oh, yes." Morgan grinned. "Can you believe my dad actually tried to pull the two weeks' notice bit with me?"

"No! Don't they have another babysitter?"

"Sure, but they have to pay her an actual wage. Anyhow, he gets like that. But he's actually happy I found a 'proper' job." Morgan said with a roll of her eyes.

"Well, one day you won't need any of these jobs anymore, proper or not."

Morgan laughed. "Right, the fame and fortune bit."

"You're still not taking it seriously? You've seen the work we've done."

"Yeah, it's just . . . a long shot. I mean, I believe you could do it, you're super talented, but I don't think I've got what it takes."

Tyler shook his head, yet his smile remained in place. "Believe me, you do. So are we still on for tonight after work? I've got the last song set to music and we can work on our debut cover song to perform here."

"You bet. Oh, customers. I'll talk to you later."

A few groups of patrons came in at the same time, all wanting warmed sandwiches. Morgan still wasn't the best at working the evil toasting machine, but she managed without burning the food or herself.

After the flurry, Morgan called Josh's house to tell him the news. However, his mother informed her he was napping.

Oh, well. She'd tell him tomorrow night. Josh had taken the night off just so they could go out and celebrate his new place. Of course it would've made more sense to take the time off after he actually moved in and they could spend the evening alone, but Morgan did appreciate the sentiment. And they definitely needed to nurture their relationship before . . . well, before yesterday, really.

They'd had a rough week. Correction: they'd had a rough couple of months. Some days she forgot what he looked like. Literally. Whenever they did get together, crappy date place or not, it was almost like meeting him all over again.

But soon they'd have a place to actually be alone together. And more often. And tomorrow was going to be spectacular. As Josh had said, "Dollars be damned!" He'd made reservations at one of the nicer restaurants in Bathurst and the weather forecast promised it might be warm enough to take a romantic stroll in the park afterward.

Morgan made her rounds with the coffee pot, listening to Tyler's music. Another customer came in – no, not a customer. It was Mel. But she looked like death warmed over.

Morgan finished tending to her customers and warily approached the counter where Mel sat. "Are you okay?"

"Oh sure, I'm swell. And by swell, I mean swollen. And by swollen, I mean I can't believe I've still got five months of this crap left. I feel like I'm going to explode."

Morgan bit her tongue, remembering that not everyone appreciated dark humor, and did not tell her friend she would be exploding soon enough. Instead, she said, "I'll get you some tea."

"Thanks."

Morgan got the beverage and studied Mel more closely as she sipped on it.

"It's nice to see you and all," Morgan said, "but you really look like you should be in bed."

Mel choked on her tea. "Well, thanks. You look good too."

"I didn't mean –"

"I know what you meant. It's something new every day it seems. Nausea, swelling, hot flashes, cold flashes, and let's not forget the wild mood swings." She ended with an appropriately maniacal laugh.

Morgan wasn't sure if it was a fake laugh or not.

"Relax," Mel said. "I'm definitely not feeling well, but I've got tonight and tomorrow night off. It'll pass. I just needed to get out of the house."

"Okay. I'm glad you came by though. We hardly ever get to spend any time together. Brilliant idea getting a job at the same place, hey?"

"Yeah, way back when we were young and naïve."

"All those months ago." Morgan placed a hand dramatically on her head and cast her eyes to the sky, expecting Mel to laugh. Instead, when she looked back, Mel was in tears.

"Shit. What's wrong now? What did I do?"

"Nothing. I told you, mood swings."

"It's more than that." Morgan eyed the customers, who seemed to be doing fine, and took a seat on the stool next to Mel. "Talk to me."

Mel dried her eyes and hiccupped. "I want to keep my baby," she said in a whisper.

"What? Are you –" *do not say insane* "– serious?"

Mel shrugged and nodded at the same time. Not helpful. Morgan had no words.

Thankfully, Mel did. "I know it's crazy, but I just can't imagine going through all this and giving my child away to strangers. *My child*."

"Um, I guess I can't really understand what you're going through . . . but how would you take care of a baby on your own?"

Morgan knew she'd said the wrong thing yet again even before Mel shot her the look. "The same way your mom did," Mel said. "I can live with my parents."

"Well, that's good." Now was not the time to point out Mel had no future or even a decent job. In fact, it was not the best time to share the news of her own decent job. Now was the time to comfort and agree, right?

"No, it's not good," Mel wailed.

Morgan cringed and patted her on the shoulder, feeling terrible. Why on earth had she been thinking about futures and jobs when her friend was going through this emotional struggle?

"Mel, it will be good. No matter what you end up doing." Now that was more like it. "Look, I've got to get back to work. But why don't you take a comfortable seat and I'll come by and chat with you some more?" Morgan suggested.

Mel sniffled and threw her arms around Morgan. "No, I'm going to go home. Thanks for listening. You made me feel better."

She hugged her back awkwardly, wondering what in the world she'd done to make her feel better.

Morgan saw her friend to the door and checked on her customers. Tyler took a break from playing and came over to where she was clearing off a table.

"What happened with Mel?" he asked.

"She got knocked up," Morgan deadpanned.

Tyler laughed. At least someone appreciated dry wit.

"Seriously," Morgan said, "I don't know. I think she's just having a tough time with it all. And I think she came to talk to the wrong person. I'm not a fan of babies."

"Make that two non-fans," Tyler said with a grimace. "My sister just had one. I don't understand the hype at all. Especially with newborns. Nothing cute about that."

"Oh, not in the slightest," Morgan agreed, remembering Matthew's early days and picturing the next two bundles of joy that were on the way.

The rest of the night was fairly slow, but tips were up. Morgan was quite pleased when she locked up for the night and left with Tyler for his place.

He usually waited for her when she closed up even though she didn't need to follow his car to get to his house. It wasn't that far from her home, and she already knew the route like the back of her hand. Better than she knew the way to Josh's house. Morgan dismissed the slightly bitter thought. It didn't matter. Because soon he'd be living somewhere else and Morgan had no doubt she'd be spending a great deal of time there.

Tyler's parents greeted her cheerily when she and Tyler came in. She stopped to chat with them and told them about her new job. They were super laidback and friendly, and Morgan always enjoyed talking to them.

As much as she loved her parents and tolerated Josh's, she couldn't help but wish her and Josh's folks could be more like them. Attitude-wise, anyway.

Downstairs, in Tyler's room, he kicked around a few piles of clothing in an attempt to tidy up as he normally did, and Morgan chuckled. His room was messy, but it was totally cool. It took up half the basement and more than half of that room space was designated for all things music.

He hadn't been lying when he'd told her the room was soundproofed. His parents had gone all out in support of his music career. They probably had an ulterior peace-for-themselves motive in mind during construction, but still. It was awesome.

Not for the first time, she wondered why Tyler's parents didn't just pay for his studio time. She'd never asked him before and decided to today.

Tyler stopped in the middle of setting up the microphone and stools. "They've offered to help me but I really want to make it on my own. Sounds cheesy, I know, but this is the most important thing in my life. I don't mind accepting my buddy's help because he owns part of the station, though. It's bro code."

"Where do I fit into bro code?" Morgan asked. "I still can't believe you're wasting your time with me."

Tyler rolled his eyes but never dropped his smile. "Quit saying that and come here."

He gestured to one of the stools and Morgan came over to sit.

"Now listen to this." Tyler sat beside her with his guitar and began to play.

She knew exactly which song of hers it was without needing to see the words. She hadn't realized she was singing along softly until it was over and he gave her an I-told-you-so look.

"Okay, I get it," Morgan said. "But I could never create that music on my own."

"Exactly. And I couldn't write the song on my own. Face it, Morgan, you and I are a team."

Morgan didn't say anything, but her mind was running full tilt after hearing her – their – song. It was getting real. A real possibility anyway.

Tyler suggested they run through the song again with her singing and make a recording of it. By the time they finished, she was overwhelmed and even more convinced they definitely had something here.

"See? I told you we'd make beautiful music together."

Morgan laughed. "Yeah, on the first day we met – well, re-met – I totally thought it was just a pickup line."

"Well, it kind of was. At the time. Don't worry," he added when he saw her shift uncomfortably, "you set me straight that same day."

Morgan heard her cell phone ringing in her bag, which she'd left across the room. "Oh, that must be Josh."

She ran to retrieve it but couldn't find it in time. However, it rang again almost immediately.

"Hello?"

"Do you have any idea how many times I've tried calling you?" Josh asked.

"Well, good morning to you too, sunshine," she said.

"My mom told me you called."

"Yeah, earlier when I was at work. What is wrong with you?"

"I'm tired, Morgan." All snappiness was gone from his voice, replaced with weariness. "I'm really, really tired."

"I know." Morgan softened her tone as well. "But just hang in there. Things will get better. I'm looking forward to tomorrow night."

"Me too. I love you, Angel."

"And I love you," she said.

Only after hanging up the phone did she realize she hadn't told Josh about her new job. Oh, well. He probably wouldn't even remember half their conversation anyhow.

"I think Winds of Change is the song we should use for our café debut."

Morgan put the phone back into her bag and turned to Tyler. "Argh. That was one of my top picks, but I've got a confession to make."

"Confess away," he said, rubbing his hands together in expectation.

She laughed. "It's not that big of a deal, but I can't whistle."

"You can't what now?"

"Okay, maybe it is a big deal."

"No, no, I'm not making fun of you, I just can't believe there's anything you can't do. Especially when it comes to music."

Morgan shrugged. "My lips just don't go that way. So we'll have to pick a different song. Or you could just do the whistling part."

"Why don't I teach you how to whistle?" Tyler suggested as she took her spot on the stool.

"Trust me, I'm hopeless. My mom is really good at whistling. She can even do that thing where you fold your tongue and put your fingers in the corners of your mouth." Morgan did so with her own tongue and fingers so her next two words were slurred. "And then . . ." She blew hard, producing nothing unless you counted a rather impressive spit bubble.

Tyler nearly fell off his stool laughing as she wiped her mouth.

"I know that whistle," he said. "It's deafening. I can't do it myself, though."

"I can't do any of them. But that's the one she tried to teach me. And believe, me she tried hard. I'm hopeless."

"Well, why don't we try the regular sort and work our way up?"

Morgan shrugged. "Your waste of time."

"I told you," Tyler said, his perma-smile gone, replaced with a look of intensity. "Nothing about you is a waste of time. Trust me?"

"I do," she said, a bit thrown off by the seriousness. "Fine then. Let's whistle our faces off."

By the time their session was through, it was safe to say another one would be in order. It was also very, very late. Babysitting was going to suck in the morning.

Regardless, Morgan left Tyler's house in high spirits. To her surprise, she had managed to whistle a few notes. Even better, babysitting was soon to be a thing of the past. And the icing on the cake was her date with Tyler – Josh – tomorrow night and the reason they were celebrating.

It couldn't happen soon enough. God only knew what Josh would think if she got his name mixed up with Tyler's aloud. As fun as the music stuff was, she wanted – and desperately needed – to spend more time with her boyfriend than she did with her music friend.

Chapter 27

In Which a Misunderstanding Occurs
Tuesday, November 28, 1995

Morgan's standard attire of T-shirts and ripped jeans wasn't going to cut it tonight. She'd taken everything out of her closet, including the dress she'd worn to prom, and tried on most of the garments in preparation for her date with Josh.

Now, piles of clothing covered her bed as she stood in front of the mirror in her outfit of choice – off-white slacks with the purple blouse she'd bought at Josh's insistence on the trip home. The shirt should have been a no-brainer. She smiled at her reflection and couldn't wait to see Josh's return smile.

Morgan had plenty of time to spare, so she went into her en suite bathroom to apply a touch of makeup and perfect her hair.

The one tube of mascara she owned had dried up, probably years ago, and the lipstick was only half applied before it was scrubbed off with a tissue. No, big night out or not, Morgan was not a makeup girl.

But she could do something with her hair. It had grown out considerably since the summer and was well past her shoulders now. Even so, her haircare routine hadn't changed. A comb and finger tousle had yet to fail her.

After a botched attempt at a swept up messy-bun and an aggravating run-in with a headband that threatened to rip out half her hair, Morgan decided to leave well enough alone.

Tinted lip gloss for her lips and a dash of leave-in conditioner for her hair was all she needed. And really, it was perfect. The end result wasn't overdone, it was just . . . shinier.

Morgan's mom called down the stairs and it was hard to hear exactly what she said, but Morgan caught the words "ready to go."

She checked the time and saw it was only seven o'clock. Josh wasn't supposed to pick her up until eight. Oh, well. She was more than ready and an extra hour with her boyfriend was certainly not something she was going to bitch about. They might need to have a chat about their communication skills, or lack of them, but that could wait for another day.

Morgan grabbed her purse and hurried upstairs.

"My goodness, what are you all dressed up for?" Morgan's mom asked.

She was wearing a much fancier outfit than Morgan and Morgan cringed. She knew her parents were going out for dinner too, because she hadn't been left with any dinner preparation chores that day, but she hoped to hell they weren't going to the same restaurant. God, that would be embarrassing. Especially with Matthew's table manners.

Morgan peered out the front window, looking for Bob. Josh's car wasn't there.

"Is Josh here?" Morgan asked.

"He'd better not be," her father said as he entered the living room. He too was all decked out in one of his best suits.

Morgan frowned. "What are you talking about? Why did you call me up if he's not here?" she asked her mom.

"We need to leave," her mom said. "Matthew's in his crib but he'll need a story before –"

"Hang on. Why is Matthew in his crib?"

Her parents gave her a strange look.

"Did you forget we were going out tonight?" her mom asked.

"No. I *am*, however, wondering what you intend on doing with your son. You know I'm going out with Josh."

"Sweetie, we told you about this banquet last week. You said you'd babysit Matthew."

"Like hell I did!"

"Language!" her dad said just as Matthew started to cry.

The next few minutes were a blur, filled with accusations and tears from everyone but her dad.

Morgan's mom went to settle Matthew and her dad went to warm up the car. Morgan was left standing by the front door, not quite sure what had just happened.

When her mom returned, they'd both calmed enough to have a reasonable discussion.

"I'm sorry about the misunderstanding, Morgan. You do look pretty. Was it an important date?"

Morgan nodded. "It *is* an important date. Can you please get another babysitter?"

"I really have to go, but go ahead and call Clarissa. Matthew's almost asleep."

Morgan didn't say anything. She just watched her mom put on her coat and leave.

She went to the kitchen to call Clarissa. It rang way too many times.

"Oh no, no, no." Realizing the machine had picked up and she was leaving a message, Morgan added, "Clarissa? This is Morgan Parker. Please call me back. An emergency has come up and I need you to babysit Matthew tonight."

She was in tears by the time she hung up.

This isn't happening. Think, Morgan, think.

She took the notepad off the fridge and went through the list of other sitters. Not home, not home, doesn't even live there anymore.

Oh, Mel! Morgan stopped crying immediately and stabbed her friend's number into the phone. Mel's mom answered.

"Hi, can I speak to Mel please?"

"Oh, Morgan. Uh, I'll tell her you called, but she can't come to the phone right now."

"What?!"

"It's nothing to be worried about, she's just under the weather."

"She's too sick to talk to me?" Morgan heard a faint retching in the background. "Oh, sorry. Never mind."

She hung up without saying goodbye and stared at the notepad of emergency contacts. 911 was looking pretty appealing right about now.

Morgan slammed her head on the table hard enough to see stars. Matthew was babbling to himself down the hall but he wasn't crying. Well, she was. Again.

With a heavy heart, she picked up the phone and dialed Josh's house.

His father answered and when she asked to speak to Josh, his response was to set the phone down and walk away. She'd only met the man once but wasn't surprised.

A moment later, Josh came on the phone and she spilled the whole story in between sobs and curses.

"Angel, settle down. It'll be okay."

"No, it won't. We needed this, Josh. You took the night off and I – I –"

Josh waited until she'd cried all the tears she had to cry before speaking. "Listen, I can probably get my shift back. Just look at it this way; in three more days I'll have my own place. You can help me decorate it. I'll give you a key and you can wait for me to come home from work and welcome me with kisses and maybe a meal."

That got a laugh out of her. "A takeout meal?"

"Or no meal at all." She could hear him smiling over the phone. "It doesn't matter. All that matters is we'll be together. Three more days," he repeated.

"Three more days," she echoed. "Aren't you disappointed about tonight?"

"Of course I am, but it's not worth shedding tears over. I'll cancel the reservation and go to work."

Morgan sighed. "I'm just so mad. Why don't you come over here? Matthew will be asleep soon and I don't give a shit if my dad finds out."

"No. We don't want to risk you getting grounded. It would only make things worse."

"I guess you're right. Thanks for understanding. I love you."

"I love you too."

Morgan went to the washroom and splashed some water on her face before dragging herself to Matthew's room. She didn't get far into reading his story before he fell asleep.

She was on her way downstairs to change when the phone rang. She ran back to the kitchen and pounced on it.

"Hello?!"

"Morgan, I just got your message. Do you still need a sitter?" Clarissa asked.

"Yes! Yes! Yes! When can you get here?"

"I'll be there in fifteen minutes. What happened? You said it was an emergency."

"Oh, that. Just a date emergency," Morgan said. "Sorry, I didn't mean to alarm you."

Clarissa laughed. "No problem. See you soon."

Thrilled, Morgan disconnected and dialed Josh's number.

"Hampton residence."

"Hello, Mrs. Hampton. Could I speak to Josh, please?"

"He's already left for work."

Morgan's heart dropped to the floor. "Oh. Thanks."

She hung up and shoved the phone across the table. Maybe she could get in the car and intercept him before he got to work. No, he'd already gotten his shift back. She'd just have to be patient, as he said, for three more days. Then everything would be all right.

Now what in the hell was she going to do tonight?

By the time Clarissa arrived, Morgan had decided to go to the café. Had she been nineteen, she probably would've gone to drown her sorrows in beer, but a cup of coffee would have to do.

The café was packed for a Tuesday night. It appeared that a group of teenagers had taken over the stage for an impromptu Karaoke night. Tyler was sitting off to the side, writing on a notepad. Morgan took off her coat and went to see if Laura needed a hand.

Rab and Trixie were at their usual table and Rab looked surprised to see Morgan. Josh must have told her about their date. Morgan shrugged and smiled at her, holding her head high. As much as she'd love to commiserate with Rab, there was no way she would do so with Trixie there.

"You look beautiful tonight," Laura commented. "What's the occasion?"

Morgan laughed mirthlessly. "There isn't one. What's going on here?" She gestured to the lounge area.

"Oh, just some kids having fun." She waved at her daughter who was dancing to the music. "Teresa's enjoying it and they're not causing any trouble. They're here to sing, not drink."

"So you don't need any help?"

"Not right now, but maybe later if you're sticking around."

"I'll be here for a while." She waved to Tyler, who had just noticed her.

On her way over to him, she passed Rab and Trixie's table again and kept her eyes straight ahead.

"Wow. You clean up real nice," Tyler said.

"Thanks. My date got canceled."

"What happened?" he asked.

"My parents. I don't want to talk about it."

"Fair enough. Why don't we get out of here? I'm not getting anywhere near that stage tonight."

"No," Morgan said. "I think I'm going to go home soon and work on my painting. I'm in a terrible mood."

"Then let me cheer you up." Tyler went to fetch another chair. "Sit down and I'll get you a coffee."

He was already gone before she could answer, so she decided to sit for a while.

When he returned with their beverages he said, "Here. Wet your whistle and then we can practice."

"Whistling? Here? No way. You've seen my attempts. I look like an idiot."

Tyler cast his eyes to the group of kids on the stage who were happily making fools of themselves and gave Morgan his best are-you-kidding-me look.

She laughed. "Point."

***

Josh turned off the radio. Bob had not come equipped with music that would soothe his soul.

He and Morgan had been looking forward to this night since . . . forever, only to have it ripped away from them by parental whim.

When Josh had called to get his shift back, he'd been told it was going to be "a slow night, so enjoy the time off." Was that a nice way of saying he wasn't needed?

So he'd left the house with no particular destination in mind.

Now he continued to drive aimlessly, making turns at random. He thought briefly of going to Morgan's, but knew it was too risky. The street had eyes.

The next thing he knew, he was driving by the café.

What the hell is Zinger doing here? She said –

He hit the brakes and half slid into an available parking spot, narrowly avoiding a collision with the car parked ahead of him. Josh snapped his seatbelt off and threw himself out the door.

The noise from the café was loud enough to be heard outside. It increased in magnitude when he pulled the front door open and scanned the crowd for Morgan.

He found her. She was sitting with that damned Tyler in a dark corner, and Josh couldn't believe his eyes. They were making kissy faces at each other and laughing.

His temper flared into a white-hot rage. But before he could yell her name, before he could charge their table and jerk pretty boy out of his seat, he saw Trixie and Rab staring at him with mouths agape.

Josh spun on his heel and pushed the door closed as hard as he could. It would have slammed if the self-closing door mechanism hadn't dampened the force of his swing.

He reached Bob and jerked the door open.

"Josh, wait!" A feminine voice called, not Morgan's.

He snapped his head toward the voice. Trixie and Rab had followed him.

Putting a hand over his face to hide his rage and lowering his head, he said, “Whatever it is you want to say, I don’t want to hear it.”

“Rab, go back inside and keep Morgan from coming out,” Trixie said.

“Why?” Rab asked.

“Because I need to talk Josh down and I don’t need to be in the middle of a fight while doing it.”

Josh got into Bob and started the engine. He put the car in gear and went to back up, but Trixie was standing right behind the car.

He rolled down the window. “Get out of my way.”

“Not until you hear what I have to say. Now you can get out and face it like a man, or I can stand here and yell through the window like a mother scolding a little boy.”

Josh leaned farther out the window. “If I get out, I’m afraid I might hurt you.”

“No you won’t. I know you. You would never hit a woman no matter how angry you are.”

Josh conceded. She was right on that point. He got out but stood between the partially open door and the car. “Okay, say your piece.”

She took a step forward, but he held up a hand for her to stop.

“Oh, Josh, my dear sweet friend, I’m so sorry you had to find out like this.”

“Find out what, exactly?”

“About him and her,” Trixie said.

“You mean Tyler and Morgan.”

“Yes, them.”

“I know about them,” Josh said, crossing his arms.

“Do you really? Do you know there are nights when you’re at work and she locks up, then they leave together?”

“It only means he hung around until closing.”

"Oh, my poor Josh, you are so naïve sometimes. I'm a woman. I can see what's in another woman's heart by the way she looks at a man," Trixie said with a sad smile.

"You're a girl who would love nothing more than for Morgan and me to break up."

"I'm not denying my feelings for you, but I can see how you're hurting. She's no good, Josh. Let's go somewhere and I'll comfort you as only a woman can," Trixie said and held out her arms invitingly.

"No. I don't need comforting."

"Can't you see that she's done with you?"

"When she is, she'll tell me. Until then, I'm not going to stop loving her. Even if she does, I don't think I'll ever stop." Josh got back in the car.

"I'm trying to help you," Trixie said as she approached the window.

"You're only trying to help yourself. We're done talking. Now move so I don't hurt you."

Trixie bowed her head and stepped slowly away from the car.

Josh put it in gear and drove off.

He needed to talk to Morgan. Storming in and yelling would not have been a good idea. It would only have made the situation worse, no matter how much he wanted to punch that slick pretty boy right in the face.

As tempting as it was, Josh had to remind himself he was an adult now. Such behavior had consequences he wasn't willing to pay.

He passed a patrol car and checked his speed. "*Merde!*" He was driving a bit too fast. Fortunately, the officer wasn't watching, or Josh wasn't going fast enough for him to bother getting out of the patrol car in the cold.

Josh didn't want to go home to call Morgan because his mother would probably hear every word he said. He was hunting for a payphone when he remembered he had a key to Cal's. He made a sharp turn and headed for the garage.

Once there, he let himself into the office and turned on the space heater under Robin's desk.

But what if what Trixie said was true? What if she really was trying to be a friend to him?

Josh dismissed the thought. If she'd stopped before offering to comfort him, her words would have held more weight.

He sat in the chair and glared at the phone, then took several deep breaths to calm down before picking up the receiver. He punched in Morgan's cell phone number and it rang and rang and rang. Finally, the recording came on telling him the user was not available and to please call back.

Or course he was going to call back. She probably couldn't hear the phone over all that noise.

After the second disconnect, he slammed the receiver on the cradle so hard he was afraid he might have broken it. "Not your phone, Josh. Calm yourself down," he muttered.

The third time Josh tried, she answered on the ninth ring. "Hello?"

"Morgan?"

"Josh! Oh my God! Where are you calling from? I didn't recognize the number."

"I'm at Cal's Garage."

"What are you doing there? Your mother told me you went to work," Morgan said.

"I took the night off so I could be with you, in case you forgot."

The connection became muffled and about all he could make out was "Josh."

"Okay, I can talk now," Morgan said. "I had to go outside. What did you say?"

Josh sighed and asked, "Why did you break our date?"

"I told you, my folks were making me babysit."

"Right! Last time I saw your brother he wasn't six feet tall with long dark hair."

"What are you talking about?" Morgan asked.

"Listen, Morgan, I love you, but if you don't want me in your life anymore, just say so."

"What ever gave you such a crazy notion?"

"How about you skipping out on our date, which I took time off for, so you could go play kissy face with pretty boy at the café?"

A pause. Then, "So you're saying I'm stupid?"

"I'm not saying you're stupid," Josh said.

"Do you think that skipping out on a date, knowing my boyfriend has the night off, to have a liaison in a highly public place is smart?"

"No, that's not smart."

"Then you're calling me stupid. Now hold on a second. How do you know I'm at the café? Your sister and *friend* are here, they couldn't have told you. Are you spying on me?" Morgan asked, her voice rising.

"It would be spying if you were caught in a secret place for a rendezvous, not sitting at a table in the café."

"Tell me how you know, Josh! Were you here?"

"It doesn't matter how I know. At least you have the decency not to lie about being at the café," Josh said bitterly.

"Why would I lie about that? I tried calling you back, but you were gone, so I came here."

"To make out with some guy in front of everyone?"

"Make out?! We were – you know what? Never mind. You're too damned nosy for your own good and too damned quick to jump to conclusions. Now I am going to ask you – one last time – how you knew I was here?"

Instead of answering, Josh said, "I'm trying not to jump to the conclusion that – Tyler – is sweeping you off your feet with promises of stardom just like Randy did to your mother."

"Joshua Hampton, you have no idea what you're talking about *or* how lucky you are the telephone is between us right now."

"We are done talking," Josh said.

"You're damned right we are," Morgan agreed.

The conversation ended with a loud bang.

Then all he heard was the dial tone.

Chapter 28

In Which Not All Goes According to Plan
Friday, December 1, 1995

Josh stood in the combined living/dining room of his place. His place, not his parents' house.

The transformation the apartment had undergone was amazing. Josh didn't know how the landlord had managed to do all the renovations since Sunday, but he had.

The musty smell was gone, the carpets had been cleaned, the wall had been repaired, and a faint aroma of fresh latex paint lingered in the air.

It was almost everything he could hope for. Except Morgan wasn't there. He hadn't seen or spoken to her since their argument on Tuesday.

He had clearly overestimated the chances of her sharing this place with him.

Josh sat on his new bed, the only piece of furniture he owned unless one counted the cardboard box he was using as a nightstand to hold his clock. The bed didn't have a headboard or footboard, those luxuries cost more than he was willing to pay. At least the delivery people had set up the bed and taken the packing material away.

His alarm clock flipped to the next minute. It was only ten after six. Too early to go to work at the grocery store but he was too tired to drag any more stuff in from his car. It wasn't a pressing matter to unload the car. The boxes hadn't been touched since Rab packed them.

Deciding to take a nap, he set his alarm and flopped onto the unmade bed.

He closed his eyes and tried to relax but couldn't. Thoughts of Morgan hounded him.

Trixie had warned him months ago, before he'd called Morgan for the very first time, that she was not in his league. Josh had thought she was teasing him as she often did.

Maybe he shouldn't have ignored her warning. He didn't think it relevant at the time because he had no intention of doing anything other than driving to Seattle with Morgan. He had no way of knowing he would develop feelings for her, never mind actually falling in love. It was a rocky start, to be sure, and he was often amazed that they'd made it as far as they did together.

Perhaps he should have realized it wasn't going to work the first time he drove Bob to her parents' house and parked the car among the nice homes and fancy vehicles. He should have quietly left, but she'd burst from the house with such an expression of joy, how could he not go in?

Her father hadn't badgered him much about his prospects that first day. But oh, how he went on about it every time Josh visited afterwards. Until he no longer visited her there.

Josh's lower class standing, crappy car, and crummy home didn't seem to bother Morgan at all. Being together had brought them joy.

The joy had drained until nothing was left.

Had Morgan's easygoing nature and low-maintenance style deceived him into believing he was good enough for her? It sure seemed that way now.

Josh sighed and gave up on sleep, deciding to put his time to better use setting up his new apartment. He wanted to at least get the bed made before his shift since he'd want to fall right into it when he returned home.

Yeah, as crappy and lonely as it might be, this was his home now.

He made his bed with the sheets he'd bought to go with the new mattress. But something was missing. Remembering his trusty wool blanket was still in Bob, he decided to go get it and bring in another load.

Josh pulled his keys from his pocket and his eyes fell on the key to Zinger. He would have to return it to Morgan. When he did, he would be admitting it was over. Sure, they hadn't officially broken up, but at this point, after not hearing from her for days, it would be only a formality.

Someone knocked on the door. His heart leapt as he scurried out of the bedroom and to the door. Could it actually be?

He opened the door only to find Trixie standing on the stoop. She was holding a foil-covered, disposable pan with a dish towel.

If Rab hadn't been standing right next to her, Josh would have closed the door and locked it.

Mustering all the courtesy he could find he said, "Why are you here?"

Trixie hefted the pan. "We thought we would bring you a little housewarming gift."

He was now aware of the aroma emanating from the pan. His stomach growled, reminding him he hadn't eaten supper yet. *Traitor.*

"Your gift may be a bit too soon." He swept an arm in an arc across the empty room. "I'm not set up for a banquet."

"Josh, at least invite us in. It's a little cold out here," Rab said. She held a paper bag in her arms.

Josh hesitated and Rab narrowed her eyes. "Ah . . . sure, won't you come in?"

"Thank you," Rab said.

Trixie smiled happily.

Josh stepped back to allow them in. "Why don't you set the dish over on the counter next to the stove?"

The two girls entered and placed their burdens on the counter.

"This is a cozy little place, Josh, but it really needs a woman's touch. Forget about Morgan and let me take care of things," Trixie offered.

Rab cleared her throat. "Not the time, Trix."

Trixie flashed her a look. "I was talking about redecorating."

"No thanks," Josh said. "I don't expect to be spending much time here except for sleeping."

"No, really," Trixie insisted. "I took a correspondence course in basic interior design. Sure, it's a rental, but there's still a lot you can do without altering the floor plan."

"Yes, but that takes money and I'm trying to save."

"You know who to call when you change your mind," Trixie said.

"Thanks for the food. What did you bring?" Josh asked, trying to change the subject.

"Spaghetti casserole." Trixie smiled at him knowingly.

"That's one of my favorite dishes. I didn't think anyplace in town made that," Josh said, tearing off the foil cover.

"I have some paper bowls and plastic utensils in the bag," Rab said, pulling them out along with a roll of paper towels.

"No restaurant involved," Trixie said. "I made it. Would you like me to get you a bowl? We even brought parmesan cheese."

"*We* made it," Rab corrected her friend. "I convinced Mom to let us use the kitchen. We have to go back and clean the kitchen before it's suppertime for Dad."

"Sure, I'll have some," Josh said when Trixie continued to hold the empty bowl expectantly. Then, remembering his manners, he said, "Would you girls like to join me? I only have the floor to sit on."

"We would love to –" Trixie started to say.

"But we *really* have to get back to the house," Rab interrupted. "Mom is in kind of a mood and we," she looked pointedly at Trixie, "don't want to get in trouble for leaving a messy kitchen."

Trixie spooned out some of the casserole for Josh. "I bet Morgan never cooked for you."

"I guess you'll never know," Josh said.

"Well, I don't care what Morgan did or didn't do. She's out of your life now. Wouldn't it be nice to have me as a roommate? I can cook and I'd take good care of you. Ordering take-out all the time will eat up all that money you're trying to save. And I could even help with the rent."

"Give it a rest, Trixie," Rab snapped. "My brother has accepted *our* housewarming gift and even thanked you for it. He's hurting right now, and he didn't throw you out on your ear. Take what you've been given and be happy with it."

Josh looked at his sister like he'd never seen her before.

Trixie stared at Rab with blinking eyes and mouth agape.

Rab addressed Josh as if nothing had happened. "Have you even called Morgan since you had your little spat?"

"No," Josh said, lowering his eyes and his voice, "and I'm not ready to discuss it with you, her, or anybody."

Trixie found her voice and said, "Hey! You just said to leave him alone, Rab."

Rab turned to her. "Please go start the car. I need to talk to my brother a moment."

Trixie hesitated then said, "You're right, Rab, we should be getting back. Good night, Josh. I'll call you later?"

Before Josh could tell her he didn't have a phone yet, Rab said, "Trixie, please."

"Yeah, sure, just don't be too long," Trixie said and left.

Josh was surprised she didn't slam the door.

"What's up?" he asked when Rab continued to stand assessing him.

"I wanted to ask you not to do anything rash, okay?"

"I'm trying not to," Josh said.

"You should talk to Morgan, if only to get some closure."

"But what if she says we're done?" Josh asked.

"Then you can start to heal and get on with your life. Just don't take up with Trixie on the rebound."

"It would be a long time before I could even think of seeing anyone else."

Rab slipped an arm around him and gave him a side hug. "Do you have someone you can talk to besides me?"

"You know I don't make friends easily. Trixie was one of my best friends, but this isn't something I can talk to her about. The few friends I did have took off. Even Shack ended up leaving for school. Maybe I should give him a call once I get a phone."

Rab stared her brother square in the face. "Oh God, no. He's the last person you need to talk to. He'd try to convince you to forget Morgan and go for some top-heavy bimbo."

"Yeah, he would." Josh chuckled softly. "You don't think I should forget about Morgan?"

Rab shrugged. "I think you need to talk to her. I don't know the whole story."

"I'll think about it."

"Look, I've got to run and try to placate Trixie. You're a pest sometimes, but you're my only brother and I love you. If you need to talk to someone, I'm here for you."

"I love you too, sis. Thanks for everything. You'd better get going."

They hugged and Rab ran out the door.

Josh locked the door behind her and went to get some casserole while it was still warm.

He sat on the hard floor eating and debating the future. The food wasn't that good, but he was hungry.

He thought about giving up on his dream of going to mechanic school but decided he didn't want to be a scrub boy the rest of his life. Without Morgan, Bathurst had little hold on him. Maybe he could return to Washington and study there. Or maybe he could advance – plan H was it? – and talk to the Canadian Forces recruiter.

That would have to wait until Monday, though. Right now the office was as closed as he feared Morgan's heart was.

Chapter 29

In Which True Colors Are Shown
Saturday, December 2, 1995

Morgan walked down the stairs to Tyler's room with a plate of cookies and smiled for the first time in days. His parents were the best. They were so . . . actually, if her mom had served up a batch of homemade cookies for her and Josh she probably would have been embarrassed.

Her smile vanished. Well, no worries about that. Josh wasn't likely to be popping over for a visit anytime soon. Every night before she went to sleep, she spent a great deal of time staring at her basement window, hoping with every fiber of her being his face would appear in it. He'd be holding a flower and his smile would be . . .

"Geez, did my mother send those down?" Tyler's voice cut through her thoughts.

She entered the room and set the plate on his desk as he got up from where he'd been reading a comic on his bed.

"At least I declined the milk," Morgan said.

He groaned. "Lovely."

"Sorry I'm late. I got carried away with my painting and then my parents just found out about my phone as I was leaving." Morgan grimaced.

"Yikes." Tyler did the clothes-kicking tidying thing before clearing off their stools in the music area.

"I had to listen to the whole responsibility lecture and I'm not sure what the point was, because the next thing my dad did was offer to get me a new phone. I told him to just cancel it. What a useless piece of junk."

"Did you tell them you smashed it?"

"Of course not. I'd still be there. I just told them I broke it. You want a cookie?" Morgan asked.

"No. Let's get to work. We won't have time to do much tonight at the café. Christmas decorating, remember?"

"I do," Morgan said as she took her seat beside him. "It might be fun. At least Laura and the new hire will be there."

"New hire? You're not quitting, are you?" Tyler asked.

"Not completely. I'll still be around to help out if she needs. The only thing I'm perma-quitting come next week is babysitting."

"Well, let's not waste time," Tyler said. "I think we should make our singing debut tonight. Ready to practice?" He pursed his lips in whistle-ready position.

"Oh, give it a rest already," Morgan snapped.

Tyler leaned back on his stool with a wounded look. "What's wrong?"

Morgan sighed. "I'm sorry. I didn't mean to be short with you. I'm just tired. And I'm really, really tired of the whistling thing. I learned how to do it a bit. Thanks for teaching me. But can we work on something else?"

Tyler scooted his stool closer and took her hand. "I'm sorry about Josh."

"What about him?" Morgan snatched her hand back.

"I was there. I know what happened. And you've been miserable ever since."

"You know what happened?" Morgan almost laughed. "Well then, please enlighten me."

"Trust me, I've been in my share of relationships that haven't ended well. It's not easy, but things will get better."

Morgan was about to set him straight on the fact she and Josh hadn't technically broken up but decided to save her breath. It was only a matter of time. Besides, she didn't want to talk about Josh.

"Do you want to go over the last set of lyrics I gave you?" she asked.

"No, I don't."

Morgan frowned. "Why not?"

He moved his stool even closer and leaned forward. Where had his grin gone? What was with the dead serious look?

"Morgan, you can't deny we have something here."

"I'm not denying it. I just suggested we work on the lyrics."

Tyler laughed, but not his usual laugh, and it ended abruptly. "I'm talking about you and me."

Oh shit. Morgan slid off the stool when he tried to take her hand again. "I'm gonna go ahead and guess you're not talking about you and me making music."

"Kind of." His grin was back but its presence was no longer welcome.

"Tyler, I'm not interested in you that way. I'm sorry. Let's just pretend this never happened before we ruin what we have here, okay?"

Tyler snorted. "What is it you think we have here?"

Morgan narrowed her eyes. "I *thought* we had a friendship and were making an album."

Tyler patted the stool. "Sit down. I want to explain something to you."

Against her better judgment, Morgan sat.

"You can write all the pretty poems you like," he said, "and I can create all the snazzy instrumentals. But it all comes down to chemistry."

"You're confusing me."

"Let me be clearer then." In one swift move, Tyler had his hand on the back of her neck and planted a kiss on her lips.

"Jesus Christ!" Morgan yelled as she shoved him away and jumped up. "Why would you do that?"

"Why would I do any of this?" he yelled back, gesturing at the stacks of papers around them. "Did you honestly think I needed your help?"

"You said you liked what I wrote," Morgan said softly, still stunned, "and my voice."

Tyler ran his hands through his hair. When he was finished, it was half out of its ponytail and looked about as crazy as he did.

"You're not irreplaceable, dear." His voice was so cold.

Tears stung Morgan's eyes. Hadn't she lost enough already? Before self-pity could envelop her, she turned and blinked the tears way. "Don't call me dear. And don't ever touch me again."

She strode over to get her carry bag and had her hand on the door when Tyler came up behind her and grabbed her arm, turning her to face him.

He might have been about to say something to her. He might have been about to kiss her again. Whatever he had planned didn't matter.

Morgan was right-handed. Tyler was holding her right arm. That also didn't matter. Her dad had taught her well.

A swift left uppercut to his throat resolved the situation.

Morgan left Tyler lying on the floor of his room, clutching his neck and doing his best to curse. On the way out, Morgan thanked Tyler's parents again for the cookies, told them it had been nice knowing them, and that their son was a dink.

Zinger didn't have a chance to warm up before she peeled out of the driveway.

Morgan's ego had taken a blow. She'd lost an important part of her life – or what she thought had been important: a friend and the music they'd been making.

But really, that punch had been so satisfying.

She briefly wondered if Josh might have been right about Tyler, then quickly decided that wasn't the case. He had no idea what the guy was like; he was just jealous.

Even though it was a bit early for her shift, Morgan went straight to the café. She was tired of being angry. She was tired of being sad. She was tired of thinking about Josh.

Of course, the first people she saw upon entering the café were Rab and Trixie. Trixie gave her the usual glare and Rab didn't look much friendlier, as had been the case for the last few days. Well, she was tired of them too.

Morgan greeted Laura and Teresa who were indulging in some Christmas cookies at the counter. Boxes of Christmas decorations were stacked behind it. After refusing the offer of a cookie and meeting the new employee – an older lady about

Laura's age – Morgan put her coat and bag in the back and donned her apron.

They'd already hung some garland around the windows and had set up a tree between the lounge area and the regular tables. Laura suggested Morgan and Teresa work on decorating the tree while she helped the new hire familiarize herself with the kitchen equipment.

Morgan wished them luck and meant it – those machines had a mind of their own.

If it wasn't for Teresa's excited chatter, Morgan would have fallen into a full-out depression. While she'd hoped Christmas decorating would lift her spirits some, all she could think of was Josh's little apartment and how empty it must be. Would he get a tree of his own? Would he decorate it with someone new?

Rab standing up caught Morgan's eye. Her moment of relief was short-lived when she realized Rab was off to the washroom and they weren't leaving as she'd hoped.

Then, out of the corner of her eye, Morgan saw Trixie waving her cup. That was new. She usually left the ordering to Rab.

Morgan ignored her until Teresa helpfully pointed out the lady needed help.

Morgan mustered a fake grin for the kid and patted her on the head before going to get the coffee pot. She did not, however, bother smiling at Trixie.

"Refill?"

"Yes, please," Trixie said, sliding her cup ever so slowly to the edge of the table. "Listen, Morgan, I wanted to offer you my sympathies."

"Who died?" Morgan deadpanned as she filled the cup.

"You know, we got off on the wrong foot, but I do feel sorry for you. I can see how upset you are. Josh was actually quite lost for a while there too."

"Can I get you anything else?" Morgan asked through gritted teeth.

"If it makes you feel any better, he's doing well now. He and I have fixed his little place up so it's a proper home. Oh, if you could only see –"

Morgan was about to dump the coffee on the troll's head when Rab's voice came from behind them. "Trixie, get up."

They both turned to find a very serious-looking Rab standing with her hands on her hips.

"Pardon me?" Trixie blinked.

"Get up," Rab repeated, her eyes locked with Trixie's.

"What for?"

"So you can leave."

Trixie laughed. "Who do you think you are, the bouncer?"

Rab slammed her hand on the table, drawing the attention of the few customers in the café. Morgan stood frozen watching the scene.

"Don't push me," Rab said. "You're going to get up and you're going to leave, or I *will* bounce your ass out of here."

Trixie's mouth opened. Then closed. Then she rose and grabbed her purse off the table. "Good luck finding a ride home."

Morgan's mouth was still hanging open when Rab turned to her.

"Now what happened with you and my brother?"

Though her voice was still all business, Rab's face had softened. She took Trixie's vacated seat and pointed at the other.

Morgan looked around to see if someone else might need coffee, or a cookie, or anything that would get her out of there. No such luck.

For the second time that day, against her better judgment, Morgan sat.

"What do you want to know?" Morgan asked. "Josh must have told you about our argument."

"Humor me," Rab said. "Pretend I don't have a stinking clue except that you ditched my brother to come here and then had a fight over the phone and haven't spoken to him since. Oh, wait. That's exactly all I know."

"I didn't ditch him," Morgan said. "I had to cancel our date because I got stuck babysitting. By the time I found a replacement sitter, he'd already left for work."

"Who told you that?"

"Your mom."

Rab frowned. "Well, she wouldn't have lied. She probably thought he'd gone to work. He couldn't get his shift back though. Did you tell Josh this?"

"I didn't get a chance to. He wouldn't listen. He just kept asking why I was at the café. Which, by the way, he shouldn't have known unless he was spying on me."

Rab raised a brow. "Spying on you? He came in here that night, and as soon as he saw you he stormed out. Trixie and I went after him and he was furious."

"So it's true about him and Trixie then?" Morgan asked.

"Of course not. Why do think I just turfed her? She was lying." Morgan didn't have a chance to react before Rab continued, "Is it true about you and Tyler?"

Morgan couldn't help but laugh. What a question for today. "If you're asking if there was anything romantic between us, the answer is no. But if you're asking if he's a snake, that's a hard yes."

Morgan waved her hand dismissively at another raised brow from Rab. "It's not important. Josh is. Honestly, Rab, I really don't know what happened the other night except that we argued."

"And it was such a terrible argument that you've decided to break up?"

Morgan frowned. "We haven't broken up, but he won't talk to me."

"You've tried to contact him?"

Morgan fiddled with the coffee pot. "Well, no. But he hasn't tried either." Even as she said it she realized how lame it sounded. She pushed the pot away and held up a hand. "Okay, you don't have to say it. I just heard myself. But everything's been different since we got home from our trip. Out there on the road, we were living the dream. Even the bad moments don't seem all that bad anymore. But here, it feels like everything is against us. Work, 'friends,'" Morgan air-quoted, "parents . . . you too?"

Rab smiled and placed her hand atop Morgan's. "No, not me. We need to do some more talking."

Chapter 30

In Which the Song Stays the Same
Saturday, December 2, 1995

Josh would have been better off working for Cal today. Shopping for a table and chair had been a bust. None of the thrift stores had any and it wasn't yard sale season.

At least he got the last of his stuff from his parents' house, and his mother had given him her old set of pots because she received new ones as an early Christmas gift.

Back at his new place, Josh finished unloading the car and pushed some of the boxes against a wall to serve as makeshift couch. He might even unpack them one day.

He was sitting on them to test their strength when someone knocked on the door. He wasn't expecting anyone, but he hefted himself off the "couch" and went to the door. When he opened it, he regretted not having looked through the peephole first.

Trixie stood outside.

Not opening the door fully, Josh squeezed outside and pulled it closed behind him. He ended up far closer to Trixie than he would have liked. Josh hoped this wouldn't take long as he was wearing only his jeans, T-shirt, and socks.

"Well, hello there, Josh. Invite me inside and you can finish getting undressed."

Snowflakes swirled around them. Josh's stocking feet melted the snow under them, making his socks soggy and cold. "Where's Rab?" he asked.

Trixie made an unhappy face and said, "I didn't bring her. I wanted to talk to you without her interference."

"We have nothing to talk about," Josh said.

"I can think of a few things, like how Morgan still hasn't spoken to you."

"Kind of hard when I don't have a phone connected."

"If she loved you, she would've found a way. Look at me; I've seen you more times in two days than she has all week," Trixie said.

"What do you want?" As soon as the words left his lips, he knew he'd said the wrong thing.

"I want you. I've always wanted you, but time after time you've refused me."

"Let's pretend I didn't just ask that. Now please go so I can get back inside. It's cold out here," Josh said.

Trixie unzipped her parka. Her shirt was mostly unbuttoned and revealed more than Josh wanted to see. "Take me inside and I'll warm you up."

Before Josh could react, she stepped forward and wrapped her parka around him, her chest pressed tightly against his, and turned her half-lidded eyes toward his.

Josh wanted to push her away. However, the small porch was slippery, and he didn't want her to fall.

"Unhand my brother right now, you Jezebel!" Rab yelled as she charged around the corner.

Trixie spun, knocking Josh against the door. The momentum of her spin caused her to stumble down the steps to land in front of Rab.

"Haven't you interfered with me enough for one day, you snot-nosed little brat?" Trixie snarled as she stood to face Rab, dusting the snow off her hands.

"You're one to talk," Rab said, "exposing yourself like that."

Josh had righted himself and edged toward them, not quite sure what to do.

"Someone has to show your brother what he's missing." Trixie threw off her parka and jerked the front of her blouse so the remaining buttons flew off. "Take a good look at these beauties, Joshua Hampton, and I dare you to tell me you don't want them."

Josh put on the brakes, slipped, and his butt hit the porch hard. "*Merde*."

Rab snatched up Trixie's parka. "For God's sake, put this back on. You're better than this."

Trixie pushed the parka and Rab away, causing the smaller girl to fall.

Rab came back up instantly and grabbed Trixie's lapels. "Get a hold of yourself, girl!"

"Girl? Girl?" Trixie lashed out, catching Rab across the face with her nails. "Take a good look! Do I look like a child to you?"

Josh was floundering trying to get to his feet. "Both of you, stop it!"

Rab stared at her friend in disbelief and touched her cheek. Blood stained her gloves. Furious now, she yanked the gloves off.

Trixie's eyes went wide. She tried to back away from Rab but wasn't fast enough.

Rab swung hard and slapped the ever-loving *merde* out of her until Trixie stumbled and fell into a snowbank.

Josh got to his feet – finally – as the two girls stared at each other, their breath forming clouds in the frigid air.

Tears formed in Trixie's eyes.

Rab stepped forward and extended a hand to her. "Enough already. Let me help you up."

Josh took a step closer but Rab held her hand up. He stopped but was prepared to intervene if hostilities resumed.

"Forget it, Rab." Trixie slapped the hand away and scrambled for her parka. "I don't need your help or your sympathy."

She stood and tugged the parka on but didn't zip it. Mascara streaked down her face as she turned to Josh. "Remember this day, Josh. One day when that little butterfly has found another flower, and you're all alone, I want you to remember you could have invited me in."

She stomped toward the front, spitting as she rounded the corner. The snow turned red where the spit landed.

"Come inside," Josh said to his sister. "Let me get you cleaned up."

"Only if you'll listen to me while you do."

"Deal. Come on."

Josh brushed off as much snow as he could. As soon as they entered the apartment, he pulled off the soaking socks. "Sit down and I'll get something to wipe your face."

Rab took off her parka and dropped it by the door before sitting on Josh's box couch.

He brought some paper towels, one of which he'd dampened, and shifted a box to sit in front of her.

"Trixie told me you weren't with her," Josh said as he dabbed at the drying blood. "How did you get here?"

"Long story. We had a fight at the café, and she took off. I guessed she was coming here, and I had to get here fast, so I drove."

"Since when did you get a car?"

"I didn't. Now stop asking questions and listen to me," Rab said.

"Okay." Josh handed her one of the dry paper towels.

"You and Morgan are both idiots. You love each other so bad it hurts but you're too stubborn to talk it out."

"I know what I saw," Josh said bitterly.

"You only saw her for a few seconds before storming out," Rab said. "Now whistle for me."

"What?"

"Just do it."

Josh whistled a few bars of a song.

"Were you blowing kisses at me?" Rab asked.

"No, I was just whistling like you told me to."

"But kissing and whistling look the same. Your girlfriend was trying to learn to whistle."

Josh frowned. "Why didn't she tell me this on the phone?"

"Why didn't you tell her you were at the café that night and saw her? I'll tell you why. You're both pig-headed," Rab said.

Josh got up and took the used towels to the kitchen. "I'm not sure what to think."

"Go. To. Her," Rab said, emphasizing each word.

"I don't know . . ."

"Go. To. Her," she repeated. "NOW. Look, I just slapped the shit out of my best friend for Morgan and you. Don't make me slap some sense into you too. Get some boots on, and let's go."

"Okay, okay. But I don't think it will do any good," Josh said.

"Ugh! Brothers!" Rab put her parka on and grabbed Josh's while he slipped into his boots.

He locked up and they trudged to the front where the cars were parked.

Josh gawked. "You came here in Zinger?"

"Yes, now get in." Rab went to the driver's side. "Shit! I locked the keys inside."

Josh smiled and pulled out his keys. "I've got it covered. I'm driving."

They switched sides and Josh drove to the café. It took every ounce of self-control he had to keep from speeding.

They parked in front of the coffee shop and got out.

"Go on. She's waiting," Rab said, making a shooing motion with her hands.

"You should come too, sis. We wouldn't be . . ."

"Shut up and go. I won't be far behind." Before he could protest any further, she said, "Once you step in, you won't even notice me."

Josh shrugged and pulled the door open. When Morgan looked up from the counter, her face lit up brighter than he had ever seen it.

She pointed to a stool and headed to the empty stage.

By time he'd gotten seated, Morgan had picked up the mic.

"This is a little song I want to dedicate to the love of my life."

She sang without music and hadn't gotten more than four words into the song when Josh recognized it. "Angel of the Morning." The same song she'd sung for him in Winnipeg.

She'd sounded great then, but here in this small café she sounded absolutely angelic. His heart soared so high he doubted it would ever return to the earth.

When she finished, everyone in the café cheered and whistled.

Josh couldn't wait any longer. He dropped his parka and marched toward the stage.

Morgan set the mic down and had no sooner stepped off the stage when Josh reached her and lifted her off her feet.

She wrapped her hands around his neck and kissed him.

Josh set her down so he could fully embrace her without breaking the kiss, scarcely registering the applause around them.

They finally broke apart and turned to find Rab with tears streaming down her face.

Morgan led Josh over to his sister and they each planted a kiss on her cheek. Morgan gave her an extra kiss on the scratched one.

"Thank you, sis," Morgan said.

Rab smiled through her happy tears and hugged her. Josh heard her whisper, "Promise me you won't name your first daughter Mary."

"I promise." Morgan laughed and turned to Josh. "Have a seat. I'll get you some coffee."

Morgan's boss came up behind them. "We've got it covered. Why don't you kids get out of here?" she said with a wink.

Morgan thanked her and turned back to Josh. "Did you bring your car?"

"No. I didn't even think about it," he said.

"Great. Just let me grab my coat and purse and we can go."

After a quick detour to drop his sister off, and another round of thank yous, Josh finally arrived home with Morgan.

"I'm sure this sounds like a line," Josh said as he unlocked the door, "but the bed is the only comfortable furniture I have to sit on right now."

"That's the best offer I've had all day," Morgan replied with a grin. "We'll try keep the funny business to a minimum."

Chapter 31

In Which Many Tears Are Shed
Sunday, December 24, 1995

"How are you not freezing?" Morgan asked after she and Mel had dashed into the store.

"Must be the extra layers," her friend replied, patting her rather large belly. "Lunch is next, right?"

"Sure." Morgan laughed. "I should probably call ahead and warn Laura."

"That's actually not a bad idea," Mel said. "Make sure they have pickles."

"Is that really a thing?" Morgan asked. "You actually crave pickles?"

"Oh, it's real. They're so . . . damn, I can't talk about them without my mouth watering. But I haven't gone so far as to put them on ice cream yet."

Morgan took her new cell phone out of her purse.

"You're not seriously calling Laura, are you?" Mel asked.

"Uh, yeah. Not about pickles. I just want to make sure Tyler's not around today."

"He's not," Mel said. "He's out of town for the holidays."

Morgan put the phone away. "Good enough for me."

"You haven't seen him at all since the, you know . . .?" Mel made a stabbing motion with her hand.

"I punched him. I didn't knife him. And no, he's been wisely cautious about keeping his distance."

"He doesn't come in all that much anymore. Last time I saw him he had another trainee with him." Mel raised her brows.

"Oh no. A girl?"

"Yeah, don't worry. I made sure to brief the poor thing."

"Hopefully she listens," Morgan said. "But enough about that creep. We're supposed to be shopping."

Morgan and Mel were making their way down King Avenue, checking out the Christmas Eve sales and focusing on the smaller gift shops that Morgan hadn't frequented in a while.

"Remember when we used to do this almost every weekend?" Mel asked as she walked over to the area dedicated to baby gifts.

"Yeah," Morgan said. "It seems like years ago, but it hasn't even been one year. And we definitely weren't shopping for stuff like this." She picked up a rattle and shook it at her friend.

"Get that thing out of my face or I'll balloon you," Mel said, nodding to the helium-filled balloons at the end of the aisle.

Morgan shuddered and put the rattle back. "You win."

"I don't know why I'm even looking at this stuff yet. It's not like I'm going to have my baby before Christmas."

Morgan picked up a teddy bear. "Yeah, but I'm still getting her something. Her first present from Auntie Morgan, received at the tender age of minus four months."

Mel, not surprisingly, broke into tears. Crying and peeing had replaced her first trimester queasiness.

"What did I do now?" Morgan asked, patting her on the shoulder.

"Nothing. I just can't believe this is really happening." Mel wiped at her face. "Morgan, I'm going to have a baby."

"Yeah, I heard."

"No. I'm going to *have* a baby." Mel made a cradling motion with her arms as tears continued to stream down her face. "I don't know what to do with an actual baby."

"You'll figure it out," Morgan said. "It's not like you're doing this on your own. Your parents will be there to help."

Mel sniffled and nodded.

It wasn't the best time to ask but there really was no best time . . . "Are you telling the father now that you're keeping it?"

Shockingly, Mel stopped crying and smiled. "Yeah. He's in town for Christmas. I'm nervous, of course, but I'll be glad not to have to carry the secret any longer."

"Excellent! So you're telling . . ."

"Him first. Nice try though. I'm going to look in the used items section. They might have some cheap maternity clothing. I've stretched this stuff all it can stretch. Meet me there when you're done?"

Morgan nodded and watched her friend waddle off. She picked up a matching teddy bear to the one she was holding, deciding to get one for her new sibling as well. Unlike Mel, her parents chose not to find out the sex of their baby.

Morgan grabbed a fire truck for Matthew and considered getting something for her other stepbrother Damian too. No, it was too late to mail it to Seattle, and the card would be good enough.

She continued through the store, ending up with a fancy paperweight for her dad and a set of stemware for her mom. She spared no expense when choosing the gifts and even splurged on a black-and-white portable TV for Rab. Her job at the law firm paid more than enough and it was Christmas, after all.

Morgan detoured to the counter more than once to set down her purchases since her arms were full. She was on her way to meet Mel when the front door opened and in came a cold gust of wind along with . . .

"Cindy?"

"Oh, Morgan." Cindy shook her golden locks free of snow and brushed off her fur coat. "I haven't seen you since my going away party."

"Yeah." Morgan began edging away. Cindy had been one of her least favorite schoolmates, and though she'd been bumped down the list of people Morgan disliked, she had no desire to chat with her. "Good to see you again," she lied.

"Aren't you supposed to be in California?" Cindy asked with her trademark high-pitched squeal.

Morgan didn't bother asking her what was so funny or correcting her on the location of her travels. Instead, she said, "I went. It was fun. How's school going?"

Cindy tilted her head and then shook it. "Great. Hey, did you hear about Mel? She got knocked up."

Mel popped her head around the corner of an aisle. "Yeah, I hear she's a total slut."

Cindy shrieked and put her hand over her heart. "I didn't . . . I don't . . ."

Morgan and Mel broke out in laughter as Cindy gave up on words and ran out the door. Another screech announced she'd slipped and landed on her ass just as the door swung shut behind her.

"Hold these," Mel said, doubled over laughing. "Now I've gotta pee."

Morgan took the clothing from her friend and continued to chuckle as she added the garments to the pile on the counter. Couldn't have happened to a nicer girl.

Morgan wandered the aisles while she waited and stopped dead in her tracks as she passed the used item section. She'd never so much as walked through the area, never mind purchased something from it, but she did now.

Thrilled beyond belief with her find, Morgan paid for everything and handed Mel her bag when she came out.

"Don't fuss at me. You can buy lunch."

They left the store and headed to the café. It was about half full, so Morgan and Mel took seats at the counter and served themselves. Morgan poured the coffee and left Mel to warm the sandwiches.

"Thanks, you two," Laura said when she'd finished with her customers. "It's on the house, of course."

"Thanks," Morgan said, although they'd be sure to leave a hefty tip. "Do you need a hand out there?"

"No. It's just the lunch hour. My parents are visiting for the holidays so Teresa's at home with them. It's almost like I'm on holiday." She laughed and took her tray of dishes to the back.

"That was just too funny what happened with Cindy," Morgan said as she and Mel settled in with their lunch.

"Don't get me started laughing again," Mel warned, biting into her pickle. "Best part is, she's not even home for a visit. She flunked out of school."

"She flunked out of interior design?"

Mel nodded. "I can't believe we used to hang out with people like that."

"Tell me about it," Morgan agreed.

"Where to next?" Mel asked.

"Wherever you want," Morgan said. "I'm shopped out."

"I think the trunk of your car agrees with you."

"Funny. I can't help it. I'm feeling Christmassy." Morgan grinned.

Mel cried.

"Oh, for – what now?"

Mel just shook her head. "This pickle is *so* good."

Morgan had no words.

"Sorry, I'm sorry." Mel grabbed a napkin and wiped her face. "You should probably take me home. I'm done shopping too and you've got to be tired of me."

"I'll never get tired of you. You're my friend. My very, very hormonal friend."

"Who would have thought we'd end up like this?"

"Not me." Again, Morgan risked a touchy topic. "What made you decide to keep the baby?"

And again, Mel's tears evaporated as a peaceful smile appeared. "I guess I kinda always knew, deep down inside. I mean I could have stayed and finished my first semester at school instead of coming straight home when I found out."

"I think you're doing the right thing. I couldn't imagine not knowing and loving my mom. But then again, I love my dad just as much. My biological father is a nice guy and all, but I don't love him." Morgan frowned. "I'm not sure what my point was."

"I think you're trying to say that love is what's important," Mel offered.

"Let's go with that." She noticed her friend's eyes getting misty again and added, "So yeah, I love my family, but I really can't wait to move out."

"Why haven't you yet?" Mel asked. "You're making enough money."

"True," Morgan said.

"Well then?"

Morgan chewed on her lip. "I don't want to sound presumptuous, but I have a feeling it would be a waste of time."

"Oh, my God. Are you and Josh moving in together?" Mel squealed.

"No, no, no. Well, he hasn't asked me to and I'm not about to invite myself. It's just . . . I spend so much time there that it feels like the next logical step. Also, what's the use in having two apartments in the meantime?"

"You're being careful, right?"

"What? Oh, you mean . . . yeah, we're being careful. Couldn't be any more careful if we tried."

"You haven't slept together yet?"

Morgan shook her head. "There've been a couple of 'almosts,' but I guess there's no rush."

"You're damned right there isn't," Mel said, sounding every bit the mom she was about to become. "You'll know when the time is right."

"Okay, enough serious stuff. I've got my second wind if you're up for more shopping."

"Sure. Just dump me at home if I start getting sobby again."

"Deal. What are you doing for Christmas tomorrow?" Morgan asked as they took their dishes to the back.

"Quiet dinner at home. No guests." She shot Morgan a look that told her in no uncertain terms it wasn't baby-daddy notification day. "What about you?"

"Josh is coming over to my house in the morning for brunch and then we're going to his parents' place for dinner later on."

"Sounds like fun," Mel said.

"Sounds like a long day," Morgan said. "But we'll be together so it'll be all right. Best part is, we're having our real Christmas after all that at his place. He's supposed to be picking up a small tree today and I'm going to bring the lights and ornaments so we can decorate it together before exchanging gifts."

"Okay, that sounds positively romantic," Mel said.

The girls made their deposits in the tip jar and wished Laura a Merry Christmas on their way out.

Just as they reached the door, it opened and there stood Cindy.

She took one look at them and scurried away.

"Damn. It would have been awesome if she'd landed on her ass again," Mel said as they watched her departure through the glass.

And sure enough, she did. Arms flailed, mouth flapped, and Cindy was deposited on the snowy ground. What was she thinking wearing stilettos in a snowstorm?

The girls laughed so hard they were both in tears.

"Santa is real and he loves me!" Morgan declared.

"I have to pee!" Mel howled.

Chapter 32

In Which the Siblings Have a Day Out
Sunday, December 24, 1995

It was almost one in the afternoon when Josh pulled into the parking lot of Burger Barn to pick up his sister.

Rab came out of the restaurant wearing a red Christmas sweater under her open parka and carrying her uniform top. She got into the car and gave him a sisterly punch on the arm before strapping in. “Thanks for picking me up.”

“No problem. Thanks for braving the crowds with me.” Josh pulled into the street and headed for the mall.

“I’m glad we’re doing this. Between work and school, I really haven’t had much time for shopping,” Rab said and tossed the uniform shirt in the back.

“It will give us a chance to catch up some too,” Josh said. “We’ve hardly seen each other since I moved out.”

“Little wonder. You’ve been busier than me. I thought Morgan would be with you today; that would have been totally cool with me. I really like her.”

“She wanted to spend the day shopping with Mel and it gives me a chance to pick up her gift. Besides, we’re spending the whole day together tomorrow.” Josh paused and glanced at his sister. “What would you think of having her as a sister-in-law?”

Rab jerked her head toward her brother. “Did you get her a ring?”

“No, not yet,” Josh said, chuckling. “Just for future consideration.”

“Well, I’d love that. I’ve seen how good she is for you.”

“In what way?”

“Besides the fact you light up every time you’re around her?” Rab thought for a moment. “The old Josh would have charged into the café and punched Tyler that night. You had the good sense to walk away, even though it took you long enough to talk to her again. I guess what I’m trying to say is you've changed since you've been with her. You've been different ever since you got back from Seattle."

"That trip changed both our lives," Josh agreed. "As for marriage, we love each other but we're still young. And I would want to have a stable income first."

"With both of you working, you would do all right," Rab said.

"She fusses about it, but I don't want her to have to work. If we're depending on two incomes, what would happen if a baby came along and she couldn't work for a while?" Josh asked.

"I would think you'd be careful until you were ready for children."

"Sure we would, but no birth control method is foolproof. Accidents can happen."

"How do you plan to manage a stable income then?" Rab asked.

"I have to get more training. It'll mean going to Moncton for school. Oulton College has an automotive technician program."

"A four-year course to be a mechanic? That seems like a lot."

"It's more like two years. Less if I take summer classes," Josh said. "I'd hoped to save enough before enrolling, but I might have to get a student loan and find work there."

Rab shrugged. "Most kids going to college get student loans."

"True, but the problem is I might have to ask our parents to help get the loan."

"That could be a problem, but since you'd be working to improve yourself, they should be okay with it," Rab said.

"It's the strings that might be attached that worry me."

"You mean like dumping Morgan?"

"That's exactly what I mean," Josh said. "You know how *Maman* is. I'm hoping that would be a point where our father would overrule."

"I'd put in a good word for you." Rab laughed. "Not that it would help much. But you don't need to be worrying about all that today. What are you getting Morgan for Christmas?"

"I already bought something."

"You already bought her something? That's a lot of initiative for you, bro," Rab said.

"I wanted to get something personalized and that meant extra time to get it engraved," Josh said.

"Can't wait to see it." Rab leaned the seat back. "God, I'm so glad the restaurant is closed tomorrow. I really need a day off. Oh, a word of warning, Trixie will be over for Christmas dinner. Will you and Morgan still come?"

Josh grimaced. "I thought you two had a falling out."

Rab laughed. "Falling out? You can't tell me you missed the full-blown catfight we had in your yard."

"I was trying not to watch too closely in case Trixie's bra failed to keep things under control."

"Well, I didn't mention it because I didn't think you wanted to hear anything about Trixie, but we're friends again. Once we had a chance to cool down, we talked a lot and sort of made up."

"I'm glad to hear that if it makes you happy," Josh said.

"Honestly, it was more for her sake than mine. I've grown up some and have more friends. She has no one else. I mean, that's partially her fault, and she's getting better, but she needs me to help her get there."

"You're sure she'll behave if Morgan and I come for dinner tomorrow?" Josh asked.

"Don't worry, big brother. I'll keep her under control."

They arrived at the mall and found the parking lot packed. After driving around for ten minutes they finally found a place to park Bob.

"Wow, what's with all the cars?" Josh asked as they trudged to the doors.

"Haven't you ever shopped on Christmas Eve before?" Rab looked stunned.

"Maybe once, but I try to avoid it," Josh said. "I'm going to the jewelry store. Meet you in the food court in an hour?"

Rab agreed and they went their separate ways.

Josh stopped at the jeweler's where he picked up the present for Morgan. He examined each half of the heart necklaces to make sure the engraving was right and paid extra to have it wrapped in fancy green paper with a bright red bow that was almost bigger than the box.

He then went to a cosmetic store and purchased a multi-color set of nail polish for his sister. After getting something for his mother and father, Josh found a store with a decent selection of toys. He wanted to buy something for Morgan's brother. He couldn't suppress a devilish grin when he selected a Sounds and Songs Activity Bus. The kid would probably like it, but if Morgan hadn't already stopped babysitting, this toy would have pushed her over the line. At least she had some relative privacy in the basement.

Finished with his shopping, he found a table where a local charity was wrapping gifts for donations. He kept an eye out for Rab as the volunteers wrapped his gifts and then he gave a generous donation. Why not? They'd saved him from buying the supplies and wrapping the gifts himself.

Josh worked his way to the food court and bought some fries and a soda while waiting for his sister. He managed to grab a table with two seats just as a familiar voice called out.

"Well, if it ain't dumbass! You home on leave?"

Josh looked up, and sure enough, it was Shack. "Merry Christmas," he said, moving his bags off the empty seat to the floor. "Doing some last-minute shopping?"

"Yeah, I had to pick up something for Monique."

"I don't think I've met her," Josh said.

"Sure, you have – she was in the Trans-Am when I came to get the Shackmobile before you left town," Shack said and plopped into the empty seat.

"Oh, her. She didn't get out of the car, so I didn't really meet her. Monique's your girlfriend now?"

"We're going to the same college so we're trying it out, kicking the tires as you might say. So, how's the army treating you, old buddy?" Shack asked, snagging a fry.

"It was the Marines, and I didn't enlist – for personal reasons."

"Never expected to see you back here," Shack said. "Speaking of girlfriends, I ran into yours the other day at Burger Barn. She sure knows how to fill out that uniform shirt."

"My girlfriend doesn't work at Burger Barn," Josh said.

"Sure she does. That hot, dark-haired sophomore you used to hang with?"

"Oh, her. Trixie's not my girlfriend, Morgan is."

"Morg's your girlfriend?" Shack's mouth fell open.

"Her name is Morgan, and yes, she's my girlfriend."

"I thought I warned you about her. She may be a carpenter's dream but good luck nailing her."

"She's not at all like you said she was," Josh said, not caring to elaborate. He also didn't bother mentioning that Morgan worked at Shack's father's law firm. He likely had never set foot in the place. He really was a dumbass. "How's school treating you?"

"It's great. Besides running into Monique, I got a spot on the hockey team – with a scholarship. I'm not first string this year, but the coach says I'll get more time on the ice next year," Shack said.

"Good for you." Josh did his best to sound enthusiastic. This guy never changed. Luckily, another thing that never changed was Shack's astuteness.

"So why'd you come back?" Shack asked. "I thought you were all gung-ho to be an American."

"I came back to be with Morgan. Hard to do that long distance."

"Listen, dumbass, you're making a big mistake. Huge. You need to ditch Morg and see if goth girl will take you back. Have you even paid attention to the rack that girl's got?"

"I'll take my chances with Morgan," Josh said, emphasizing her full name.

"Okay, but if you shrivel up from lack of use, don't blame me." Shack got up and scanned the crowd. "Hey, I gotta go. Good seeing you, buddy."

"Good seeing you too, Shack. You and Monique have a happy holiday."

Shack grinned big. "I sure hope to, if you know what I mean. Hey, you think you can give the Shackmobile a once-over before I head back to school?"

"I'm not working at Cal's anymore, sorry."

Shack shrugged and left without bothering to ask where Josh actually was working, or if he even had a job.

Josh shook his head as he watched him walk away. He wasn't sure who he felt sorrier for – Shack for being Shack, or Monique for being with him.

He sat and sipped his soda until Rab found him and plopped into the open seat. "Wow, I'm beat. Remind me why I had to go shopping right after a long shift?"

"Last shopping day before Christmas, maybe?" Josh said and picked up another fry.

"Now I'm hungry. Would you please be a sweet big brother and get me a monster cookie?"

"What kind would you like? Chocolate chip?"

"No. I'd love one of the sugar cookies with the green sprinkles shaped like a Christmas tree," Rab said.

"*Merde*! I almost forgot. I need to get a Christmas tree."

"How could you forget? Every store has one or more on display."

"It's that time of year. They blend in with the background," Josh said, standing up and pushing the last of his fries toward his sister. "One cookie coming up."

He dashed to the cookie stand and came back with two of the sugar cookies. Sitting down again, he asked, "What do you think, Rab, should I get a real or artificial tree?"

"Why do you need a tree anyway?"

"Morgan and I plan to decorate it tomorrow night after the family visits."

"Ooh, in that case get a real one. The artificial ones are really expensive anyway, and they'll be selling the real ones at a discount now."

"That's a good idea."

"Go buy a tree stand. I'll hold down the fort," Rab said as she took a big bite of her cookie.

"I'll be right back!" Josh said as he got up to hurry off.

"Take your time," Rab called after him. "I need to sit for awhile."

Josh checked three stores before he found one that still had a tree stand. By the time he returned to the food court, Rab was ready to go. She agreed to ride around with him looking for a tree, to lend him her expert advice.

The first two lots they stopped at had only weird-shaped or withered trees, so they drove on. When they arrived at the last place in town that sold trees, the lights were off and no one was in the booth. A sign on the window read, "All remaining trees are free."

Like the other two lots, most of the trees were already losing needles or were misshapen. However, they found one lonely tree in reasonable shape that stood only about five feet high. Josh pushed a five-dollar bill through the door to the shack.

Since they only had a few feet of twine, Josh put the base of the tree into the trunk and tied the trunk down.

It was well after seven o'clock when Josh dropped Rab off at home.

"Shit, I'm going to have to hurry up and get changed for Mass," Rab said.

Sure enough, their mom was peering out the kitchen window and didn't look happy.

"Tell *Maman* I'm going to go the midnight Mass," Josh said.

Rab eyed him. "You'd better bring a used candle tomorrow to prove you were there."

"I'd go with you tonight, but I imagine Trixie will be there," Josh said, knowing the excuse was lame. Truth was, he'd been considering it, but he simply didn't want to go. He should have taken Morgan up on the offer of spending Christmas Eve at her house.

"You imagine right," Rab said as she got out of the car. "Thanks for taking me shopping."

"Anytime, sis. See you tomorrow. Merry Christmas."

He watched as she headed to the door their mother had already opened and decided he'd made the right choices for his evening.

Josh drove home with his tiny tree, looking forward to tomorrow *after* the family visits were done.

Chapter 33

In Which Christmas Thankfully Comes But Once a Year
Monday, December 25, 1995

"Try again?" Morgan's mom suggested.

Morgan sucked on her finger where she'd burned it trying to save the blackened cinnamon rolls from the oven.

"That was the third time," Morgan said, glowering at the appliance. "There's something wrong with that thing."

Her mom laughed and grabbed an oven mitt to carry the pan to the trash. "You'll get it. How about you let me use the oven for the quiche first? You still have a bit of mixture left."

"I don't think I did that part right either. Aren't they supposed to be . . . fluffier?" Morgan asked as the pucks landed in the garbage can.

"We'll try the next batch together," her mom said. "You should put some calamine lotion on that finger."

Morgan nodded and went to the washroom to do so. Silly idea, really, trying to bake cinnamon rolls. She should have just opened the can of cranberry sauce instead.

After tending to her finger, Morgan wiped the flour from the striped turtleneck she'd received for Christmas and fiddled with her hair yet again. She'd tied it back with a big red bow in the spirit of the holidays but was still on the fence about the new look. Maybe it was the shirt that made her neck look so long and her shoulders so bony . . .

The doorbell rang and Morgan ran from the bathroom yelling, "I'll get it!"

She flung the front door open and threw her arms around Josh, pulling the door shut so they could have a proper Christmas kiss before joining the rest of the family.

"Merry Christmas," Josh said breathlessly when they broke apart.

"Merry Christmas," Morgan replied. "What is that?"

Josh removed the plastic grocery bag covering a slightly squashed package to inspect its contents. “It was a salmon cheese ball and crackers.”

“Did it survive?”

“Sure, it’s just a bit tossed now.” He handed her the tray with the dented lid. “You look beautiful.”

“Thanks. You look handsome . . . as always,” she added with a grin, referring to Josh’s trusty button-down green shirt.

“What? It’s Christmas.” He grinned back. “At least I left my hat in the car.”

“Who’s the present for?” Morgan asked, noticing the gift-wrapped box he had tucked under his arm.

“Matthew. You don’t get yours until tonight.”

“I can’t wait,” Morgan said. “Come on in. Matthew’s still tearing through the rest of his presents in the living room.”

Josh followed her into the house and took his shoes off.

“Morgan, you have a phone call,” her mom called from the kitchen.

“Make yourself comfortable,” she told Josh, pointing to the living room where her dad was sitting in a suit and tie while Matthew flew around in his pjs, waving bits of shredded wrapping paper.

She left him to the wolves and took her call in the kitchen.

“Randy,” her mom mouthed before handing her the phone.

“Merry Christmas,” Morgan said in lieu of a hello.

“Merry Christmas, Munchkin.”

Morgan talked to her biological father for a bit until the phone was handed off to her stepbrother Damian. She was only half-listening; her attention was focused on the living room and what her dad was saying to Josh. He’d better not be grilling him about future plans again. It was impossible to hear over Matthew’s screeching.

“Sorry, it’s a nuthouse here,” Morgan said when she realized Randy was back on the phone and she’d missed what he said. “Tell Lisa Merry Christmas as well and thanks for calling.”

They exchanged goodbyes and Morgan hung up feeling a bit guilty. Just a year ago she would have been over the moon excited to receive a call from the man at Christmas. Of course, she wouldn't have been talking to the rest of his family because she hadn't known they'd existed . . .

"You okay?" Morgan's mom asked.

"Oh, yeah. Just thinking."

"You want to try the cinnamon rolls again?"

"In a minute. I've got to see what Dad's doing to Josh first."

Her mom laughed and took the quiche out of the oven with one hand while smoothing out her dress with the other. Morgan was never going to be a housewife.

"What's going on in here?" Morgan asked as she entered the living room.

Her dad looked as if he'd been caught with his hand in the cookie jar. She must have been correct in her assumption. He knew better than to pester Josh when she was around.

Josh sat on the floor beside Matthew as he tore into his present. Josh didn't look at all disturbed. In fact, he looked strangely satisfied.

"Your father and I were just talking about schooling," Josh said.

Before Morgan could chastise her dad, Matthew bellowed at the top of his lungs, "Jos!"

"Now what's this?" her dad asked, getting up from his chair to inspect the newest present. "A Sights and Sounds Activity Bus?"

Morgan stifled a laugh. That thing looked loud.

"Well, it looks like the batteries aren't included," her dad said with mock disappointment. "We'll have to pick up some more before –"

"Got 'em right here, sir," Josh said, pulling a package of batteries from the pocket of his jeans.

Morgan snorted and ran back into the kitchen before she completely lost it. The look on her dad's face was priceless.

Her final attempt at cinnamon rolls produced semi-edible results. They were still flat, but not burned or undercooked. Morgan's mom helped her fluff them up a bit and they finished setting the table to the sounds of Matthew's new toy. It was loud, it was annoying, but it was all worth it. Every time Morgan poked her head around the corner, her dad was chasing Matthew around asking if he could play with it but each attempt was thwarted by either her brother or Josh.

By the time they sat down to brunch, her dad's hair was not so immaculately styled. It looked like he'd been pulling on it.

Josh declined the offer of a mimosa, but Morgan accepted hers with glee. He'd be sorry later, she was sure.

"How was church last night?" her dad asked Josh.

"It was good, but Christmas service is always special."

"Too bad you didn't come over for dinner," Morgan said. "You could have met Gran."

"I hope to meet her one day soon. Didn't you say she lives close to Cal's?"

"She does," Morgan said.

"We're awfully disappointed you won't be coming to see your other grandparents," her dad said, referring to his parents who lived a couple of hours away. "It's only once a year, you know."

"Right, but I have plans," Morgan said. "I spoke to them last night and they understood."

"There's still time to change your mind, you know," her dad persisted. "We're not leaving until late this afternoon."

"I won't change my mind," she said. "I'll see you when you get back tomorrow. Tell them I send my love."

The rest of the meal dragged on. Everyone was kind enough to try one of Morgan's cinnamon rolls and they all pretended to like them. Except for Matthew. He spit it right out and Morgan had to agree. They tasted like shit.

After the meal, Josh returned to the living room with Matthew and Morgan's dad while she and her mom cleaned up.

By the time they had finished, Morgan couldn't wait to get the hell out of there. That toy Josh bought Matthew was migraine-inducing and she had a feeling it would go missing shortly after they left.

"One down," Morgan declared once she and Josh were out the door.

"And one to go," Josh said as he loaded Morgan's plastic tote with tree decorations and gifts into Bob's trunk.

"Oh, wait. I've got to get Rab's present out of there." She lifted the lid and pulled out the package, then considered the fruitcake her parents had sent with her. "Should we just toss this in there? It's kinda embarrassing."

"What's embarrassing about a fruitcake?" Josh asked.

Morgan shrugged. "It seems cliché. Also, they only sent it because I screwed up the cinnamon rolls."

Josh put his arms around her and kissed her. "I don't love you because of your cooking skills."

Morgan laughed. "Thank God for that."

The drive to Josh's parents' house went way too quickly. Morgan wished she would have brought her pack of cigarettes, or at least snatched another mimosa, as they pulled into the driveway.

"Any chance they're serving wine?" she asked.

"Not even the slightest," Josh said. "Come on. I made it through the morning with your dad."

"Nice call on the toy."

"It made me happy."

They laughed their way to the door where Josh's mother stood waiting to greet them. She looked like she was dressed for work. All that was missing was the name tag.

"*Maman,*" Josh greeted her with a kiss on her cheek.

"Merry Christmas, Mrs. Hampton," Morgan said and handed her the fruitcake.

Even though it was freezing out, the woman took her time eyeing Morgan and the fruitcake before nodding and allowing them into the house.

"Everyone's in the living room waiting to open gifts," she said as they took off their coats and shoes. "What would you like to drink?"

"Soda's fine," Josh answered for them both.

Morgan blinked hard to prevent an eye roll.

Armed with glasses of cola, Morgan and Josh made their way to the living room.

"Merry Christmas," Rab greeted them from the couch where she sat with Trixie.

"Merry Christmas," Morgan and Josh said together.

Josh's father sat in a recliner by the tree. "Welcome. Have a seat," he said, waving to the one open chair and the end of the couch.

Morgan panicked but Josh led her to the chair and perched on the edge of it beside her.

Trixie had yet to say a word, but Morgan refused to face her full on.

Rab and Josh talked a bit about her boyfriend David, who was coming over after dinner. Morgan counted the ticks as the minutes dragged by, hoping to hell they wouldn't still be there when he arrived.

When Josh's mother came in and took the final seat on the couch next to Trixie, it was time for presents. Rab and Josh were in charge of doling them out.

Morgan hadn't been expecting any gifts and was surprised when Josh presented her with an early one from himself while Rab gave her one "From the Hampton household."

Present opening was done like in most households with a flurry of wrapping paper and exclamations of delight.

Morgan thanked Rab for the fluffy socks and Josh for the nice journal and pen as he opened a set of towels from his parents. She couldn't help but make comparisons to her own family's Christmas, where there was just so much more of everything. Her room at home was littered with piles of clothing, art supplies, and silly impulse-buy gifts that she had yet to take out of their packages.

In all honesty, she found this more enjoyable. Well, not all of the company, but the relative simplicity of it.

Rab's squeal of delight did bring a big smile to Morgan's face when she unwrapped the gift she'd given her.

"What is that?" Josh's father asked.

"It's a TV!" Rab exclaimed.

As Trixie eyed the TV, Morgan had a chance to take a proper look at her while she was distracted. Her roots were showing, and she had cut her hair since the last time she'd darkened the café's door. Ah, a redhead. That explained a bit. She really needed to fix that hair. And get a larger shirt.

The room had fallen strangely silent, and Morgan realized Josh's parents were looking at her. What had she missed?

"Uh, it's just a portable black-and-white TV," she said.

"It's terrific! Thanks, Morgan." Rab came over to hug her and present opening was declared over.

They all took their seats in the dining room. Josh's father sat at the head of the table, his mother at the foot, and Josh directed Morgan to a chair beside him. Rab and Trixie sat on the other side.

Morgan was wondering where the food was, but she didn't have to wonder long. Heads were bowed and Morgan stared at her plate while Josh's mother said a blessing. Then Rab left to begin bringing the dishes in one by one, serving her father before he passed them to Josh and then around the table.

Weird. But the food was good, and Morgan was now entirely certain she wouldn't have room for another bite that day. Wine, maybe, but there was no sign of it here just as Josh had promised.

The worst part was when dinner was over and Rab and Josh were tasked with cleaning up.

Josh sensed her panic and whispered in her ear, "If I help, we get out of here quicker."

This gave her the fortitude to spend the next half hour in the living room "visiting" with Josh's parents and Trixie.

Josh's father asked Morgan a few questions about how her family was celebrating the holidays and she couldn't for the life of her remember what her responses were.

Josh's mother ignored Morgan completely and focused on fawning all over Trixie, complimenting her hairstyle and choice of outfit. That settled it. The woman was bonkers.

When Josh appeared in the doorway to rescue her, Morgan was on her feet in a flash and nearly forgot to say goodbye to everyone before said feet were being shoved into shoes at the door. She called out a general farewell and Merry Christmas to everyone and was outside by the time Josh tapped her on the shoulder and handed her her coat.

She chuckled. "It was hot in there?"

Josh helped her put it on and kissed her while he did up the zipper. "Very. Let's get out of here."

Chapter 34

In Which They Reach Home
Monday, December 25, 1995

Josh watched Morgan as she studied the scrawny tree.

"Got it at the last minute, you say?" she asked, but it was more a statement.

"You don't like it," Josh said.

Morgan smiled and shook her head. "It's our first Christmas tree and I think it's beautiful. Ready to decorate?"

"Where do we start?" Josh asked.

Morgan dragged the tote of ornaments she'd brought to the middle of the room. "You've never decorated a tree?"

"I tried to help once, but *Maman* is very particular about how the tree should look. *Very* particular," Josh said. "Rab has the patience to help her, but not me, so this will be a learning experience."

"Let's start with the lights." Morgan dug through the box and pulled out a tangled mess of multicolored lights. "Help me unravel these."

Josh pulled the two chairs over from his recently acquired kitchen table so they could sit and untangle the lights. They'd only just begun when he leaned over and gave her a kiss.

"Stop that or we'll never get this decorated," Morgan said and laughed.

"Sure we will." He kissed her nose and ducked back before she could swat him.

"Not while it's still Christmas."

"I'll try to behave, but it's so hard with you sitting there looking so beautiful," Josh said. "You going to let your hair stay long?"

"I haven't decided yet. I kind of like the look, but it takes more fussing with."

Josh ran his hand through his hair, which hadn't been cut since summer. "I know what you mean."

"Oh, hey. I think we've got it," Morgan said and stretched out a length of cord.

"Do we wrap the tree now?"

"We could, but it's easier to test the lights if they're not on the tree." Morgan plugged an end into the socket.

They didn't light up.

"Is there some sort to time delay?" Josh asked.

"Nope. There must be a broken bulb in the line somewhere."

"So, what do we do?"

"If we're very lucky, we just go down the line and look for one that's shattered," she said.

Each started at one of the ends and searched.

"No such luck," Josh said.

"Rats. Okay, now we change them one at a time until the lights come on." She pulled out a box of bulbs and handed one to Josh.

"Shouldn't we unplug it while changing them?" he asked.

"Probably. But if we're careful not to touch the base while taking the bulb out or putting it in, we should be fine."

Morgan hummed a song while she went merrily along changing bulbs. She must have changed three bulbs for every one Josh changed.

They got lucky and the lights came on after Josh changed his third bulb.

"Awesome," Morgan said and clapped. "Now I want you to feed it to me slowly while I wrap the tree."

"Okay, Angel, wrap away."

After the lights were on, Morgan gave him a silver tinsel garland and had him wrap it around the tree. Her eyes were lit with mirth and she bit her lip as he struggled to get it even.

Josh knew it wasn't perfect – *Maman's* trees were perfect – but loved the way she didn't chide him or redo it.

Morgan took a gold garland and wrapped it in the opposite direction so the two crossed.

Finally, it was time to add the ornaments.

"These look like they're very old," Josh said as he gingerly removed an ornament from its tissue paper wrapping.

"They are. Grandma gave these to Mom and that's what we used until she and Dad decided to go with a more modern look. I like these better."

"Me too," Josh agreed.

Between the two of them, they placed all the ornaments on the tree and decided to bring a few from the back to fill in the visible side more. The last item to come out of the box was an angel for the top of the tree.

Josh added the finishing touch and they stood with their arms around each other admiring their work.

"See, with a little work, any tree can be beautiful," Morgan said.

"You're the creative one of this team."

Morgan rewarded him with a kiss.

"Let's get the presents under the tree," Josh suggested.

Morgan pulled his from the bottom of the tote while Josh went into his bedroom to get hers.

Morgan's eyes went wide when she saw her present. "Ooh, so tiny," she said.

Josh put it under the tree with the other two presents then stood as straight and tall as he could. "Big things come in small packages."

"Promises, promises." Morgan chuckled and snapped a couple pictures with a disposable camera.

"Where's the camera you got for your birthday?" Josh asked as he returned the chairs to the kitchen table.

"Too many damned bells and whistles. I suppose one day I'll actually have to learn how to use it. Now go stand by the tree."

Josh did as she asked. She took a few more pictures and they changed places. When he was done, she bent over to snatch up the little package and shook it next to her ear. "Hmm, it has a slight rattle. Can we open them now?"

"Sure. You want to do it at the table or just plop on the floor?"

"Floor. Now get down here," Morgan said.

"As you wish, my love." He sat next to her. "Should I formally hand it to you?"

"Pfft. Like I'd give it back to you now that it's in my hands. Possession is nine-tenths of the law, you know."

"Working at a law firm has made you a lawyer now?" Josh asked.

"As if." She tried tugging the ribbon but that only made the knot tighter, so she pushed the ribbon off.

Josh watched her with love filling his heart.

She showed no mercy with the wrapping. Whatever was left she wadded into a foil ball and tossed across the room at the garbage can. She opened the box and lifted out the two chains. Tears welled in her eyes as she saw their names engraved, one on each heart.

"There's one for each of us, to remind us we're only whole when we're together," Josh said.

Morgan placed the box in her lap and wrapped her arms around him. He could feel tears wet his neck as she said, "Oh, Josh, I love you so much."

He kissed her ear and whispered, "You own my heart, Angel."

She pulled away and wiped her eyes. She took the necklace with his name on it and fastened it around her neck then slipped the other one over his head. "Now open mine."

She handed him the first package in a gift bag.

Josh pulled out the tissue paper and dropped it to the floor. He laughed with delight when he saw a Bathurst High Phantoms ball cap identical to the one he'd lost on the ferry. "Oh Morgan, did you brave the halls of high school to get this?"

"No, I found it in a consignment shop. I don't think it's ever been worn."

He immediately put in on his head. "Has now."

She shoved the larger, gift-wrapped present at him. "This one's better."

Josh took his time opening the package as she chewed on her lip and watched.

"Oh." The cover of the photo album held a display shot from their trip – the one of the two of them kissing in front of Zinger. For a moment he could only stare at it, falling back through time and reliving the moments.

Josh leaned over to kiss Morgan, but she shook her head. "Open it."

He did and stared in awe as he flipped through page after page of their lives starting with his "last night in Canada" after he'd given her the first disposable camera. It was more than just photos; Morgan had added her own sketches, paintings, and poems to the story.

"On second thought," she said, interrupting his perusal, "maybe that can wait. Can we get off the floor now? It's freezing."

"Sure." Josh set down the album and stood to offer her a hand. They let the packaging lie on the floor where it had fallen, and embraced. "Thank you," he said and kissed her.

"Mmm. Now that's better. What do you have to drink, handsome?" Morgan asked.

"What goes well with French toast? Red wine or white wine?"

"You have wine? Oh, thank God! How'd you get it?"

"Well, I know someone who can obtain Cinnamon Schnapps, so I figured she could get a couple bottles of wine," Josh said.

"Mel to the rescue." Morgan smacked her hand on her head. "Why didn't I think of that?"

"I'm glad you didn't. Now I get to ration it," Josh teased.

"Funny. Back to the question of which kind. French toast uses eggs, right?"

"They're one of the main ingredients."

"Well, eggs are white, so we'll go with white wine," Morgan said.

Josh took a bottle of Copper Moon Pinot Grigio from the fridge. He carried it and a pair of glasses to the table where Morgan had replaced the chairs.

"Don't mind the glasses. They're the finest juice glasses I could find at the antique store," Josh said.

"If you don't stop talking and pour, I'm going to die of thirst."

"By your command." Josh twisted the top off and poured.

Morgan raised her glass in a toast. "To us."

"To us, my love. Merry Christmas."

They kissed before clinking their glasses.

"Now what about this French toast?" Morgan asked after taking a healthy swallow.

"I was about to cook some up. You want to help?"

"Not if we plan to eat it. You ate my cinnamon roll."

"You have a point, but you can watch," Josh said.

She wandered over and leaned against the sink as he put a cast iron frying pan on the stove to warm up.

He cracked a couple of eggs into a bowl and added a splash of milk before beating them with a fork. "The secret to French toast is to make sure the egg yolk and white are good and blended."

"I'll take your word for it," Morgan said. "How about I set the table?"

Josh agreed and finished mixing the batter. Morgan set the table in record time, as he didn't own many dishes, and sat down to pour more wine while Josh cooked the toast two slices at a time.

Before long he had a stack of toast and brought it to the table.

"Ladies first," Josh said as he set the plate down.

"Don't have to tell me twice. This smells delicious."

They each took a couple of slices and found they were hungrier than they'd thought they'd be after eating all day.

"That was delicious," Morgan said, leaning back in her chair. "Thank you."

"My pleasure," Josh said. "I'll just rinse these dishes. They can be washed later." He motioned to an ancient TV on a box. "Then I suppose we could see if there's a good movie on."

"God!" Morgan said and plopped her head on her arms. "I think we watched enough movies the last few months to last us years. I'd rather do the dishes."

"I'd rather sit and smooch," he said.

"That's an even better idea." Morgan brought her plate over to the sink. "I don't think we've spent a whole day together since, well, September."

Josh was silent for a minute as Morgan watched him rinse the dishes.

"What's wrong?" she asked.

Josh sighed. "I'm thinking about starting school next fall."

"Well, that's good, right?"

"It would be in Moncton. I know it's not that far, but I'd only be able to come home on the weekends."

"Obviously, it's not ideal, but we've been through a lot. I'm sure we could deal with a few years of school." She thought for a minute. "Where would you stay when you came home though?"

"I'd keep this place," Josh said, gathering his nerve.

"Just for the weekends? It seems like a waste of money."

"It wouldn't be a waste, Angel. Not if someone else used it during the week."

"What are you saying, Josh?" Morgan asked, puzzled.

Josh took a deep breath and kept his eyes on the sink. "What I'm saying is I'd like you to share this apartment with me. We could set you up a bedroom in the spare room."

"That won't be necessary."

Josh looked up, confused, and saw the sly smile on her face.

Without another word, they left the dishes in the sink and paused for a kiss in the doorway to the bedroom where Josh had hung mistletoe.

He knew then that they were finally home.

Join Morgan and Josh as their journey continues with Fork in the Road, Book Three of The Winding Road Series. Coming late 2022.

About the Authors

Canadian, multi-genre author Kerri Davidson currently lives in Elbow, Saskatchewan with her husband Travis. She has lived in numerous other locations throughout Saskatchewan and Manitoba. She used to list all the communities in her bio but has finally run out of room.

A reluctant vegetarian, she loves vodka, potato chips, all animals, and some humans.

You can find her published works at Bagoflettuce.com as well as your favorite online stores.

Author website: KerriDavidsonBooks.com
Twitter: @bagoflettuce

Mark Gelinas was born in New England but didn't stay there long. As an Air Force dependent and while in the Navy, he lived throughout the United States and Canada. During his Navy career, he enjoyed three tours as an instructor. This prepared him for later work as a technical writer.

While enlisted, he wrote shorter pieces for various magazines. In 2005, NaNoWriMo showed him he could write longer pieces.

Mark now lives in Georgia with his wife, Kate, his youngest daughter, and cats. His writing career continues.

Twitter: @Elderac

Bee and Badger Books

CPSIA information can be obtained
at www.ICGtesting.com
Printed in the USA
BVHW062258070122
625487BV00002B/3